50
Tales of Magic, Monsters and Men

50 Tales of Magic, Monsters and Men

RUPA

Published by
Rupa Publications India Pvt. Ltd 2023
7/16, Ansari Road, Daryaganj
New Delhi 110002

Sales centres:
Bengaluru Chennai
Hyderabad Jaipur Kathmandu
Kolkata Mumbai Prayagraj

P-ISBN: 978-93-5702-855-4
E-ISBN: 978-93-5702-847-9

Second impression 2024

10 9 8 7 6 5 4 3 2

Printed in India

Contents

Introduction

Magic has always fascinated humanity. Throughout history, people from different corners of the world have spun intricate tales of enchantment, monsters and extraordinary men and women. These stories have been passed down through generations, each narrative reflecting the unique culture, beliefs and folklore of its source. In *50 Greatest Tales of Magic, Monsters and Men*, we embark on an enchanting journey through a kaleidoscope of ancient lores and legends from diverse countries, unveiling the rich tapestry of human imagination that spans continents and millennia.

In the pages of this book, you will encounter an array of captivating tales, each carefully selected to represent the depth and breadth of human storytelling. These stories hail from Japan, Russia, India, Ireland, Hawaii, Greece, Mexico, Nordic countries and beyond, offering a remarkable exploration of the myriad ways in which humans have harnessed the power of narrative to express their deepest fears, desires and dreams.

Throughout history, storytelling has been a universal medium for preserving cultural heritage, shaping identity and imparting wisdom. These stories are the threads that bind generations, acting as a bridge between the past and the present. Delving into these narratives, you will discover that, while their cultural origins may be distinct, they often share strikingly similar themes, characters and motifs. Such commonalities underscore the timeless nature of human experience, as well as the shared human fascination with the supernatural and the extraordinary.

From the mystical depths of Japan's seas, where the Dragon King rules in his underwater palace, to the frozen landscapes of Russia, where the Baba Yaga dwells in her bone hut, we'll encounter a diverse array of magical creatures and beings. In India, the enchanting world of the Puranas and the epics is rich with gods, demons and battles that echo through the annals of time. In Ireland, the land of enchanting leprechauns and the legendary Banshee, the destinies of mythical monsters and daring heroes intertwine.

The Pacific paradise of Hawaii offers a unique perspective on the supernatural, with Pele, the volcanic goddess, and her fiery wrath contrasting the serene beauty of the islands. The cradle of democracy, Greece, boasts a plethora of legends, featuring the epic exploits of Hercules, the riveting dynamics between their gods and goddesses, and the enigmatic oracle of Delphi. Mexico's ancient myths and legends are woven into the tapestry of Mesoamerican culture, with the feathered serpent Quetzalcoatl and the filth-eating goddess Tlazolteotl capturing the imaginations of its people. Venturing north to the Nordic countries, we encounter the fearsome Norse monster, the wolf Fenris, and his father, the mischievous and cunning Loki.

Each of these cultural narratives holds its own unique charm, revealing the distinct worldviews and values of the societies that created them. Together, they form an awe-inspiring mosaic of human creativity and wonder. Often told around campfires, in ancient temples or within the cozy confines of homes, they have managed to endure through centuries and traverse continents. They have been adapted, reimagined and embellished, yet their core essence remains untouched.

50 Greatest Tales of Magic, Monsters and Men does not merely serve as a compilation of stories but also as a testament to the common threads that weave through the world's cultures. It is a celebration of the shared human longing for magic, the fear of the unknown, and the enduring quest for heroes and heroines who can inspire us to face life's challenges with courage and resilience.

This book invites you to explore closely the eternal struggle between good and evil, the universal complexity of moral choices and the significance of legends in shaping a society's collective consciousness. At the same time, it encourages you to embrace the diversity of human cultures, serving as a window into the beliefs, values and traditions of the people who have crafted these narratives. It offers you the opportunity to traverse the boundaries of time and space and immerse yourself in the enchanting, thrilling and heartwarming narratives that have captivated the human spirit for generations. Whether you are a seasoned mythologist, a lover of folklore or a curious explorer of the unknown, it will ignite your imagination and keep you enchanted from start to finish.

As you delve into the stories that follow, let yourself be carried away on a magical carpet ride, guided by the voices of storytellers from around the world. With *50 Greatest Tales of Magic, Monsters and Men*, we embark on a voyage to the very heart of humanity's most captivating stories, where magic, monsters and men converge in a symphony of timeless wonder.

1

The Birth-Time of the Gods

(Japanese)

Before time was, and while yet the world was uncreated, chaos reigned. The earth and the waters, the light and the darkness, the stars and the firmament, were intermingled in a vapoury liquid. All things were formless and confused. No creature existed; phantom shapes moved as clouds on the ruffled surface of a sea. It was the birth-time of the gods. The first deity sprang from an immense bulrush-bud, which rose, spear-like, in the midst of the boundless disorder. Other gods were born, but three generations passed before the actual separation of the atmosphere from the more solid earth. Finally, where the tip of the bulrush points upward, the Heavenly Spirits appeared.

From this time their kingdom was divided from the lower world where chaos still prevailed. To the fourth pair of gods it was given to create the earth. These two beings were the powerful God of the Air, Izanagi, and the fair Goddess of the Clouds, Izanami. From them sprang all life.

Now Izanagi and Izanami wandered on the Floating Bridge of Heaven. This bridge spanned the gulf between heaven and the unformed world; it was upheld in the air, and it stood secure. The God of the Air spoke to the Goddess of the Clouds: 'There must needs be a kingdom beneath us, let us visit it.' When he had so said, he plunged his jewelled spear into the seething mass below. The drops that fell from the point of the spear congealed and became the island of Onogoro. Thereupon the Earth-Makers descended, and called up a high mountain peak, on whose summit could rest one end of the Heavenly Bridge, and around which the whole world should revolve.

The Wisdom of the Heavenly Spirit had decreed that Izanagi should be a man, and Izanami a woman, and these two deities decided to wed and dwell together on the earth. But, as befitted their august birth, the wooing must be solemn. Izanagi skirted the base of the mountain to the right, Izanami turned to the left. When the Goddess of the Clouds saw the God of the Air approaching afar off, she cried, enraptured: 'Ah, what a fair and lovely youth!' Then Izanagi exclaimed, 'Ah, what a fair and lovely maiden!' As they met, they clasped hands, and the marriage was accomplished. But, for some unknown cause, the union did not prove as happy as the god and goddess had hoped. They continued their work of creation, but Awaji, the island that rose from the deep, was little more than a barren waste, and their first-born son, Hiruko, was a weakling. The Earth-Makers placed him in a little boat woven of reeds, and left him to the mercy of wind and tide.

In deep grief, Izanagi and Izanami recrossed the Floating Bridge, and came to the place where the Heavenly Spirits hold eternal audience. From them they learned that Izanagi should have been the first to speak, when the gods met round the base of the Pillar of Earth. They must woo and wed anew. On their return to earth, Izanagi, as before, went to the right, and Izanami to the left of the mountain, but now, when they met, Izanagi exclaimed: 'Ah, what a fair and lovely maiden!' and Izanami joyfully responded, 'Ah, what a fair and lovely youth!' They clasped hands once more, and their happiness began. They created the eight large islands of the Kingdom of Japan; first the luxuriant Island of the Dragon-fly, the great Yamato; then Tsukushi, the White-Sun Youth; Iyo, the Lovely Princess, and many more. The rocky islets of the archipelago were formed by the foam of the rolling breakers as they dashed on the coast-lines of the islands already created. Thus China and the remaining lands and continents of the world came into existence.

Now were born to Izanagi and Izanami, the Ruler of the Rivers, the Deity of the Mountains, and, later, the God of the Trees, and a goddess to whom was entrusted the care of tender plants and herbs.

Then Izanagi and Izanami said: 'We have created the mighty Kingdom of the Eight Islands, with mountains, rivers, and trees; yet another divinity there must be, who shall guard and rule this fair world.'

As they spoke, a daughter was born to them. Her beauty was dazzling, and her regal bearing betokened that her throne should be set high above the clouds. She was none other than Ama-terasu, The Heaven-Illuminating Spirit. Izanagi and Izanami rejoiced greatly when they beheld her face, and exclaimed, 'Our daughter shall dwell in the Blue Plain of High Heaven, and from there she shall direct the universe.' So they led her to the summit of the mountain, and over the wondrous bridge. The Heavenly Spirits were joyful when they saw Ama-terasu, and said: 'You shall mount into the soft blue of the sky, your brilliancy shall illumine, and your sweet smile shall gladden, the Eternal Land, and all the world. Fleecy clouds shall be your handmaidens, and sparkling dewdrops your messengers of peace.'

The next child of Izanagi and Izanami was a son, and as he also was beautiful, with the dream-like beauty of the evening, they placed him in the heavens, as co-ruler with his sister Ama-terasu. His name was Tsuku-yomi, the Moon-God. The god Susa-no-o is another son of the two deities who wooed and wed around the base of the Pillar of Earth. Unlike his brother and his sister, he was fond of the shadow and the gloom. When he wept, the grass on the mountainside withered, the flowers were blighted, and men died. Izanagi had little joy in this son, nevertheless he made him ruler of the ocean.

Now that the world was created, the happy life of the God of the Air and the Goddess of the Clouds was over. The consumer, the God of Fire, was born, and Izanami died. She vanished into the deep solitudes of the Kingdom of the Trees, in the country of Kii, and disappeared thence into the lower regions.

Izanagi was sorely troubled because Izanami had been taken from him, and he descended in pursuit of her to the portals of the shadowy kingdom where sunshine is unknown. Izanami would fain have left that place to rejoin Izanagi on the beautiful earth. Her spirit came to meet him, and in urgent and tender words besought him not to seek her in those cavernous regions. But the bold god would not be warned. He pressed forward, and, by the light struck from his comb, he sought for his loved one long and earnestly. Grim forms rose to confront him, but he passed them by with kingly disdain. Sounds as of the wailing of lost souls struck his ear, but still he persisted. After endless search, he found his Izanami lying in an attitude of untold despair, but so changed was she, that he gazed intently into her eyes ere he could recognize her. Izanami was angry that Izanagi had not listened to her commands, for she knew how fruitless would be his efforts. Without the sanction of the ruler of the Underworld, she could not return to earth, and this consent she had tried in vain to obtain.

Izanagi, hard pressed by the eight monsters who guard the Land of Gloom, had to flee for his life. He defended himself valiantly with his sword; then he threw down his head-dress, and it was transformed into bunches of purple grapes; he also cast behind him the comb, by means of which he had obtained light, and from it sprang tender shoots of bamboo. While the monsters eagerly devoured the luscious grapes and tender shoots, Izanagi gained the broad flight of steps which led back to earth. At the top he paused and cried to Izanami: 'All hope of our reunion is now at an end. Our separation must be eternal.'

Stretching far beyond Izanagi lay the ocean, and on its surface was reflected the face of his well-beloved daughter, Ama-terasu. She seemed to speak, and beseech him to purify himself in the great waters of the sea. As he bathed, his wounds were healed, and a sense of infinite peace stole over him.

The life-work of the Earth-Maker was done. He bestowed the world upon his children, and afterwards crossed, for the last time, the many-coloured Bridge of Heaven. The God of the Air now spends his days with the Heaven-Illuminating Spirit in her sun-glorious palace.

2

The Vision of Tsunu

(Japanese)

When the five tall pine trees on the windy heights of Mionoseki were but tiny shoots, there lived in the Kingdom of the Islands a pious man. His home was in a remote hamlet surrounded by mountains and great forests of pine. Tsunu had a wife and sons and daughters. He was a woodman, and his days were spent in the forest and on the hillsides. In summer he was up at cock-crow, and worked patiently, in the soft light under the pines, until nightfall. Then, with his burden of logs and branches, he went slowly homeward. After the evening meal, he would tell some old story or legend. Tsunu was never weary of relating the wondrous tales of the Land of the Gods. Best of all he loved to speak of Fuji-yama, the mountain that stood so near his home.

In times gone by, there was no mountain where now the sacred peak reaches up to the sky; only a far-stretching plain bathed in sunlight all day. The peasants in the district were astonished, one morning, to behold a mighty hill where before had been the open plain. It had sprung up in a single night, while they slept. Flames and huge stones were hurled from its summit; the peasants feared that the demons from the Underworld had come to wreak vengeance upon them. But for many generations there have been peace and silence on the heights. The good Sun-Goddess loves Fuji-yama. Every evening she lingers on his summit, and when at last she leaves him, his lofty crest is bathed in soft purple light. In the evening the Matchless Mountain seems to rise higher and higher into the skies, until no mortal can tell the place of his rest. Golden clouds enfold Fuji-yama in the early morning. Pilgrims come from far and near, to gain blessing and health for themselves and their families from the sacred mountain.

On the self-same night that Fuji-yama rose out of the earth, a strange thing happened in the mountainous district near Kyōto. The inhabitants were awakened by a terrible roar, which continued throughout the night. In the morning every mountain had disappeared; not one of the hills that they loved was to be seen. A blue lake lay before them. It was none other than the lute-shaped Lake Biwa. The mountains had, in truth, travelled under the earth for more than a hundred miles, and now form the sacred Fuji-yama.

As Tsunu stepped out of his hut in the morning, his eyes sought the Mountain of the Gods. He saw the golden clouds, and the beautiful story was in his mind as he went to his work.

One day the woodman wandered farther than usual into the forest. At noon he was in a very lonely spot. The air was soft and sweet, the sky so blue that he looked long at it, and then took a deep breath. Tsunu was happy.

Now his eye fell on a little fox who watched him curiously from the bushes; The creature ran away when it saw that the man's attention had been attracted. Tsunu thought, 'I will follow the little fox and see where she goes.' Off he started in pursuit. He soon came to a bamboo thicket. The smooth slender stems waved dreamily, the pale green leaves still sparkled with the morning dew. But it was not this which caused the woodman to stand spellbound. On a plot of mossy grass beyond the thicket, sat two maidens of surpassing beauty. They were partly shaded by the waving bamboos, but their faces were lit up by the sunlight.

Not a word came from their lips, yet Tsunu knew that the voices of both must be sweet as the cooing of the wild dove.

The maidens were graceful as the slender willow, they were fair as the blossom of the cherry tree. Slowly they moved the chess-men which lay before them on the grass. Tsunu hardly dared to breathe, lest he should disturb them. The breeze caught their long hair, the sunlight played upon it... The sun still shone... The chess-men were still slowly moved to and fro... The woodman gazed enraptured.

'But now,' thought Tsunu, 'I must return, and tell those at home of the beautiful maidens.' Alas, his knees were stiff and weak. 'Surely I have stood here for many hours,' he said. He leaned for support upon his axe; it crumbled into dust. Looking down, he saw that a flowing white beard hung from his chin.

For many hours the poor woodman tried in vain to reach his home. Fatigued and wearied, he came at last to a hut. But all was changed. Strange faces peered curiously at him. The speech of the people was unfamiliar. 'Where are my wife and my children?' he cried. But no one knew his name.

Finally, the poor woodman came to understand that seven generations had passed since he bade farewell to his dear ones in the early morning. While he had gazed at the beautiful maidens, his wife, his children, and his children's children, had lived and died.

The few remaining years of Tsunu's life were spent as a pious pilgrim to Fuji-yama, his well-loved mountain.

Since his death he has been honoured as a saint who brings prosperity to the people of his native country.

3

Vrigu and Agni

(*Indian*)

Once upon a time in the days when the Bharata princes ruled over India there lived a mighty rishi named Vrigu. And his wisdom and powers were such that men said that the god Brahmadeva had created him out of the fire, when Varuna the sea god made a great sacrifice. At this same time, there lived a most beautiful maiden named Puloma, the fame of whose loveliness spread throughout the whole empire of the Bharatas. When she grew to full womanhood her father offered her in marriage to Vrigu the rishi. Vrigu accepted her hand. And thus the wisest and the loveliest in all the land were united in wedlock.

They lived together happily and after several months Puloma was about to bear her lord a son. But before the child's birth the great sage went to bathe in a holy river. In his absence there came to his hermitage a demon king named Paulama. When Puloma was quite a child her father had promised her hand to the demon king. But afterwards, hearing the fame of the rishi Vrigu, he broke his promise and gave her in marriage to the great sage. Paulama in vain urged that he was betrothed to Puloma. But her father treated him with scorn. At last the demon king went away in anger, vowing that his disgrace would one day be avenged. Day after day he hid himself near Vrigu's hermitage, until at last, seeing that Vrigu had gone to a distant river, the demon king boldly entered the hermitage and asked Puloma to give him food. The rishi's beautiful wife suspected no evil and welcoming the betrothed of her childhood, offered him for food the fruits of the forest. But as Paulama ate, his longing for Puloma grew and so also grew his hatred for Vrigu. 'I shall carry her off,' he muttered to himself, 'and thus I shall avenge my dishonour and win for myself the wife whom Vrigu tore away from my arms.' But before he did so, he entered an inner room where a sacred fire burnt always day and night. 'O fire god Agni,' he said, 'the lady Puloma was once my affianced bride. Vrigu took her from me by trickery. But she was given to me first, therefore tell me, I pray you, whether she is not now my lawful wife.' Agni at first did not answer. He would gladly have said that Paulama had a just claim. But he feared that if he spoke thus, Vrigu's curse would fall upon and destroy him. So after thinking deeply he said, 'O demon king, it is true that Puloma was your affianced bride, but she never became your wife. She went through the marriage ceremony with the rishi Vrigu. She is therefore Vrigu's wife and not yours.'

The demon king grew angry and paying no heed to the words of Agni, took the shape of a boar, and throwing Puloma across his back galloped at full speed through the forest. As he galloped he met the rishi Vrigu, who was returning from the sacred river where he had gone to bathe. When the great sage saw that the wild boar carried on his back his beautiful bride he cursed the boar as he ran. Instantly the boar was consumed and became a heap of ashes. Puloma fell to the ground and lay unconscious.

When Puloma had recovered from the fall Vrigu asked her who had pointed out their hermitage to the demon king Paulama, so that he might curse him. 'It was Agni,' answered Puloma weeping, for she thought that Agni had aided Paulama. Then Vrigu's wrath blazed up like a forest fire and he cursed Agni saying, 'Henceforth everything that you touch will be consumed.' Agni was very angry at the curse for he had in no way merited it.

And he would have cursed Vrigu in turn, had Vrigu not been one of the race of the Brahmans whom he respected. So Agni went far away into a distant cave and hid himself. And because mankind had no longer any fire they could no longer offer sacrifices to the gods, nor did the gods receive any honour from them. At last in great distress the rishis and the Immortals met. 'O Immortals' said the rishis, 'we can no longer serve you, owing to the flight of Agni. Let us therefore pray to the god Brahmadeva and perhaps he may help us.' Together, therefore, the rishis and the Immortals went to the throne of the god Brahmadeva and told him how Vrigu had cursed Agni the fire god, and how in his wrath Agni had hidden himself from mankind.

On hearing their tale, the god Brahmadeva sent a messenger to call Agni the fire god to him. And Agni came into his presence and told Brahmadeva how Vrigu had cursed him without reason. But Brahmadeva answered Agni with soothing words. 'The curse of Vrigu,' said Brahmadeva, 'cannot be removed. But I shall turn his curse into a blessing. Henceforth, Agni, all that is vile you will consume with your flames. But all that is pure will remain. Thus all that passes through fire will be purified.' And Agni hearing these words was comforted. He no longer hid himself in a distant cave, but lived in his former dwelling. And mankind used Agni as of old in their sacrifices. The Immortals were happy because of the honour which they received and the rishis because they once again could offer sacrifices. And because of the happiness of the Immortals and the power of the rishis mankind grew daily happier. And in after years they spoke of this time as the golden age.

4

Strong Desire and the Red Sorcerer

(Native American)

There was a man called Odshedoph, or the Child of Strong Desires, who had a wife and one son. He had withdrawn his family from the village, where they had spent the winter, to the neighborhood of a distant forest, where game abounded. This wood was a day's travel from his winter home, and under its ample shadow the wife fixed the lodge, while the husband went out to hunt. Early in the evening he returned with a deer, and, being weary and athirst, he asked his son, whom he called Strong Desire, to go to the river for some water. The son replied that it was dark, and he was afraid. His father still urged him, saying that his mother, as well as himself, was tired, and the distance to the water very short. But no persuasion could overcome the young man's reluctance. He refused to go.

'Ah, my son,' said the father, at last, 'if you are afraid to go to the river, you will never kill the Red Head.'

The stripling was deeply vexed by this observation; it seemed to touch him to the very quick. He mused in silence. He refused to eat, and made no reply when spoken to. He sat by the lodge door all the night through, looking up at the stars, and sighing like one sorely distressed.

The next day he asked his mother to dress the skin of the deer, and to make it into moccasins for him, while he busied himself in preparing a bow and arrows.

As soon as these were in readiness, he left the lodge one morning, at sunrise, without saying a word to his father or mother. As he passed along, he fired one of his arrows into the air, which fell westward. He took that course, and coming to the spot where the arrow had fallen, he was rejoiced to find it piercing the heart of a deer. He refreshed himself with a meal of the venison, and the next morning he fired another arrow. Following its course, after traveling all day he found that he had transfixed another deer. In this manner he fired four arrows, and every evening he discovered that he had killed a deer.

By a strange oversight, he left the arrows sticking in the carcasses, and passed on without withdrawing them. Having in this way no arrow for the fifth day, he was in great distress at night for the want of food.

At last he threw himself upon the earth in despair, concluding that he might as well perish there as go further. But he had not lain long before he heard a hollow rumbling noise, in the ground beneath him, like that of an earthquake moving slowly along.

He sprang up, and discovered at a distance the figure of a human being, walking with a stick. He looked attentively, and saw that the figure was walking in a wide beaten path in a prairie, leading from a dusky lodge to a lake, whose waters were black and turbid.

To his surprise, this lodge, which had not been in view when he cast himself upon the ground, was now near at hand. He approached a little nearer, and concealed himself; and in a moment he discovered that the figure was no other than that of the terrible witch, the little old woman who makes war. Her path to the lake was perfectly smooth and solid, and the noise Strong Desire had heard was caused by the striking of her walking staff upon the ground. The top of this staff was decorated with a string of the toes and bills of birds of every kind, who, at every stroke of the stick, fluttered and sung their various notes in concert.

She entered her lodge and laid off her mantle, which was entirely composed of the scalps of women.

Before folding it, she shook it several times, and at every shake the scalps uttered loud shouts of laughter, in which the old hag joined. The boy, who lingered at the door, was greatly alarmed, but he uttered no cry.

After laying by the cloak, she came directly to him. Looking at him steadily, she informed him that she had known him from the time he had left his father's lodge, and had watched his movements. She told him not to fear or despair, for she would be his protector and friend. She invited him into her lodge, and gave him a supper. During the repast, she questioned him as to his motives for visiting her. He related his history, stated the manner in which he had been disgraced, and the difficulties he labored under.

'Now tell me truly,' said the little old woman who makes war, 'you were afraid to go to the water in the dark.'

'I was,' Strong Desire answered, promptly.

As he replied, the hag waved her staff. The birds set up a clamorous cry, and the mantle shook violently as all the scalps burst into a hideous shout of laughter.

'And are you afraid now,' she asked again.

'I am,' again answered Strong Desire, without hesitation.

'But you are not afraid to speak the truth,' rejoined the little old woman. 'You will be a brave man yet.'

She cheered him with the assurance of her friendship, and began at once to exercise her power upon him. His hair being very short, she took a great leaden comb, and after drawing it through his locks several times, they became of a handsome length like those of a beautiful young woman. She then proceeded to dress him as a female, furnishing him with the necessary garments, and tinting his face with colors of the most charming dye. She gave him, too, a bowl of shining metal. She directed him to put in his girdle a blade of scented sword-grass, and to proceed the next morning to the banks of the lake, which was no other than that over which the Red Head reigned. Now Hah-Undo-Tah, or the Red Head, was a most powerful sorcerer, living upon an island in the center of his realm of water, and he was the terror of all the country. She informed him that there would be many Indians upon the island, who, as soon as they saw him use the shining bowl to drink with, would come and solicit him to be their wife, and to take him over to the island. These offers he was to refuse, and to say that he had come a great distance to be the wife of the Red Head, and that if the chief could not seek her for himself, she would return to her village. She said, that as soon as the Red Head heard of this he would come for her in his own canoe, in which she must embark.

'On reaching the shore,' added the little old woman, 'you must consent to be his wife; and in the evening you are to induce him to take a walk out of the village, and when you have reached a lonesome spot, use the first opportunity to cut off his head with the blade of grass.'

She also gave Strong Desire general advice how he was to conduct himself to sustain his assumed character of a woman. His fear would scarcely permit him to consent to engage in an adventure attended with so much danger; but the recollection of his father's looks and reproaches of the want of courage, decided him.

Early in the morning he left the lodge of the little old woman who makes war, which was clouded in a heavy brackish fog, so thick and heavy to breathe, that he with difficulty made his way forth. When he turned to look back for it, it was gone.

He took the hard beaten path to the banks of the lake, and made for the water at a point directly opposite the Red Head's lodge.

Where he now stood it was beautiful day. The heavens were

clear, and the sun shone out as brightly to Strong Desire as on the first morning when he had put forth his little head from the door of his father's lodge. He had not been long there, sauntering along the beach, when he displayed the glittering bowl by dipping water from the lake. Very soon a number of canoes came off from the island. The men admired his dress, and were charmed with his beauty, and almost with one voice they all made proposals of marriage. These, Strong Desire promptly declined.

When this was reported to Red Head, he ordered his royal bark to be launched by his chosen men of the oar, and crossed over to see this wonderful girl. As they approached the shore, Strong Desire saw that the ribs of the sorcerer's canoe were formed of living rattlesnakes, whose heads pointed outward to guard him from his enemies. Being invited, he had no sooner stepped into the canoe, than they began to hiss and rattle furiously, which put him in a great fright; but the magician spoke to them, when they became pacified and quiet. Shortly after they were at the landing upon the island. The marriage took place immediately; and the bride made presents of various valuables which had been furnished her by the old witch who inhabited the cloudy lodge.

As they were sitting in the lodge, surrounded by the friends and relatives, the mother of the Red Head regarded the face of her new daughter-in-law for a long time with fixed attention. From this scrutiny she was convinced that this singular and hasty marriage boded no good to her son. She drew him aside, and disclosed to him her suspicions. This can be no female, said she; she has the figure and manners, the countenance, and more especially the eyes, are beyond a doubt those of a man. Her husband rejected her suspicions, and rebuked her severely for entertaining such notions of her own daughter-in-law. She still urged her doubts, which so vexed the husband that he broke his pipe-stem in her face, and called her an owl.

This act astonished the company, who sought an explanation;

and it was no sooner given, than the mock bride, rising with an air of offended dignity, informed the Red Head that after receiving so gross an affront from his relatives she could not think of remaining with him as his wife, but should forthwith return to her own friends.

With a toss of the head, like that of an angry female, Strong Desire left the lodge, followed by Red Head, and walked away until he came to the beach of the island, near the spot where they had first landed. Red Head entreated him to remain, urging every motive, and making all sorts of magnificent promises—none of which seemed to make the least impression. Strong Desire, Red Head thought, was very hard-hearted. During these appeals they had seated themselves upon the ground, and Red Head, in great affliction, reclined his head upon his fancied wife's lap. Strong Desire now changed his manner, was very kind and soothing, and suggested in the most winning accent that if Red Head would sleep soundly for awhile he might possibly dream himself out of all his troubles. Red Head, delighted at so happy a prospect, said that he would fall asleep immediately.

'You have killed a good many men in your time, Red Head,' said Strong Desire, by way of suggesting an agreeable train of ideas to the sorcerer.

'Hundreds,' answered Red Head; 'and what is better, now that I am fairly settled in life by this happy marriage, I shall be able to give my whole attention to massacre.'

'And you will kill hundreds more,' interposed Strong Desire, in the most insinuating manner imaginable.

'Just so, my dear,' Red Head replied, with a great leer; 'thousands. There will be no end to my delicious murders. I love dearly to kill people. I would like to kill you if you were not my wife.'

'There, there,' said Strong Desire, with the coaxing air of a little coquette, 'go to sleep; that's a good Red Head.'

No other subject of conversation occurring to the chief, now that he had exhausted the delightful topic of wholesale murder, he straightway fell into a deep sleep.

The chance so anxiously sought for had come; and Strong Desire, with a smiling eye, drawing his blade of grass with lightning swiftness once across the neck of the Red Head, severed the huge and wicked head from the body.

In a moment, stripping off his woman's dress, underneath which he had all along worn his male attire, Strong Desire seized the bleeding trophy, plunged into the lake, and swam safely over to the main shore. He had scarcely reached it, when, looking back, he saw amid the darkness the torches of persons come out in search of the new married couple. He listened until they had found the headless body, and he heard their piercing shrieks of rage and sorrow as he took his way to the lodge of his kind adviser.

The little old woman who makes war was in an excellent humor, and she received Strong Desire with rejoicing. She admired his prudence, and assured him his bravery should never be questioned again. Lifting up the head, which she gazed upon with vast delight, she said he need only have brought the scalp. Cutting off a lock of the hair for herself, she told him he might now return with the head, which would be evidence of an achievement that would cause his own people to respect him.

'In your way home,' added the little old woman, 'you will meet with but one difficulty. Maunkahkeesh, the Spirit of the Earth, requires an offering or sacrifice from all of her sons who perform extraordinary deeds. As you walk along in a prairie there will be an earthquake; the earth will open and divide the prairie in the middle. Take this partridge and throw it into the opening, and instantly spring over it.'

With many thanks to the little old witch, who had so faithfully befriended him, Strong Desire took leave of her, and having, by the course pointed out, safely passed the earthquake, he arrived near his own village. He secretly hid his precious trophy.

On entering the village, he found that his parents had returned from the place of their spring encampment by the wood-side, and that they were in heavy sorrowing for their son, whom they supposed to be lost. One and another of the young men had presented themselves to the disconsolate parents, and said, 'Look up, I am your son;' but when they looked up, they beheld not the familiar face of Strong Desire.

Having been often deceived in this manner, when their own son in truth presented himself they sat with their heads down, and with their eyes nearly blinded with weeping. It was some time before they could be prevailed upon to bestow a glance upon him. It was still longer before they could recognize him as their son who had refused to draw water from the river, at night, for fear, for his countenance was no longer that of a timid stripling; it was that of a man who has seen and done great things, and who has the heart to do greater still.

When he recounted his adventures they believed him mad. The young men laughed at him—him, Strong Desire—who feared to walk to the river at night-time.

He left the lodge, and ere their laughter had ceased, returned with his trophy. He held aloft the head of the Red Sorcerer, with the great ghastly leer which lighted it up before his last sleep, at prospect of a thousand future murders, fresh upon it. It was easily recognized, and the young men who had scoffed at Strong Desire shrunk into the corners out of sight. Strong Desire had conquered the terrible Red Head! All doubts of the truth of his adventures were dispelled.

He was greeted with joy, and placed among the first warriors of the nation. He finally became a chief, and his family were ever after respected and esteemed.

5

Huitzilopochtli, the War-God

(Mexican)

Huitzilopochtli occupied in the Aztec pantheon a place similar to that of Mars in the Roman. His origin is obscure, but the myth relating to it is distinctly original in character. It recounts how, under the shadow of the mountain of Coatepec, near the Toltec city of Tollan, there dwelt a pious widow called Coatlicue, the mother of a tribe of Indians called Centzonuitznaua, who had a daughter called Coyolxauhqui, and who daily repaired to a small hill with the intention of offering up prayers to the gods in a penitent spirit of piety. Whilst occupied in her devotions one day she was surprised by a small ball of brilliantly coloured feathers falling upon her from on high. She was pleased by the bright variety of its hues, and placed it in her bosom, intending to offer it up to the sun-god. Some time afterwards she learnt that she was to become the mother of another child. Her sons, hearing of this, rained abuse upon her, being incited to humiliate her in every possible way by their sister Coyolxauhqui.

Coatlicue went about in fear and anxiety; but the spirit of her unborn infant came and spoke to her and gave her words of encouragement, soothing her troubled heart. Her sons, however, were resolved to wipe out what they considered an insult to their race by the death of their mother, and took counsel with one another to slay her. They attired themselves in their war-gear, and arranged their hair after the manner of warriors going to battle. But one of their number, Quauitlicac, relented, and confessed the perfidy of his brothers to the still unborn Huitzilopochtli, who replied to him: 'O brother, hearken attentively to what I have to say to you. I am fully informed of what is about to happen.' With the intention of slaying their mother, the Indians went in search of her. At their head marched their sister, Coyolxauhqui. They were armed to the teeth, and carried bundles of darts with which they intended to kill the luckless Coatlicue.

Quauitlicac climbed the mountain to acquaint Huitzilopochtli with the news that his brothers were approaching to kill their mother.

'Mark well where they are at,' replied the infant god. 'To what place have they advanced?'

'To Tzompantitlan,' responded Quauitlicac.

Later on Huitzilopochtli asked: 'Where may they be now?'

'At Coaxalco,' was the reply.

Once more Huitzilopochtli asked to what point his enemies had advanced.

'They are now at Petlac,' Quauitlicac replied.

After a little while Quauitlicac informed Huitzilopochtli that the Centzonuitznaua were at hand under the leadership of Coyolxauhqui. At the moment of the enemy's arrival Huitzilopochtli was born, flourishing a shield and spear of a blue colour. He was painted, his head was surmounted by a panache, and his left leg was covered with feathers. He shattered Coyolxauhqui with a flash of serpentine lightning, and then gave chase to the Centzonuitznaua, whom he pursued four times round the mountain. They did not attempt to defend themselves, but fled incontinently. Many perished in the waters of the adjoining lake, to which they had rushed in their despair. All were slain save a few who escaped to a place called Uitzlampa, where they surrendered to Huitzilopochtli and gave up their arms.

The name Huitzilopochtli signifies 'Humming-bird to the left,' from the circumstance that the god wore the feathers of the humming-bird, or *colibri*, on his left leg. From this it has been inferred that he was a humming-bird totem. The explanation of Huitzilopochtli's origin is a little deeper than this, however. Among the American tribes, especially those of the northern continent, the serpent is regarded with the deepest veneration as the symbol of wisdom and magic. From these sources come success in war. The serpent also typifies the lightning, the symbol of the divine spear, the apotheosis of warlike might. Fragments of serpents are regarded as powerful war-physic among many tribes. Atatarho, a mythical wizard-king of the Iroquois, was clothed with living serpents as with a robe, and his myth throws light on one of the names of Huitzilopochtli's mother, Coatlantona (Robe of Serpents). Huitzilopochtli's image was surrounded by serpents, and rested on serpent-shaped supporters. His sceptre was a single snake, and his great drum was of serpent-skin.

In American mythology the serpent is closely associated with the bird. Thus the name of the god Quetzalcoatl is translatable as 'Feathered Serpent,' and many similar cases where the conception of bird and serpent have been unified could be adduced. Huitzilopochtli is undoubtedly one of these. We may regard him as a god the primary conception of whom arose from the idea of the serpent, the symbol of warlike wisdom and might, the symbol of the warrior's dart or spear, and the humming-bird, the harbinger of summer, type of the season when the snake or lightning god has power over the crops.

Huitzilopochtli was usually represented as wearing on his head a waving panache or plume of humming-birds' feathers. His face and limbs were striped with bars of blue, and in his right hand he carried four spears. His left hand bore his shield, on the surface of which were displayed five tufts of down, arranged in the form of a quincunx. The shield was made with reeds, covered with eagle's down. The spear he brandished was also tipped with tufts of down instead of flint. These weapons were placed in the hands of those who as captives engaged in the sacrificial fight, for in the Aztec mind Huitzilopochtli symbolized the warrior's death on the gladiatorial stone of combat. As has been said, Huitzilopochtli was war-god of the Aztecs, and was supposed to have led them to the site of Mexico from their original home in the north. The city of Mexico took its name from one of its districts, which was designated by a title of Huitzilopochtli's, Mexitli (Hare of the Aloes).

The War-God as Fertilizer

But Huitzilopochtli was not a war-god alone. As the serpent-god of lightning he had a connection with summer, the season of lightning, and therefore had dominion to some extent over the crops and fruits of the earth. The Algonquian Indians of North America believed that the rattlesnake could raise ruinous storms or grant favourable breezes. They alluded to it also as the symbol of life, for the serpent has a phallic significance because of its similarity to the symbol of generation and fructification. With some American tribes also, notably the Pueblo Indians of Arizona, the serpent has a solar significance, and with tail in mouth symbolizes the annual round of the sun. The Nahua believed that Huitzilopochtli could grant them fair weather for the fructification of their crops, and they placed an image of Tlaloc, the rain-god, near him, so that, if necessary, the war-god could compel the rain-maker to exert his pluvial powers or to abstain from the creation of floods. We must, in considering the nature of this deity, bear well in mind the connection in the Nahua consciousness between the pantheon, war, and the food-supply. If war was not waged annually the gods must go without flesh food and perish, and if the gods succumbed the crops would fail, and famine would destroy the race. So it was small wonder that Huitzilopochtli was one of the chief gods of Mexico.

Huitzilopochtli's principal festival was the Toxcatl, celebrated immediately after the Toxcatl festival of Tezcatlipoca, to which it bore a strong resemblance. Festivals of the god were held in May and December, at the latter of which an image of him, moulded in dough kneaded with the blood of sacrificed children, was pierced by the presiding priest with an arrow—an act significant of the death of Huitzilopochtli until his resurrection in the next year.

Strangely enough, when the absolute supremacy of Tezcatlipoca is remembered, the high-priest of Huitzilopochtli, the Mexicatl Teohuatzin, was considered to be the religious head of the Mexican priesthood. The priests of Huitzilopochtli held office by right of descent, and their primate exacted absolute obedience from the priesthoods of all the other deities, being regarded as next to the monarch himself in power and dominion.

6

Tlazolteotl

(Mexican)

Tlazolteotl (God of Ordure), or Tlaelquani (Filth-eater), was called by the Mexicans the earth-goddess because she was the eradicator of sins, to whose priests the people went to make confession so that they might be absolved from their misdeeds. Sin was symbolized by the Mexicans as excrement. Confession covered only the sins of immorality. But if Tlazolteotl was the goddess of confession, she was also the patroness of desire and luxury. It was, however, as a deity whose chief office was the eradication of human sin that she was pre-eminent. The process by which this was supposed to be effected is quaintly described by Sahagun in the twelfth chapter of his first book. The penitent addressed the confessor as follows: 'Sir, I desire to approach that most powerful god, the protector of all, that is to say, Tezcatlipoca. I desire to tell him my sins in secret.' The confessor replied: 'Be happy, my son: that which thou wishest to do will be to thy good and advantage.' The confessor then opened the divinatory book known as the Tonalamatl (that is, the Book of the Calendar) and acquainted the applicant with the day which appeared the most suitable for his confession. The day having arrived, the penitent provided himself with a mat, copal gum to burn as incense, and wood whereon to burn it. If he was a person high in office the priest repaired to his house, but in the case of lesser people the confession took place in the dwelling of the priest. Having lighted the fire and burned the incense, the penitent addressed the fire in the following terms: 'Thou, lord, who art the father and mother of the gods, and the most ancient of them all, thy servant, thy slave bows before thee. Weeping, he approaches thee in great distress. He comes plunged in grief, because he has been buried in sin, having backslidden, and partaken of those vices and evil delights which merit death. O master most compassionate, who art the upholder and defence of all, receive the penitence and anguish of thy slave and vassal.'

This prayer having concluded, the confessor then turned to the penitent and thus addressed him: 'My son, thou art come into the presence of that god who is the protector and upholder of all; thou art come to him to confess thy evil vices and thy hidden uncleannesses; thou art come to him to unbosom the secrets of thy heart. Take care that thou omit nothing from the catalogue of thy sins in the presence of our lord who is called Tezcatlipoca. It is certain that thou art before him who is invisible and impalpable, thou who art not worthy to be seen before him, or to speak with him...'

The allusions to Tezcatlipoca are, of course, to him in the shape of Tlazolteotl. Having listened to a sermon by the confessor, the penitent then confessed his misdeeds, after which the confessor said: 'My son, thou hast before our lord god confessed in his presence thy evil actions. I wish to say in his name that thou hast an obligation to make. At the time when the goddesses called Ciuapipiltin descend to earth during the celebration of the feast of the goddesses of carnal things, whom they name Ixcuiname, thou shalt fast during four days, punishing thy stomach and thy mouth. When the day of the feast of the Ixcuiname arrives thou shalt scarify thy tongue with the small thorns of the osier (called *teocalcacatl* or *tlazotl*), and if that is not sufficient thou shalt do likewise to thine ears, the whole for penitence, for the remission of thy sin, and as a meritorious act.

Thou wilt apply to thy tongue the middle of a spine of maguey, and thou wilt scarify thy shoulders... That done, thy sins will be pardoned.'

If the sins of the penitent were not very grave the priest would enjoin upon him a fast of a more or less prolonged nature. Only old men confessed crimes *in veneribus*, as the punishment for such was death, and younger men had no desire to risk the penalty involved, although the priests were enjoined to strict secrecy.

Father Burgoa describes very fully a ceremony of this kind which came under his notice in 1652 in the Zapotec village of San Francisco de Cajonos. He encountered on a tour of inspection an old native *cacique*, or chief, of great refinement of manners and of a stately presence, who dressed in costly garments after the Spanish fashion, and who was regarded by the Indians with much veneration. This man came to the priest for the purpose of reporting upon the progress in things spiritual and temporal in his village. Burgoa recognized his urbanity and wonderful command of the Spanish language, but perceived by certain signs that he had been taught to look for by long experience that the man was a pagan. He communicated his suspicions to the vicar of the village, but met with such assurances of the *cacique's* soundness of faith that he believed himself to be in error for once. Shortly afterwards, however, a wandering Spaniard perceived the chief in a retired place in the mountains performing idolatrous ceremonies, and aroused the monks, two of whom accompanied him to the spot where the *cacique* had been seen indulging in his heathenish practices. They found on the altar 'feathers of many colours, sprinkled with blood which the Indians had drawn from the veins under their tongues and behind their ears, incense spoons and remains of copal, and in the middle a horrible stone figure, which was the god to whom they had offered this sacrifice in expiation of their sins, while they made their confessions to the blasphemous priests, and cast off their sins in the following manner: they had woven a kind of dish out of a strong herb, specially gathered for this purpose, and casting this before the priest, said to him that they came to beg mercy of their god, and pardon for their sins that they had committed during that year, and that they brought them all carefully enumerated. They then drew out of a cloth pairs of thin threads made of dry maize husks, that they had tied two by two in the middle with a knot, by which they represented their sins. They laid these threads on the dishes of grass, and over them pierced their veins, and let the blood trickle upon them, and the priest took these offerings to the idol, and in a long speech he begged the god to forgive these, his sons, their sins which were brought to him, and to permit them to be joyful and hold feasts to him as their god and lord. Then the priest came back to those who had confessed, delivered a long discourse on the ceremonies they had still to perform, and told them that the god had pardoned them and that they might be glad again and sin anew.'

7

One-Eyed Likho

(Russian)

Once upon a time there was a smith. 'Well now,' says he, 'I've never set eyes on any harm. They say there's evil (*likho*) in the world. I'll go and seek me out evil.' So he went and had a goodish drink, and then started in search of evil. On the way he met a tailor.

'Good day,' says the Tailor.

'Good day.'

'Where are you going?' asks the Tailor.

'Well, brother, everybody says there is evil on earth. But I've never seen any, so I'm going to look for it.'

'Let's go together. I'm a thriving man, too, and have seen no evil; let's go and have a hunt for some.'

Well, they walked and walked till they reached a dark, dense forest. In it they found a small path, and along it they went—along the narrow path. They walked and walked along the path, and at last they saw a large cottage standing before them. It was night; there was nowhere else to go to. 'Look here,' they say, 'let's go into that cottage.' In they went. There was nobody there. All looked bare and squalid. They sat down, and remained sitting there some time. Presently in came a tall woman, lank, crooked, with only one eye.

'Ah!' says she, 'I've visitors. Good day to you.'

'Good day, grandmother. We've come to pass the night under your roof.'

'Very good: I shall have something to sup on.'

Thereupon they were greatly terrified. As for her, she went and fetched a great heap of firewood. She brought in the heap of firewood, flung it into the stove, and set it alight. Then she went up to the two men, took one of them—the Tailor—cut his throat, trussed him, and put him in the oven.

Meantime the Smith sat there, thinking, 'What's to be done? how's one to save one's life?' When she had finished her supper, the Smith looked at the oven and said:

'Granny, I'm a smith.'

'What can you forge?'

'Anything.'

'Make me an eye.'

'Good,' says he; 'but have you got any cord? I must tie you up, or you won't keep still. I shall have to hammer your eye in.'

She went and fetched two cords, one rather thin, the other thicker. Well, he bound her with the one which was thinnest.

'Now then, granny,' says he, 'just turn over.' She turned over, and broke the cord.

'That won't do, granny,' says he; 'that cord doesn't suit.'

He took the thick cord, and tied her up with it famously.

'Now then, turn away, granny!' says he. She turned and twisted, but didn't break the cord. Then he took an awl, heated it red-hot, and applied it to her eye—her sound one. At the same moment he caught up a hatchet, and hammered away vigorously with the back of it at the awl. She struggled like anything, and broke the cord; then she went and sat down at the threshold.

'Ah, villain!' she cried. 'You sha'n't get away from me now!'

He saw that he was in an evil plight again. There he sat, thinking, 'What's to be done?'

By-and-by the sheep came home from afield, and she drove them into her cottage for the night. Well, the Smith spent the night there, too. In the morning she got up to let the sheep out.

He took his sheep-skin pelisse and turned it inside out so that the wool was outside, passed his arms through its sleeves, and pulled it well over him, and crept up to her as he had been a sheep. She let the flock go out one at a time, catching hold of each by the wool on its back, and shoving it out. Well, he came creeping up like the rest. She caught hold of the wool on his back and shoved him out. But as soon as she had shoved him out, he stood up and cried:

'Farewell, Likho! I have suffered much evil (*likha*) at your hands. Now you can do nothing to me.'

'Wait a bit!' she replied; 'you shall endure still more. You haven't escaped yet!'

The Smith went back through the forest along the narrow path. Presently he saw a golden-handled hatchet sticking in a tree, and he felt a strong desire to seize it. Well, he did seize that hatchet, and his hand stuck fast to it. What was to be done? There was no freeing it anyhow. He gave a look behind him. There was Likho coming after him, and crying:

'There you are, villain! you've not got off yet!'

The Smith pulled out a small knife which he had in his pocket, and began hacking away at his hand—cut it clean off and ran away. When he reached his village, he immediately began to show his arm as a proof that he had seen Likho at last.

'Look,' says he, 'that's the state of things. Here am I,' says he, 'without my hand. And as for my comrade, she's eaten him up entirely.'

8

The Strange Banana Skin

(Hawaiian)

Kukali, according to the folk-lore of Hawaii, was born at Kalapana, the most southerly point of the largest island of the Hawaiian group. Kukali lived hundreds of years ago in the days of the migrations of Polynesians from one group of islands to another throughout the length and breadth of the great Pacific Ocean. He visited strange lands, now known under the general name, Kahiki, or Tahiti. Here he killed the great bird Halulu, found the deep bottomless pit in which was a pool of the fabled water of life, married the sister of Halulu, and returned to his old home. All this he accomplished through the wonderful power of a banana skin.

Kukali's father was a priest, or kahuna, of great wisdom and ability, who taught his children how to exercise strange and magical powers. To Kukali he gave a banana with the impressive charge to preserve the skin whenever he ate the fruit, and be careful that it was always under his control. He taught Kukali the wisdom of the makers of canoes and also how to select the fine-grained lava for stone knives and hatchets, and fashion the blade to the best shape. He instructed the young man in the prayers and incantations of greatest efficacy and showed him charms which would be more powerful than any charms his enemies might use in attempting to destroy him, and taught him those omens which were too powerful to be overcome. Thus Kukali became a wizard, having great confidence in his ability to meet the craft of the wise men of distant islands.

Kukali went inland through the forests and up the mountains, carrying no food save the banana which his father had given him. Hunger came, and he carefully stripped back the skin and ate the banana, folding the skin once more together. In a little while the skin was filled with fruit. Again and again he ate, and as his hunger was satisfied the fruit always again filled the skin, which he was careful never to throw away or lose.

The fever of sea-roving was in the blood of the Hawaiian people in those days, and Kukali's heart burned within him with the desire to visit the far-away lands about which other men told marvelous tales and from which came strangers like to the Hawaiians in many ways.

After a while he went to the forests and selected trees approved by the omens, and with many prayers fashioned a great canoe in which to embark upon his journey. The story is not told of the days passed on the great stretches of water as he sailed on and on, guided by the sun in the day and the stars in the night, until he came to the strange lands about which he had dreamed for years.

His canoe was drawn up on the shore and he lay down for rest. Before falling asleep he secreted his magic banana in his *malo*, or loin-cloth, and then gave himself to deep slumber. His rest was troubled with strange dreams, but his weariness was great and his eyes heavy, and he could not arouse himself to meet the dangers which were swiftly surrounding him.

A great bird which lived on human flesh was the god of the land to which he had come. The name of the bird was Halulu. Each feather of its wings was provided with talons and seemed to be endowed with human powers. Nothing like this bird was ever known or seen in the beautiful Hawaiian Islands. But here in the mysterious foreign land it had its deep valley, walled in like the valley of the Arabian Nights, over which the great bird hovered looking into the depths for food. A strong wind always attended the coming of Halulu when he sought the valley for his victims.

Kukali was lifted on the wings of the bird-god and carried to this hole and quietly laid on the ground to finish his hour of deep sleep.

When Kukali awoke he found himself in the shut-in valley with many companions who had been captured by the great bird and placed in this prison hole. They had been without food and were very weak. Now and then one of the number would lie down to die. Halulu, the bird-god, would perch on a tree which grew on the edge of the precipice and let down its wing to sweep across the floor of the valley and pick up the victims lying on the ground. Those who were strong could escape the feathers as they brushed over the bottom and hide in the crevices in the walls, but day by day the weakest of the prisoners were lifted out and prepared for Halulu's feast.

Kukali pitied the helpless state of his fellow-prisoners and prepared his best incantations and prayers to help him overcome the great bird. He took his wonderful banana and fed all the people until they were very strong. He taught them how to seek stones best fitted for the manufacture of knives and hatchets. Then for days they worked until they were all well armed with sharp stone weapons.

While Kukali and his fellow-prisoners were making preparation for the final struggle, the bird-god had often come to his perch and put his wing down into the valley, brushing the feathers back and forth to catch his prey.

Frequently the search was fruitless. At last he became very impatient, and sent his strongest feathers along the precipitous walls, seeking for victims.

Kukali and his companions then ran out from their hiding-places and fought the strong feathers, cutting them off and chopping them into small pieces.

Halulu cried out with pain and anger, and sent feather after feather into the prison. Soon one wing was entirely destroyed. Then the other wing was broken to pieces and the bird-god in his insane wrath put down a strong leg armed with great talons. Kukali uttered mighty invocations and prepared sacred charms for the protection of his friends.

After a fierce battle they cut off the leg and destroyed the talons. Then came the struggle with the remaining leg and claws, but Kukali's friends had become very bold. They fearlessly gathered around this enemy, hacking and pulling until the bird-god, screaming with pain, fell into the pit among the prisoners, who quickly cut the body into fragments.

The prisoners made steps in the walls, and by the aid of vines climbed out of their prison. When they had fully escaped, they gathered great piles of branches and trunks of trees and threw them into the prison until the body of the bird-god was covered. Fire was thrown down and Halulu was burned to ashes. Thus Kukali taught by his charms that Halulu could be completely destroyed.

But two of the breast feathers of the burning Halulu flew away to his sister, who lived in a great hole which had no bottom. The name of this sister was Namakaeha. She belonged to the family of Pele, the goddess of volcanic fires, who had journeyed to Hawaii and taken up her home in the crater of the volcano Kilauea.

Namakaeha smelled smoke on the feathers which came to her, and knew that her brother was dead. She also knew that he could have been conquered only by one possessing great magical powers. So she called to his people: 'Who is the great *kupua* (wizard) who has killed my brother? Oh, my people, keep careful watch.'

Kukali was exploring all parts of the strange land in which he had already found marvelous adventures. By and by he came to the great pit in which Namakaeha lived. He could not see the bottom, so he told his companions he was going down to see what mysteries were concealed in this hole without a bottom. They made a rope of the hau tree bark. Fastening one end around his body he ordered his friends to let him down. Uttering prayers and incantations he went down and down until, owing to counter incantations of Namakaeha's priests, who had been watching, the rope broke and he fell.

Down he went swiftly, but, remembering the prayer which a falling man must use to keep him from injury, he cried, 'O Ku! guard my life!'

In the ancient Hawaiian mythology there was frequent mention of 'the water of life.' Sometimes the sick bathed in it and were healed. Sometimes it was sprinkled upon the unconscious, bringing them back to life. Kukali's incantation was of great power, for it threw him into a pool of the water of life and he was saved.

One of the *kahuna*s (priests) caring for Namakaeha was a very great wizard. He saw the wonderful preservation of Kukali and became his friend. He warned Kukali against eating anything that was ripe, because it would be poison, and even the most powerful charms could not save him.

Kukali thanked him and went out among the people. He had carefully preserved his wonderful banana skin, and was able to eat apparently ripe fruit and yet be perfectly safe.

The kahunas of Namakaeha tried to overcome him and destroy him, but he conquered them, killed those who were bad, and entered into friendship with those who were good.

At last he came to the place where the great chiefess dwelt. Here he was tested in many ways.

He accepted the fruits offered him, but always ate the food in his magic banana. Thus he preserved his strength and conquered even the chiefess and married her. After living with her for a time he began to long for his old home in Hawaii. Then he persuaded her to do as her relative Pele had already done, and the family, taking their large canoe, sailed away to Hawaii, their future home.

9

The Three Daughters of the King of the East, and the Son of a King in Erin

(Irish)

There was once a king in Erin, and he had an only son. While this son was a little child his mother died.

After a time the king married and had a second son.

The two boys grew up together; and as the elder was far handsomer and better than the younger, the queen became jealous, and was for banishing him out of her sight.

The king's castle stood near the shore of Loch Erne, and three swans came every day to be in the water and swim in the lake. The elder brother used to go fishing; and once when he sat at the side of the water, the three swans made young women of themselves, came to where he sat, and talked to the king's son.

The queen had a boy minding cows in the place, and when he went home that night he told about what he had seen,—that there were three young women at the lake, and the king's son was talking to the three that day. Next morning the queen called the cowboy to her, and said: 'Here is a pin of slumber; and do you stick it in the clothes of the king's son before the young women come, and when they go away, take out the pin and bring it back to me.'

That day when the cowboy saw the three young women coming, he went near and threw the pin, which stuck in the clothes of the king's son. That instant he fell asleep on the ground.

When the young women came, one of them took a towel, dipped it in the cold water of the lake, and rubbed his face; but she could not rouse him. When their time came to go, they were crying and lamenting because the young man was asleep; and one of the three put a gold pin in his bosom, so that when he woke up he would find it and keep her in mind.

After they had gone a couple of hours, the cowboy came up, took out the sleeping-pin, and hurried off. The king's son woke up without delay; and finding the gold pin in his bosom, he knew the young woman had come to see him.

Next day he fished and waited again. When the cowboy saw the young women coming out of the lake, he stole up a second time, and threw the pin, which stuck in his clothes, and that moment he was drowsy and fell asleep. When the young women came he was lying on the ground asleep. One of them rubbed him with a towel dipped in the water of the lake; but no matter what she did, he slept on, and when they had to go, she put a gold ring in his bosom. When the sisters were leaving the lake, and had put on their swan-skins and become swans, they all flew around him and flapped their wings in his face to know could they rouse him; but there was no use in trying.

After they had gone, the cowboy came and took out the sleeping-pin. When the king's son was awake he put his hand in his bosom, found the keepsake, and knew that the sisters had come to him.

When he went fishing the third day, he called up the cowboy and said: 'I fall asleep every day. I know something is done to me. Now do you tell me all. In time I'll reward you well. I know my stepmother sends something by you that takes my senses away.'

'I would tell,' said the cowboy, 'but I'm in dread my mistress might kill or banish me.'

'She will not, for I'll put you in the way she'll not harm you. You see my fishing-bag here? Now throw the pin, which I know you have, towards me, and hit the bag.'

The cowboy did as he was told, and threw the pin into the fishing-bag, where it remained without harm to any one. The cowboy went back to his cattle, and the prince fished on as before. The three swans were out in the middle of the lake swimming around for themselves in the water, and the prince moved on, fishing, till he came to a bend in the shore. On one side of him a tongue of land ran out into the lake. The swans came to the shore, leaving the piece of land between themselves and the prince. Then they took off their swan-skins, were young women, and bathed in the lake.

After that they came out, put on the dress of young women, and went to where the king's son was fishing.

He spoke to them, and asked where were they from, in what place were they born, and why were they swans.

They said: 'We are three sisters, daughters of the king of the East, and we have two brothers. Our mother died, and our father married again, and had two other daughters; and these two are not so good looking nor so well favoured as we, and their mother was in dread they wouldn't get such fine husbands as we, so she enchanted us, and now we are going about the world from lake to lake in the form of swans.'

Then the eldest of the three sisters said to the king's son: 'What kind are you, and where were you born?'

'I was born in Erin,' said he; 'and when I was a little boy my mother died, my father married again and had a second son, and that son wasn't to the eye what I was, and my stepmother was for banishing me from my father's house because she thought her own son was not so good as I was, and I am fishing here every day by the lake to keep out of her sight.'

'Well,' said the eldest sister, 'I thought you were a king's son, and so I came to you in my own form to know could we go on in the world together.'

'I don't know yet what to do,' said the king's son.

'Well, be sure of your mind to-morrow, for that will be the last day for me here.'

When the cowboy was going home, the king's son gave him the sleeping-pin for the stepmother. When he had driven in the cattle, the cowboy told the queen that the young man had fallen asleep as on the two other days.

But there was an old witch in the place who was wandering about the lake that day. She saw everything, went to the queen, and told her how the three swans had made young women of themselves, and talked with her stepson.

When the queen heard the old witch, she fell into a terrible rage at the cowboy for telling her a lie, and banished him out of her sight forever. Then she got another cowboy, and sent him off with the sleeping-pin next day. When he came near the lake, the king's son tried to drive him off; but the cowboy threw the sleeping-pin into his clothes, and he fell down near the edge of the water without sight or sense.

The three sisters came, and found him sleeping. They rubbed him, and threw water on his face, but they could not wake him. And the three were lamenting sorely, for they had brought a swan's skin with them that day, so the king's son might make a swan of himself and fly away with them, for this was their last day at that place; but they could do nothing now, for he lay there dead asleep on the ground before them.

The eldest sister pulled out her handkerchief, and the falling tears dropped on it. Then she took a knife, and cut one of the nipples from her breast. The second sister wrote on the handkerchief: 'Keep this in mind till you get more account from us.' They put it in his bosom and went away.

As soon as the sisters had gone, the cowboy came, drew out the pin, and hurried away. The stepmother was always trying to banish the king's son, hoping that something might happen to him, and her own son be the heir. So now he went off and wandered away through Erin, always inquiring for the eldest sister, but never could find her.

At the end of seven years he came home, and was fishing at the side of Loch Erne again, when a swan flew up to him and said: 'Your love is lying on her death-bed, unless you go to save her. She is bleeding from the breast, and you must go to her now. Go straight to the East!'

The king's son went straight to the East, and on the way there rose up storm and fog against him; but they did not stop him. He was going on always, and when he was three weeks' journey from his father's castle he stumbled one dark, misty day and fell over a ditch. When he rose up there stood on the other side of the ditch before him a little horse, all bridled and saddled, with a whip on the saddle. The horse spoke up and said: 'If you are the king's son, I was sent here to meet you, and carry you to the castle of the king of the East. There is a young woman at the castle who thinks it long till she sees you. Now ask me no questions, for I'm not at liberty to talk to you till I bring you to the East.'

'I suppose we are to be a long time going?' said the king's son.

'Don't trouble yourself about the going; I'll take you safely. Sit on my back now, and be sure you're a good rider, and you'll not be long on the road. This is my last word.'

They went on, and were going always; and as he travelled, the prince met the wind that was before him, and the wind that blew behind could not come up with him. When he was hungry the pommel of the saddle opened, and he found the best of eating inside.

They went on sweeping over the world for two weeks, and when they were near the East the horse said: 'Get down from my back now, for it's tired I am.'

'How far are we from the castle?' asked the king's son.

'Five days' journey,' answered the horse. 'When you come to the castle, don't stop a moment till you ask where the young woman is lying; and tell them to be sure to give good stabling and food to the horse. Come and see me yourself every day. If you don't, there will be nothing for me but fasting; and that's what I don't like.'

When the king's son came to the castle it was evening. The two younger sisters welcomed him. (These were two of the swans at the lake in Erin, and now at home by the enchantment of their stepmother. They were swans in the daytime, and women only at night, so as not to be under the eye of young men when these came to see the stepmother's own daughters.) They said: 'Our sister is on an island, and we'll go to her.' They got a boat for the young man, and went with him to where their sister was lying. They said to her: 'The son of the king of Erin is here.'

'Let him come in, that I may look at him,' said she.

The king's son went in, and when she saw him she was glad. 'Have you anything that belongs to me?' asked she.

'I have.'

'Then throw it on my breast.'

He threw the handkerchief on her breast and went away. Next day she rose from the bed as well as ever. On the third day after his arrival, the son of the king of Erin married the eldest daughter of the king of the East, and the stepmother's enchantment was destroyed; and there was the grandest wedding that ever was seen in that kingdom.

The king's son, thinking only of his bride, forgot all about the horse that had brought him over the long road. When at last he went to see him, the stable was empty; the horse had gone. And neither his father in Erin nor the stepmother came to his mind, he was living so pleasantly in the East. But after he had been there a long time, and a son and a daughter had been born to him, he remembered his father. Then he made up his mind not to let the stepmother's son be heir to the kingdom in place of himself. So taking his wife and children, he left the East and travelled to Erin. He stopped on the road, and sent word to the father that he was coming.

When the stepmother heard the news, a great weakness came on her. She fell into a fit and died.

The king's son waited in a convenient place till the funeral was over, and then he came to the castle and lived with his father. He was not long in the place when he sent messengers to know could they find the cowboy that the stepmother banished for telling about the sleeping-pin. They brought the cowboy to the castle, and the king made him his coachman.

The cowboy was not twelve months in his new place before he married. Then the king's son gave him a fine piece of land to live on, with six cows and four horses. There was not a happier man in the kingdom than the cowboy. When the father died, the king's son became king in Erin himself.

10

The Palace of the Ocean-Bed

(Japanese)

Ho-wori, Prince Fire-Fade, the son of Ninigi, was a great hunter. He caught 'things rough of hair and things soft of hair.' His elder brother Ho-deri, Prince Fire-Flash, was a fisher who caught 'things broad of fin and things narrow of fin.' But, often, when the wind blew and the waves ran high, he would spend hours on the sea and catch no fish. When the Storm God was abroad, Ho-deri had to stay at home, while at nightfall Ho-wori returned laden with spoil from the mountains. Ho-deri spoke to his brother, and said: 'I would have your bow and arrows and become a hunter. You shall have my fish-hook.' At first Ho-wori would not consent, but finally the exchange was made.

Now Prince Fire-Flash was no hunter. He could not track the game, nor run swiftly, nor take good aim. Day after day Prince Fire-Fade went out to sea. In vain he threw his line; he caught no fish. Moreover, one day, he lost his brother's fish-hook. Then Ho-deri came to Ho-wori, and said: 'There is the luck of the mountain and there is the luck of the sea. Let each restore to the other his luck.' Ho-wori replied: 'I did not catch a single fish with your hook, and now it is lost in the sea.' The elder brother was very angry, and, with many hard words, demanded the return of his treasure. Prince Fire-Fade was unhappy. He broke in pieces his good sword and made five hundred fish-hooks which he offered to his brother. But this did not appease the wrath of Prince

Fire-Flash, who still raged and asked for his own hook.

Ho-wori could find neither comfort nor help. He sat one day by the shore and heaved a deep sigh. The Old Man of the Sea heard the sigh, and asked the cause of his sorrow. Ho-wori told him of the loss of the fish-hook, and of his brother's displeasure. Thereupon the wise man promised to give his help. He plaited strips of bamboo so tightly together that the water could not pass through, and fashioned therewith a stout little boat. Into this boat Ho-wori jumped, and was carried far out to sea.

After a time, as the old man had foretold, his boat began to sink. Deeper and deeper it sank, until at last he came to a glittering palace of fishes' scales. In front of it was a well, shaded by a great cassia tree. Prince Fire-Fade sat among the wide-spreading branches. He looked down, and saw a maiden approach the well; in her hand she carried a jewelled bowl. She was the lovely Toyo-tama, Peerless Jewel, the daughter of Wata-tsu-mi, the Sea-King. Ho-wori was spellbound by her strange wave-like beauty, her long flowing hair, her soft deep blue eyes. The maiden stooped to fill her bowl. Suddenly, she saw the reflection of Prince Fire-Fade in the water; she dropped the precious bowl, and it fell in a thousand pieces. Toyo-tama hastened to her father, and exclaimed, 'A man, with the grace and beauty of a god, sits in the branches of the cassia tree. I have seen his picture in the waters of the well.' The Sea-King knew that it must be the great hunter, Prince Fire-Fade.

Then Wata-tsu-mi went forth and stood under the cassia tree. He looked up to Ho-wori, and said: 'Come down, O Son of the Gods, and enter my Palace of the Ocean-Bed.' Ho-wori obeyed, and was led into the palace and seated on a throne of sea-asses' skins. A banquet was prepared in his honour. The *hashi* were delicate branches of coral, and the plates were of silvery mother-of-pearl. The clear-rock wine was sipped from cup-shaped ocean blooms with long slender stalks. Ho-wori thought that never before had there been such a banquet. When it was ended he went with Toyo-tama to the roof of the palace. Dimly, through the blue waters that moved above, he could discern the Sun-Goddess. He saw the mountains and valleys of ocean, the waving forests of tall sea-plants, the homes of the *shaké* and the *kani*.

Ho-wori told Wata-tsu-mi of the loss of the fish-hook. Then the Sea-King called all his subjects together and questioned them. No fish knew aught of the hook, but, said the lobster: 'As I sat one day in my crevice among the rocks, the *tai* passed near me. His mouth was swollen, and he went by without giving me greeting.' Wata-tsu-mi then noticed that the tai had not answered his summons. A messenger, fleet of fin, was sent to fetch him. When the tai appeared, the lost fish-hook was found in his poor wounded mouth. It was restored to Ho-wori, and he was happy. Toyo-tama became his bride, and they lived together in the cool fish-scale palace.

Prince Fire-Fade came to understand the secrets of the ocean, the cause of its anger, the cause of its joy. The Storm-Spirit of the upper sea did not rule in the ocean-bed, and night after night Ho-wori was rocked to sleep by the gentle motion of the waters.

Many tides had ebbed and flowed, when, in the quiet of the night, Ho-wori heaved a deep sigh. Toyo-tama was troubled, and told her father that, as Ho-wori dreamt of his home on the earth, a great longing had come over him to visit it once more. Then Wata-tsu-mi gave into Ho-wori's hands two great jewels, the one to rule the flow, the other to rule the ebb of the tide. He spoke thus: 'Return to earth on the head of my trusted sea-dragon. Restore the lost fish-hook to Ho-deri. If he is still wroth with you, bring forth the tide-flowing jewel, and the waters shall cover him. If he asks your forgiveness, bring forth the tide-ebbing jewel, and it shall be well with him.'

Ho-wori left the Palace of the Ocean-Bed, and was carried swiftly to his own land.

As he set foot on the shore, he ungirded his sword, and tied it round the neck of the sea-dragon. Then he said: 'Take this to the Sea-King as a token of my love and gratitude.'

11

Sif, the Golden-Haired

(Norse)

Sif, Thor's wife, was very vain of a magnificent head of long golden hair which covered her from head to foot like a brilliant veil; and as she too was a symbol of the earth, her hair was said to represent the long grass, or the golden grain covering the Northern harvest fields. Thor was very proud of his wife's beautiful hair; imagine his dismay, therefore, upon waking one morning, to find her shorn, and as bald and denuded of ornament as the earth when the grain has been garnered, and nothing but the stubble remains! In his anger, Thor sprang to his feet, vowing he would punish the perpetrator of this outrage, whom he immediately and rightly conjectured to be Loki, the arch-plotter, ever on the look-out for some evil deed to perform. Seizing his hammer, Thor went in search of Loki, who attempted to evade the irate god by changing his form. But it was all to no purpose; Thor soon overtook him, and without more ado caught him by the throat, and almost strangled him ere he yielded to his imploring signs and relaxed his powerful grip. When he could draw his breath, Loki begged forgiveness, but all his entreaties were vain, until he promised to procure for Sif a new head of hair, as beautiful as the first, and as luxuriant in growth.

And thence for Sif new tresses I'll bring
Of gold, ere the daylight's gone,
So that she shall liken a field in spring,

With its yellow-flowered garment on.

The Dwarfs, Oehlenschläger (Pigott's tr.).

Then Thor consented to let the traitor go; so Loki rapidly crept down into the bowels of the earth, where Svart-alfa-heim was situated, to beg the dwarf Dvalin to fashion not only the precious hair, but a present for Odin and Frey, whose anger he wished to disarm.

His request was favourably received and the dwarf fashioned the spear Gungnir, which never failed in its aim, and the ship Skidbladnir, which, always wafted by favourable winds, could sail through the air as well as on the water, and which had this further magic property, that although it could contain the gods and all their steeds, it could be folded up into the very smallest compass and thrust in one's pocket. Lastly, he spun the finest golden thread, from which he fashioned the hair required for Sif, declaring that as soon as it touched her head it would grow fast there and become as her own.

Though they now seem dead, let them touch but her head,
Each hair shall the life-moisture fill;
Nor shall malice nor spell henceforward prevail
Sif's tresses to work aught of ill.

The Dwarfs, Oehlenschläger (Pigott's tr.).

Loki was so pleased with these proofs of the dwarfs' skill that he declared the son of Ivald to be the most clever of smiths—words which were overheard by Brock, another dwarf, who exclaimed that he was sure his brother Sindri could produce three objects which would surpass those which Loki held, not only in intrinsic value, but also in magical properties. Loki immediately challenged the dwarf to show his skill, wagering his head against Brock's on the result of the undertaking.

Sindri, apprised of the wager, accepted Brock's offer to blow the bellows, warning him, however, that he must work persistently and not for a moment relax his efforts if he wished him to succeed; then he threw some gold in the fire, and went out to bespeak the favour of the hidden powers. During his absence Brock diligently plied the bellows, while Loki, hoping to make him pause, changed himself into a gadfly and cruelly stung his hand. In spite of the pain, the dwarf kept on blowing, and when Sindri returned, he drew out of the fire an enormous wild boar, called Gullin-bursti, because of its golden bristles, which had the power of radiating light as it flitted across the sky, for it could travel through the air with marvellous velocity.

And now, strange to tell, from the roaring fire
Came the golden-haired Gullinbörst,
To serve as a charger the sun-god Frey,
Sure, of all wild boars this the first.

The Dwarfs, Oehlenschläger (Pigott's tr.).

This first piece of work successfully completed, Sindri flung some more gold on the fire and bade his brother resume blowing, while he again went out to secure magic assistance. This time Loki, still disguised as a gadfly, stung the dwarf on his cheek; but in spite of the pain Brock worked on, and when Sindri returned, he triumphantly drew out of the flames the magic ring Draupnir, the emblem of fertility, from which eight similar rings dropped every ninth night.

They worked it and turned it with wondrous skill,
Till they gave it the virtue rare,
That each thrice third night from its rim there fell
Eight rings, as their parent fair.

The Dwarfs, Oehlenschläger (Pigott's tr.).

Now a lump of iron was cast in the flames, and with renewed caution not to forfeit their success by inattention, Sindri passed out, leaving Brock to ply the bellows as before. Loki was now in desperation and he prepared for a final effort. This time, still in the guise of the gadfly, he stung the dwarf above the eye until the blood began to flow in such a stream, that it prevented his seeing what he was doing. Hastily raising his hand for a second, Brock dashed aside the stream of blood; but short as was the interruption it had worked irreparable harm, and when Sindri drew his work out of the fire he uttered an exclamation of disappointment for the hammer he had fashioned was short in the handle.

> Then the dwarf raised his hand to his brow for the smart,
> Ere the iron well out was beat,
> And they found that the haft by an inch was too short,
> But to alter it then 'twas too late.
>
> *The Dwarfs, Oehlenschläger (Pigott's tr.).*

Notwithstanding this mishap, Brock was sure of winning the wager and he did not hesitate to present himself before the gods in Asgard, where he gave Odin the ring Draupnir, Frey the boar Gullin-bursti, and Thor the hammer Miölnir, whose power none could resist.

Loki in turn gave the spear Gungnir to Odin, the ship Skidbladnir to Frey, and the golden hair to Thor; but although the latter immediately grew upon Sif's head and was unanimously declared more beautiful than her own locks had ever been, the gods decreed that Brock had won the wager, on the ground that the hammer Miölnir, in Thor's hands, would prove invaluable against the frost giants on the last day.

> And at their head came Thor,
> Shouldering his hammer, which the giants know.
>
> *Balder Dead (Matthew Arnold).*

In order to save his head, Loki fled precipitately, but was overtaken by Thor, who brought him back and handed him over to Brock, telling him, however, that although Loki's head was rightfully his, he must not touch his neck. Hindered from obtaining full vengeance, the dwarf determined to punish Loki by sewing his lips together, and as his sword would not pierce them, he borrowed his brother's awl for the purpose. However, Loki, after enduring the gods' gibes in silence for a little while, managed to cut the string and soon after was as loquacious as ever.

In spite of his redoubtable hammer, Thor was not held in dread as the injurious god of the storm, who destroyed peaceful homesteads and ruined the harvest by sudden hail-storms and cloud-bursts. The Northmen fancied he hurled it only against ice giants and rocky walls, reducing the latter to powder to fertilize the earth and make it yield plentiful fruit to the tillers of the soil.

In Germany, where the eastern storms are always cold and blighting, while the western bring warm rains and mild weather, Thor was supposed to journey always from west to east, to wage war against the evil spirits which would fain have enveloped the country in impenetrable veils of mist and have bound it in icy fetters.

12

Koshchei the Deathless

(Russian)

In a certain country there once lived a king, and he had three sons, all of them grown up. All of a sudden Koshchei the Deathless carried off their mother. Then the eldest son craved his father's blessing, that he might go and look for his mother. His father gave him his blessing, and he went off and disappeared, leaving no trace behind. The second son waited and waited, then he too obtained his father's blessing—and he also disappeared. Then the youngest son, Prince Ivan, said to his father, 'Father, give me your blessing, and let me go and look for my mother.'

But his father would not let him go, saying, 'Your brothers are no more; if you likewise go away, I shall die of grief.'

'Not so, father. But if you bless me I shall go; and if you do not bless me I shall go.'

So his father gave him his blessing.

Prince Ivan went to choose a steed, but every one that he laid his hand upon gave way under it. He could not find a steed to suit him, so he wandered with drooping brow along the road and about the town. Suddenly there appeared an old woman, who asked:

'Why hangs your brow so low, Prince Ivan?'

'Be off, old crone,' he replied. 'If I put you on one of my hands, and give it a slap with the other, there'll be a little wet left, that's all.' The old woman ran down a by-street, came to meet him a second time, and said:

'Good day, Prince Ivan! why hangs your brow so low?'

Then he thought:

'Why does this old woman ask me? Mightn't she be of use to me?'—and he replied:

'Well, mother! because I cannot get myself a good steed.'

'Silly fellow!' she cried, 'to suffer, and not to ask the old woman's help! Come along with me.'

She took him to a hill, showed him a certain spot, and said:

'Dig up that piece of ground.'

Prince Ivan dug it up and saw an iron plate with twelve padlocks on it. He immediately broke off the padlocks, tore open a door, and followed a path leading underground. There, fastened with twelve chains, stood a heroic steed which evidently heard the approaching steps of a rider worthy to mount it, and so began to neigh and to struggle, until it broke all twelve of its chains. Then Prince Ivan put on armour fit for a hero, and bridled the horse, and saddled it with a Circassian saddle. And he gave the old woman money, and said to her:

'Forgive me, mother, and bless me!' then he mounted his steed and rode away.

Long time did he ride; at last he came to a mountain—a tremendously high mountain, and so steep that it was utterly impossible to get up it. Presently his brothers came that way. They all greeted each other, and rode on together, till they came to an iron rock a hundred and fifty poods in weight, and on it was this inscription, 'Whosoever will fling this rock against the mountain, to him will a way be opened.' The two elder brothers were unable to lift the rock, but Prince Ivan at the first try flung it against the mountain—and immediately there appeared a ladder leading up the mountain side.

Prince Ivan dismounted, let some drops of blood run from his little finger into a glass, gave it to his brothers, and said:

'If the blood in this glass turns black, tarry here no longer: that will mean that I am about to die.' Then he took leave of them and went his way.

He mounted the hill. What did not he see there? All sorts of trees were there, all sorts of fruits, all sorts of birds! Long did Prince Ivan walk on; at last he came to a house, a huge house! In it lived a king's daughter who had been carried off by Koshchei the Deathless. Prince Ivan walked round the enclosure, but could not see any doors. The king's daughter saw there was some one there, came on to the balcony, and called out to him, 'See, there is a chink in the enclosure; touch it with your little finger, and it will become a door.'

What she said turned out to be true. Prince Ivan went into the house, and the maiden received him kindly, gave him to eat and to drink, and then began to question him. He told her how he had come to rescue his mother from Koshchei the Deathless. Then the maiden said:

'It will be difficult for you to get at your mother, Prince Ivan. You see, Koshchei is not mortal: he will kill you. He often comes here to see me. There is his sword, fifty poods in weight. Can you lift it? If so, you may venture to go.'

Not only did Prince Ivan lift the sword, but he tossed it high in the air. So he went on his way again.

By-and-by he came to a second house. He knew now where to look for the door, and he entered in. There was his mother. With tears did they embrace each other.

Here also did he try his strength, heaving aloft a ball which weighed some fifteen hundred poods. The time came for Koshchei the Deathless to arrive. The mother hid away her son. Suddenly Koshchei the Deathless entered the house and cried out, 'Phou, Phou! A Russian bone one usen't to hear with one's ears, or see with one's eyes, but now a Russian bone has come to the house! Who has been with you? Wasn't it your son?'

'What are you talking about, God bless you! You've been flying through Russia, and got the air up your nostrils, that's why you fancy it's here,' answered Prince Ivan's mother, and then she drew nigh to Koshchei, addressed him in terms of affection, asked him about one thing and another, and at last said:

'Whereabouts is your death, O Koshchei?'

'My death,' he replied, 'is in such a place. There stands an oak, and under the oak is a casket, and in the casket is a hare, and in the hare is a duck, and in the duck is an egg, and in the egg is my death.'

Having thus spoken, Koshchei the Deathless tarried there a little longer, and then flew away.

The time came—Prince Ivan received his mother's blessing, and went to look for Koshchei's death. He went on his way a long time without eating or drinking; at last he felt mortally hungry, and thought, 'If only something would come my way!' Suddenly there appeared a young wolf; he determined to kill it. But out from a hole sprang the she wolf, and said, 'Don't hurt my little one; I'll do you a good turn.' Very good! Prince Ivan let the young wolf go. On he went and saw a crow. 'Stop a bit,' he thought, 'here I shall get a mouthful.' He loaded his gun and was going to shoot, but the crow exclaimed, 'Don't hurt me; I'll do you a good turn.'

Prince Ivan thought the matter over and spared the crow. Then he went farther, and came to a sea and stood still on the shore. At that moment a young pike suddenly jumped out of the water and fell on the strand. He caught hold of it, and thought—for he was half dead with hunger—'Now I shall have something to eat.' All of a sudden appeared a pike and said, 'Don't hurt my little one, Prince Ivan; I'll do you a good turn.' And so he spared the little pike also.

But how was he to cross the sea? He sat down on the shore and meditated. But the pike knew quite well what he was thinking about, and laid herself right across the sea. Prince Ivan walked along her back, as if he were going over a bridge, and came to the oak where Koshchei's death was. There he found the casket and opened it—out jumped the hare and ran away. How was the hare to be stopped?

Prince Ivan was terribly frightened at having let the hare escape, and gave himself up to gloomy thoughts; but a wolf, the one he had refrained from killing, rushed after the hare, caught it, and brought it to Prince Ivan. With great delight he seized the hare, cut it open—and had such a fright! Out popped the duck and flew away. He fired after it, but shot all on one side, so again he gave himself up to his thoughts. Suddenly there appeared the crow with her little crows, and set off after the duck, and caught it, and brought it to Prince Ivan. The Prince was greatly pleased and got hold of the egg. Then he went on his way. But when he came to the sea, he began washing the egg, and let it drop into the water. However was he to get it out of the water? an immeasurable depth! Again the Prince gave himself up to dejection.

Suddenly the sea became violently agitated, and the pike brought him the egg. Moreover it stretched itself across the sea. Prince Ivan walked along it to the other side, and then he set out again for his mother's. When he got there, they greeted each other lovingly, and then she hid him again as before. Presently in flew Koshchei the Deathless and said:

'Phoo, Phoo! No Russian bone can the ear hear nor the eye see, but there's a smell of Russia here!'

'What are you talking about, Koshchei? There's no one with me,' replied Prince Ivan's mother.

A second time spake Koshchei and said, 'I feel rather unwell.'

Then Prince Ivan began squeezing the egg, and thereupon Koshchei the Deathless bent double. At last Prince Ivan came out from his hiding-place, held up the egg and said, 'There is your death, O Koshchei the Deathless!'

Then Koshchei fell on his knees before him, saying, 'Don't kill me, Prince Ivan! Let's be friends! All the world will lie at our feet.'

But these words had no weight with Prince Ivan. He smashed the egg, and Koshchei the Deathless died.

Ivan and his mother took all they wanted and started homewards. On their way they came to where the King's daughter was whom Ivan had seen on his way, and they took her with them too. They went further, and came to the hill where Ivan's brothers were still waiting for him. Then the maiden said, 'Prince Ivan! do go back to my house. I have forgotten a marriage robe, a diamond ring, and a pair of seamless shoes.'

He consented to do so, but in the mean time he let his mother go down the ladder, as well as the Princess—whom it had been settled he was to marry when they got home. They were received by his brothers, who then set to work and cut away the ladder, so that he himself would not be able to get down. And they used such threats to his mother and the Princess, that they made them promise not to tell about Prince Ivan when they got home. And after a time they reached their native country. Their father was delighted at seeing his wife and his two sons, but still he was grieved about the other one, Prince Ivan.

But Prince Ivan returned to the home of his betrothed, and got the wedding dress, and the ring, and the seamless shoes. Then he came back to the mountain and tossed the ring from one hand to the other. Immediately there appeared twelve strong youths, who said:

'What are your commands?'

'Carry me down from this hill.'

The youths immediately carried him down. Prince Ivan put the ring on his finger—they disappeared.

Then he went on to his own country, and arrived at the city

in which his father and brothers lived.

There he took up his quarters in the house of an old woman, and asked her:

'What news is there, mother, in your country?'

'What news, lad? You see our Queen was kept in prison by Koshchei the Deathless. Her three sons went to look for her, and two of them found her and came back, but the third, Prince Ivan, has disappeared, and no one knows where he is. The King is very unhappy about him. And those two Princes and their mother brought a certain Princess back with them; and the eldest son wants to marry her, but she declares he must fetch her her betrothal ring first, or get one made just as she wants it. But although they have made a public proclamation about it, no one has been found to do it yet.'

'Well, mother, go and tell the King that you will make one. I'll manage it for you,' said Prince Ivan.

So the old woman immediately dressed herself, and hastened to the King, and said:

'Please, your Majesty, I will make the wedding ring.'

'Make it, then, make it, mother! Such people as you are welcome,' said the King. 'But if you don't make it, off goes your head!'

The old woman was dreadfully frightened; she ran home, and told Prince Ivan to set to work at the ring. But Ivan lay down to sleep, troubling himself very little about it. The ring was there all the time. So he only laughed at the old woman, but she was trembling all over, and crying, and scolding him.

'As for you,' she said, 'you're out of the scrape; but you've done for me, fool that I was!'

The old woman cried and cried until she fell asleep. Early in the morning Prince Ivan got up and awakened her, saying:

'Get up, mother, and go out! take them the ring, and mind, don't accept more than one ducat for it. If anyone asks who made the ring, say you made it yourself; don't say a word about me.'

The old woman was overjoyed and carried off the ring. The bride was delighted with it.

'Just what I wanted,' she said. So they gave the old woman a dish full of gold, but she took only one ducat.

'Why do you take so little?' said the King.

'What good would a lot do me, your Majesty? if I want some more afterwards, you'll give it me.'

Having said this the old woman went away.

Time passed, and the news spread abroad that the bride had told her lover to fetch her her wedding-dress or else to get one made, just such a one as she wanted. Well, the old woman, thanks to Prince Ivan's aid, succeeded in this matter too, and took her the wedding-dress. And afterwards she took her the seamless shoes also, and would only accept one ducat each time and always said that she had made the things herself.

Well, the people heard that there would be a wedding at the palace on such-and-such a day. And the day they all anxiously awaited came at last. Then Prince Ivan said to the old woman:

'Look here, mother! when the bride is just going to be married, let me know.'

The old woman didn't let the time go by unheeded.

Then Ivan immediately put on his princely raiment, and went out of the house.

'See, mother, this is what I'm really like!' says he.

The old woman fell at his feet.

'Pray forgive me for scolding you,' said she.

'God be with you,' said he. So he went into the church and, finding his brothers had not yet arrived, he stood up alongside of the bride and got married to her. Then he and she were escorted back to the palace, and as they went along, the proper bridegroom, his eldest brother, met them. But when he saw that his bride and Prince Ivan were being escorted home together, he turned back again ignominiously.

As to the King, he was delighted to see Prince Ivan again, and when he had learnt all about the treachery of his brothers, after the wedding feast had been solemnized, he banished the two elder princes, but he made Ivan heir to the throne.

13

The Baba Yaga

(Russian)

Once upon a time there was an old couple. The husband lost his wife and married again. But he had a daughter by the first marriage, a young girl, and she found no favour in the eyes of her evil stepmother, who used to beat her, and consider how she could get her killed outright. One day the father went away somewhere or other, so the stepmother said to the girl, 'Go to your aunt, my sister, and ask her for a needle and thread to make you a shift.'

Now that aunt was a Baba Yaga. Well, the girl was no fool, so she went to a real aunt of hers first, and says she:

'Good morning, auntie!'

'Good morning, my dear! what have you come for?'

'Mother has sent me to her sister, to ask for a needle and thread to make me a shift.'

Then her aunt instructed her what to do. 'There is a birch-tree there, niece, which would hit you in the eye—you must tie a ribbon round it; there are doors which would creak and bang—you must pour oil on their hinges; there are dogs which would tear you in pieces—you must throw them these rolls; there is a cat which would scratch your eyes out—you must give it a piece of bacon.'

So the girl went away, and walked and walked, till she came to the place. There stood a hut, and in it sat weaving the Baba

Yaga, the Bony-shanks.

'Good morning, auntie,' says the girl.

'Good morning, my dear,' replies the Baba Yaga.

'Mother has sent me to ask you for a needle and thread to make me a shift.'

'Very well; sit down and weave a little in the meantime.'

So the girl sat down behind the loom, and the Baba Yaga went outside, and said to her servant-maid:

'Go and heat the bath, and get my niece washed; and mind you look sharp after her. I want to breakfast off her.'

Well, the girl sat there in such a fright that she was as much dead as alive. Presently she spoke imploringly to the servant-maid, saying:

'Kinswoman dear, do please wet the firewood instead of making it burn; and fetch the water for the bath in a sieve.' And she made her a present of a handkerchief.

The Baba Yaga waited awhile; then she came to the window and asked:

'Are you weaving, niece? are you weaving, my dear?'

'Oh yes, dear aunt, I'm weaving.' So the Baba Yaga went away again, and the girl gave the Cat a piece of bacon, and asked:

'Is there no way of escaping from here?'

'Here's a comb for you and a towel,' said the Cat; 'take them, and be off. The Baba Yaga will pursue you, but you must lay your ear on the ground, and when you hear that she is close at hand, first of all throw down the towel. It will become a wide, wide river. And if the Baba Yaga gets across the river, and tries to catch you, then you must lay your ear on the ground again, and when you hear that she is close at hand, throw down the comb. It will become a dense, dense forest; through that she won't be able to force her way anyhow.'

The girl took the towel and the comb and fled. The dogs would have rent her, but she threw them the rolls, and they let her go by; the doors would have begun to bang, but she poured oil on their hinges, and they let her pass through; the birch-tree would have poked her eyes out, but she tied the ribbon around it, and it let her pass on. And the Cat sat down to the loom, and worked away; muddled everything about, if it didn't do much weaving. Up came the Baba Yaga to the window, and asked:

'Are you weaving, niece? are you weaving, my dear?'

'I'm weaving, dear aunt, I'm weaving,' gruffly replied the Cat.

The Baba Yaga rushed into the hut, saw that the girl was gone, and took to beating the Cat, and abusing it for not having scratched the girl's eyes out. 'Long as I've served you,' said the Cat, 'you've never given me so much as a bone; but she gave me bacon.' Then the Baba Yaga pounced upon the dogs, on the doors, on the birch-tree, and on the servant-maid, and set to work to abuse them all, and to knock them about. Then the dogs said to her, 'Long as we've served you, you've never so much as pitched us a burnt crust; but she gave us rolls to eat.' And the doors said, 'Long as we've served you, you've never poured even a drop of water on our hinges; but she poured oil on us.' The birch-tree said, 'Long as I've served you, you've never tied a single thread round me; but she fastened a ribbon around me.' And the servant-maid said, 'Long as I've served you, you've never given me so much as a rag; but she gave me a handkerchief.'

The Baba Yaga, bony of limb, quickly jumped into her mortar, sent it flying along with the pestle, sweeping away the while all traces of its flight with a broom, and set off in pursuit of the girl. Then the girl put her ear to the ground, and when she heard that the Baba Yaga was chasing her, and was now close at hand, she flung down the towel. And it became a wide, such a wide river! Up came the Baba Yaga to the river, and gnashed her teeth with spite; then she went home for her oxen, and drove them to the river. The oxen drank up every drop of the river, and then the Baba Yaga began the pursuit anew. But the girl put her ear to the ground again, and when she heard that the Baba Yaga was near, she flung down the comb, and instantly a forest sprang up, such an awfully thick one! The Baba Yaga began gnawing away at it, but however hard she worked, she couldn't gnaw her way through it, so she had to go back again.

But by this time the girl's father had returned home, and he asked:

'Where's my daughter?'

'She's gone to her aunt's,' replied her stepmother.

Soon afterwards the girl herself came running home.

'Where have you been?' asked her father.

'Ah, father!' she said, 'mother sent me to aunt's to ask for a needle and thread to make me a shift. But aunt's a Baba Yaga, and she wanted to eat me!'

'And how did you get away, daughter?'

'Why like this,' said the girl, and explained the whole matter. As soon as her father had heard all about it, he became wroth with his wife, and shot her. But he and his daughter lived on and flourished, and everything went well with them.

14

Pelops, the Hero of the Peloponnesos

(*Greek*)

Some of the heroes famed in Greek song and story, and whose descendants lived in Greece, had come from foreign countries, many of them from Asia Minor. Greece and Asia Minor had always been closely connected. Travellers from each were in the habit of visiting the other country. Sometimes they traded together and sometimes made war on each other.

One of the most powerful kingdoms of Asia Minor was Phrygia, and it was ruled by a king of the name of Tantalos, who had at first governed wisely and in the fear of the gods. He was made arrogant by prosperity, and at length grew so overbearing and cruel even to his own son, Pelops, that the gods determined to make an example of him. They sent him living to Tartaros, the portion of Hades reserved for the very worst offenders, there to endure a terrible punishment forever.

He was placed up to his waist in the midst of running water, clear and cool, under hanging boughs laden with lovely fruit. Yet he could not reach the water or the fruit, and was always faint with hunger and thirst. Whenever he bent down to get a drink of water it rapidly rushed away from him, and if he lifted up his hand to pluck some of the ripe fragrant fruit, a sudden gust of wind tossed the branches high up into the air. Poor Tantalos never came nearer than this to quenching his thirst or satisfying his hunger.

To make his misery more unbearable, a huge block of rock was poised above his head, so lightly that it moved with every breeze, and he was in perpetual fear of its falling down on him. Pelops, the son whom he had abused in childhood, became a great favourite with the gods, and they wished to make up to him for his father's cruelty. They gave him a shoulder of ivory to replace the shoulder of which his father had deprived him. When he grew up the gods helped him to leave his native land, where he had been ill-treated, and they guided him across the Ægean Sea, and around the southern point of Greece to Elis, where Herakles had cleaned out the stables of Augeias. The capital of Elis was the city of Pisa, where a king ruled who had a beautiful daughter named Hippodameia. She must have been very fond of sports and athletics, for her name means 'The Tamer of Horses.'

Hippodameia had many suitors, but her father, Oenomaos, had heard that he would be dethroned by his daughter's husband, and so he did not wish her to marry. He was very warlike, being a son of Ares, the God of War, and he determined to kill all the suitors. So he proposed a chariot race with each of the wooers, and promised that the one who succeeded in winning the race should have his daughter in marriage; on the other hand, if the suitor lost the race he should be put to death by the king.

Oenomaos was a famous charioteer, and he had steeds which were swifter than the wind. The race-course began at Pisa, and stretched as far as the Isthmus of Corinth to the altar of Poseidon. Oenomaos believed in himself and in his own skill. So great was his self-reliance, and so sure was he of the swiftness of his horses, that whenever a suitor came along he let him go ahead with his chariot drawn by four horses, while he himself first sacrificed a ram to Zeus, and only at the end of the ceremony mounted his chariot, having as driver, Myrtilos, and being armed with a strong spear. Then he would overtake the suitor and kill him. Thus he had already killed a great many.

Pelops, on his arrival at Pisa, saw Hippodameia, and at once had a strong desire to make her his wife. When he saw that he could not conquer Oenomaos by fair means he planned a trick. He secretly approached the king's charioteer, Myrtilos, and said to him: 'Myrtilos, hear what I have to say to thee. Help me to win the race and I will give thee half the kingdom when I become King of Pisa.'

Hippodameia, too, who greatly admired the young man, advised the charioteer to lend them his aid. Myrtilos accepted the proposal of Pelops. On the day of the race Oenomaos again waited to sacrifice a ram to Zeus, leaving Pelops to drive on ahead, and only mounted his chariot after the offering was over, being sure that he should overtake the suitor as he had done with the others.

But suddenly a wheel flew off from the king's chariot, and Oenomaos fell to the ground, hurting himself badly. Myrtilos had removed the pin which held the wheel on to the axle. Thus Pelops reached the Isthmus before the king and won the race.

Oenomaos died of his injuries, and Pelops married Hippodameia, and took possession of the kingdom. Then Myrtilos demanded half the kingdom as it had been promised him by Pelops. But Pelops carried him to the sea and cast him into it. On account of this crime the descendants of Pelops, the Pelopides, had to suffer many misfortunes. Crime and craft may answer an immediate purpose, but they are followed by divine wrath.

Pelops instituted the famous Olympic games, which were celebrated every fourth year, and lasted five days. And he did many other things which were of great use to his people. In honour of Pelops, the great peninsula, south of the Isthmus of Corinth, was called Peloponnesos, which means Pelops' Island. The name was not quite correct at the time, for the land was not an island but a peninsula. But after all these thousands of years it has curiously come to pass that the old name is a true one, for it was only a few years ago that the Isthmus of Corinth was cut in two, and the Peloponnesos was in truth made an island.

15

He of the Little Shell

(Native American)

Once upon a time, all the people of a certain country had died, excepting two helpless children, a baby boy and a little girl.

When their parents died, these children were asleep. The little girl, who was the elder, was the first to awake. She looked around her, but seeing nobody beside her little brother, who lay smiling in his dreams, she quietly resumed her bed.

At the end of ten days her brother moved, without opening his eyes.

At the end of ten days more he changed his position, lying on the other side, and in this way he kept on sleeping for a long time; and pleasant, too, must have been his dreams, for his little sister never looked at him that he was not quite a little heaven of smiles and flashing lights, which beamed about his head and filled the lodge with a strange splendor.

The girl soon grew to be a woman, but the boy increased in stature very slowly. It was a long time before he could even creep, and he was well advanced in years before he could stand alone. When he was able to walk, his sister made him a little bow and arrows, and hung around his neck a small shell, saying:

'You shall be called Dais-Imid, or He of the Little Shell.'

Every day he would go out with his little bow, shooting at the small birds. The first bird he killed was a tom-tit. His sister was highly pleased when he took it to her. She carefully prepared and stuffed it, and put it away for him.

The next day he killed a red squirrel. His sister preserved this, too. The third day he killed a partridge, and this they had for their evening meal.

After this he acquired more courage, and would venture some distance from home. His skill and success as a hunter daily increased, and he killed the deer, bear, moose, and other large animals inhabiting the forest.

At last, although so very small of stature, he became a great hunter, and all that he shot he brought home and shared with his sister; and whenever he entered the lodge, a light beamed about his head and filled the place with a strange splendor.

He had now arrived at the years of manhood, but he still remained a perfect infant in size.

One day, walking about in quest of game, he came to a small lake.

It was in the winter season; and upon the ice of the lake he saw a man of giant height, employed killing beavers.

Comparing himself with this great man, he felt that he was no bigger than an insect. He seated himself on the shore and watched his movements.

When the large man had killed many beavers, he put them on a hand-sled which he had, and pursued his way home. When he saw him retire, the dwarf hunter followed, and, wielding his magic shell, he cut off the tail of one of the beavers, and ran home with the prize.

The giant, on reaching his lodge with his sled-load of beavers, was surprised to find one of them shorn of its tail.

The next day the little hero of the shell went to the same lake. The giant, who had been busy there for some time, had already loaded his sled and commenced his return; but running nimbly forward and overtaking him, he succeeded in securing another of the beaver-tails.

'I wonder,' said the giant, on reaching his lodge and overlooking his beavers, 'what dog it is that has thus cheated me. Could I meet him, I would make his flesh quiver at the point of my javelin.'

The giant forgot that he had taken these very beavers out of a beaver-dam which belonged to the little shell-man and his sister, without permission.

The next day he pursued his hunting at the bea ver-dam near the lake, and he was again followed by the little man with the shell.

This time the giant was so nimble in his movements that he had nearly reached home before the Shell, make the best speed he could, could overtake him; but he was just in time to clip another beaver's tail before the sled slipped into the lodge.

The giant would have been a patient giant, indeed, if his anger had not been violent at these constant tricks played upon him. What vexed him most, was, that he could not get a sight of his enemy. Sharp eyes he would have needed to do so, inasmuch as he of the little shell had the gift of making himself invisible whenever he chose.

The giant, giving vent to his feelings with many loud rumbling words, looked sharply around to see whether he could discover any tracks. He could find none. The unknown had stepped too lightly to leave the slightest mark behind.

The next day the giant resolved to disappoint his mysterious follower by going to the beaver-dam very early; and accordingly, when the little shell man came to the place he found the fresh traces of his work, but the giant had already gone away. He followed hard upon his tracks, but he failed to overtake him. When he of the little shell came in sight of the lodge, the stranger was in front of it, employed in skinning his beavers.

As Dais-Imid stood looking at him—for he had been all this

time invisible—he thought:

'I will let him have a view of me.'

Presently the man, who proved to be no less a personage than the celebrated giant, Manabozho, looked up and saw him.

After regarding him with attention, 'Who are you, little man?' said Manabozho. 'I have a mind to kill you.'

The little hero of the shell replied:

'If you were to try to kill me you could not do it.'

With this speech of the little man, Manabozho grabbed at him; but when he thought to have had him in his hand, he was gone.

'Where are you now, little man?' cried Manabozho.

'Here, under your girdle,' answered the shell-dwarf; at which giant Manabozho, thinking to crush him, slapped down his great hand with all his might; but on unloosing his girdle he was disappointed at finding no dwarf there.

'Where are you now, little man?' he cried again, in a greater rage than ever.

'In your right nostril!' the dwarf replied; whereupon the giant Manabozho seized himself by the finger and thumb at the place, and gave it a violent tweak; but as he immediately heard the voice of the dwarf at a distance upon the ground, he was sat isfied that he had only pulled his own nose to no purpose.

'Good-by, Manabozho,' said the voice of the invisible dwarf. 'Count your beaver-tails, and you will find that I have taken another for my sister;' for he of the little shell never, in his wanderings or pastimes, forgot his sister and her wishes. 'Good-by, beaver-man!'

And as he went away he made himself visible once more, and a light beamed about his head and lit the air around him with a strange splendor; a circumstance which Manabozho, who was at times quite thick-headed and dull of apprehension, could no way understand.

When Dais-Imid returned home, he told his sister that the time drew nigh when they must separate.

'I must go away,' said Dais-Imid, 'it is my fate. You, too,' he added, 'must go away soon. Tell me where you would wish to dwell.'

She said, 'I would like to go to the place of the breaking of daylight. I have always loved the East. The earliest glimpses of light are from that quarter, and it is to my mind the most beautiful part of the heavens. After I get there, my brother, whenever you see the clouds, in that direction, of various colors, you may think that your sister is painting her face.'

'And I,' said he, 'I, my sister, shall live on the mountains and rocks. There I can see you at the earliest hour; there are the streams of water clear; the air is pure, and the golden lights will shine ever around my head, and I shall ever be called "Puck-Ininee, or the Little Wild Man of the Mountains." But,' he resumed, 'before we part forever, I must go and try to find what manitoes rule the earth, and see which of them will be friendly to us.'

He left his sister and traveled over the surface of the globe, and then went far down into the earth.

He had been treated well wherever he went. At last he came to a giant manito, who had a large kettle which was forever boiling. The giant, who was a first cousin to Manabozho, and had already heard of the tricks which Dais-Imid had played upon his kinsman, regarded him with a stern look, and, catching him up in his hand, he threw him unceremoniously into the kettle.

It was evidently the giant's intention to drown Dais-Imid; in which he was mistaken, for by means of his magic shell, little Dais, in less than a second's time, bailed the water to the bottom, leaped from the kettle, and ran away unharmed.

He returned to his sister and related his rovings and adventures. He finished his story by addressing her thus:

'My sister there is a manito at each of the four corners of

the earth. There is also one above them, far in the sky, a Great Being who assigns to you, and to me, and to all of us, where we must go. And last,' he continued, 'there is another and wicked one who lives deep down in the earth. It will be our lot to escape out of his reach. We must now separate. When the winds blow from the four corners of the earth, you must then go. They will carry you to the place you wish. I go to the rocks and mountains, where my kindred will ever delight to dwell.'

Dais-Imid then took his ball-stick and commenced running up a high mountain, and a bright light shone about his head all the way, and he kept singing as he went:

Blow, winds, blow! my sister lingers
For her dwelling in the sky,
Where the morn, with rosy fingers,
Shall her cheeks with vermil dye.

There my earliest views directed,
Shall from her their color take,
And her smiles, through clouds reflected,
Guide me on by wood or lake.

While I range the highest mountains,
Sport in valleys green and low,
Or, beside our Indian fountains,
Raise my tiny hip-hallo.

Presently the winds blew, and, as Dais-Imid had predicted, his sister was borne by them to the eastern sky, where she has ever since lived, and her name is now the Morning Star.

16

Deucalion and Pyrrha

(Greek)

While the men of the Age of Bronze still dwelt upon the earth reports of their wickedness were carried to Jupiter. The god decided to verify the reports by coming to earth himself in the form of a man, and everywhere he went he found that the reports were much milder than the truth.

One evening in the late twilight he entered the inhospitable shelter of the Arcadian King Lycaon, who was famed for his wild conduct. By several signs he let it be known that he was a god, and the crowd dropped to their knees; but Lycaon made light of the pious prayers.

'Let us see,' he said, 'whether he is a mortal or a god.'

Thereupon he decided to destroy the guest that night while he lay in slumber, not expecting death. But before doing so he killed a poor hostage whom the Molossians had sent to him, cooked the half-living limbs in boiling water or broiled them over a fire, and placed them on the table before the guest for his evening meal.

But Jupiter, who knew all this, left the table and sent a raging fire over the castle of the godless man. Frightened, the king fled into the open field. The first cry he uttered was a howl; his garments changed to fur; his arms to legs; he was transformed into a bloodthirsty wolf.

Jupiter returned to Olympus, held counsel with the gods and

decided to destroy the reckless race of men. At first he wanted to turn his lightnings over all the earth, but the fear that the ether would take fire and destroy the axle of the universe restrained him. He laid aside the thunderbolt which the Cyclops had fashioned for him, and decided to send rain from heaven over all the earth and so destroy the race of mortals.

Immediately the North Wind and all the other cloud-scattering winds were locked in the cave of Aeolus, and only the South Wind sent out. The latter descended upon the earth; his frightful face was covered with darkness; his beard was heavy with clouds; from his white hair ran the flood; mists lay upon his brow; from his bosom dropped the water. The South Wind grasped the heavens, seized in his hands the surrounding clouds and began to squeeze them. The thunder rolled; floods of rain burst from the heavens. The standing corn was bent to the earth; destroyed was the hope of the farmer; destroyed the weary work of a whole year.

Even Neptune, god of the sea, came to the assistance of his brother Jupiter in the work of destruction. He called all the rivers together and said, 'Give full rein to your torrents; enter houses; break through all dams!'

They followed his command, and Neptune himself struck the earth with his trident and let the flood enter. Then the waters streamed over the open meadows, covered the fields, dislodged trees, temples and houses. Wherever a palace stood, its gables were soon covered with water and the highest turrets were hidden in the torrent. Sea and earth were no longer divided; all was flood—an unbroken stretch of water.

Men tried to save themselves as best they could; some climbed the high mountains; others entered boats and rowed, now over the roofs of the fallen houses, now over the hills of their ruined vineyards. Fish swam among the branches of the highest trees; the wild boar was caught in the flood; people were swept away by the water and those whom the flood spared died of hunger on the barren mountains.

One high mountain in the country of Phocis still raised two peaks above the surrounding waters. It was the great Mount Parnassus. Toward this floated a boat containing Deucalion, the son of Prometheus, and his wife Pyrrha. No man, no woman, had ever been found who surpassed these in righteousness and piety. When, therefore, Jupiter, looking down from heaven upon the earth, saw that only a single pair of mortals remained of the many thousand times a thousand, both blameless, both devoted servants of the gods, he sent forth the North Wind, recalled the clouds, and once again separated the earth from the heavens and the heavens from the earth.

Even Neptune, lord of the sea, laid down his trident and calmed the flood. The ocean resumed its banks; the rivers returned to their beds; forests stretched their slime-covered tree-tops out of the deep; hills followed; finally stretches of level land appeared and the earth was as before.

Deucalion looked around him. The country was laid waste; it was wrapped in the silence of the grave. Tears rolled down his cheeks and he said to his wife, Pyrrha, 'Beloved, solitary companion of my life, as far as I can see through all the surrounding country, I can discover no living creature. We two must people the earth; all the rest have been drowned by the flood. But even we are not yet certain of our lives. Every cloud that I see strikes terror to my soul. And even if danger is past, what shall we do alone on the forsaken earth? Oh, that my father Prometheus had taught me the art of creating men and breathing life into them!'

Then the two began to weep. They threw themselves on their knees before the half-destroyed altar of the goddess Themis, and began to pray, saying, 'Tell us, O goddess, by what means we can replace the race that has disappeared? Oh, help the earth to new life.'

'Leave my altar,' sounded the voice of the goddess. 'Uncover your heads, ungird your garments and cast the bones of your mother behind you.'

For a long time Deucalion and Pyrrha wondered over the puzzling words of the goddess. Pyrrha was the first to break the silence. 'Pardon me, O noble goddess,' she said, 'if I do not obey you and cannot consent to scatter the bones of my mother.'

Then Deucalion had a happy thought. He comforted his wife. 'Either my reason deceives me,' he said, 'or the command of the goddess is good and involves no impiety. The great mother of all of us is the Earth; her bones are the stones, and these, Pyrrha, we will cast behind us!'

Both mistrusted this interpretation of the words, but what harm would it do to try? Thereupon they uncovered their heads, ungirded their garments and began casting stones behind them.

Then a wonderful thing happened. The stone began to lose its hardness, became malleable, grew and took form—not definite at once, but rude figures such as an artist first hews out of the rough marble. Whatever was moist or earthy in the stones was changed into flesh; the harder parts became bones; the veins in the rock remained as veins in the bodies. Thus, in a little while, with the aid of the gods, the stones which Deucalion threw assumed the form of men; those which Pyrrha threw, the form of women.

This homely origin the race of men does not deny; they are a hardy people, accustomed to work. Every moment of the day they remember from what sturdy stock they have sprung.

17

The Churning of the Ocean

(Indian)

Once upon a time in the youth of the world there stood to the north of India a mighty mountain named Mount Meru. Its summit shone so brightly that the sun's rays, when they struck it, shivered and fell away. One day the lesser gods gathered in council upon its peak, for they wished to obtain the ambrosia which would make them immortal like the three supreme gods, Vishnu, Brahmadeva and Shiva. Now the jar in which the ambrosia was kept lay at the bottom of the ocean and none of the lesser gods could conceive a plan by which they could obtain possession of it. As they sat in council, there came to them the great god Vishnu, and the lesser gods asked him for his advice. Vishnu answered them, saying, 'Call the demons to your aid and churn the ocean. When you have churned it, not only will you get the ambrosia, but you will get a great store of jewels and other precious things besides.'

The lesser gods followed the counsel of Vishnu, left the summit of Mount Meru and withdrew to another great mountain named Mount Mandara. Its peak was not resplendent like that of Mount Meru. Its sides were covered with dense forests, through which roamed elephants and lions, tigers and leopards. The lesser gods seized the great mountain and tried to uproot it so that they might churn the ocean with it, as the Lord Vishnu had advised. But although they strove their utmost, the great mass of Mount Mandara moved not a hair's breadth. The celestials, finding their strength unequal to the task, sought out the great gods Vishnu and Brahmadeva. 'Great lords,' they said, 'tell us, we pray you, how we may uproot Mandara Mountain, for without it we cannot churn the ocean and win the ambrosia.' Lord Vishnu called to him Vasuki the king of the snake people and said to him, 'O Snake King, the command that I lay upon you is this. Go with the lesser gods and help them uproot Mandara Mountain.' Vasuki, the king of the snake people, obeyed Lord Vishnu, and going with the lesser gods to Mount Mandara, he fastened round it his endless coils. Then pressing them against the base of the mountain he tore it up by the roots. Together the Snake King and the lesser gods rolled the mountain to the shores of the ocean. 'Lord Ocean,' they said, 'we desire the ambrosia which lies fathoms deep below your surface. And to win it we shall churn your water with the Mandara Mountain.' 'As you will,' said the ocean. 'Give me but a draught of the ambrosia and I will gladly allow you to churn my waters.'

Hearing the words of the ocean the lesser gods were glad, and, as the Lord Vishnu had advised them, they bade the demons join them. Then gods and demons went together to the king of the tortoises. They found him in his palace and said to him. 'O Tortoise King, come to our aid, we pray you. For we have resolved to churn the ocean with Mount Mandara that we may win the ambrosia. But if we place Mount Mandara on the bottom of the ocean it will sink into the sands. Come, therefore, O King of the Tortoises, and lie at the bottom of the ocean. For if you bear it on your mighty back, we shall be able to pull Mount Mandara to and fro and so churn the ocean.' The Tortoise King consented, and with the gods and the demons walked to the shores of the ocean. When they had reached the edge of the water, the god Indra, the chief of the lesser gods, by means of many cunning instruments, placed Mount Mandara upon the back of the king of the tortoises. Bearing this mighty burden the king of the tortoises entered the ocean, and walked along its bottom until he reached the deepest part. Then Vasuki the Snake King swam out across the surface of the water until he reached the spot where the top of Mount Mandara stood high above the waves. Coiling himself round the great mountain he bade the lesser gods hold him by the tail and the demons hold his head. Demons and gods seized him as he bade them, and pulling him backwards and forwards they began to churn the ocean. Great masses of foam rose upon the waters. Clouds of vapour issued from the mouth of the Snake King Vasuki and scorched the faces of the demons who pulled the Snake King's head. Then rising higher the vapour descended in cooling rain to refresh the lesser gods. And the forest flowers torn from the sides of Mount Mandara by the coils of the Snake King were wafted abroad by the winds and fell softly upon their faces. The gods and demons pulled the mountain summit backwards and forwards through the air so swiftly that the forests upon it caught fire. But the god Indra opened the windows of heaven and the rain fell in torrents on the fire and extinguished it. Yet although gods and demons toiled without ceasing until their strength was spent, nothing rose from the surface of the ocean. The lesser gods and the demons then went to the court of Brahmadeva and said, 'O father of the gods, we are exhausted with labour and can work no more, yet the ambrosia has not been won.' Brahmadeva begged the Lord Vishnu to give the gods and demons greater strength, that they might continue the churning. This the Lord Vishnu did, and they swung Mount Mandara to and fro until the foam of the churned ocean rose almost higher than the great mountain itself. At last a pale yellow disk began slowly to rise from the ocean. It rose right out of the waters high into the sky, and, ever since, as the moon, has at night time shed its pale light over the earth. Next there rose from the waters an elephant larger than mortal mind could have imagined. Two enormous white tusks stretched many yards in front of him. His eyes were like red ponds, and his trunk seemed to rival in length the great coils of the Snake King himself. Indra called the mighty beast to him and soothing it with his hand, said, 'You shall be known hereafter as Airavat and shall be my servant always.' Still the churning continued and there rose from the sea the prettiest maid who had ever been seen in the three worlds. Her long black lashes drooped upon a pair of rosy cheeks. Her hair curled in golden rings over an ivory forehead. Her eyes were bluer than the sky above. Indra called her to him. 'You shall hereafter be called Rambha,' he said, 'and you shall be chief among my dancing girls.'

Harder still the gods and demons toiled at the churning, until there rose from the waters the most awful vision of beauty that eyes human or divine had ever seen. From a perfect face two eyes of deepest grey looked out. They gazed unblinking into space. But so grave was their expression and so full of wisdom that neither demon nor god, except Vishnu alone, dared meet their look. A moment later, amid an awed hush, Vishnu stepped forward and took the lovely woman by the hand. 'You shall be called Lakshmi,' he said, 'and you shall be my queen.'

Backwards and forwards swung Mount Mandara. Then from a distance the gods and demons saw a fair woman coming towards them. In each hand she carried a jar, but when she came close, they saw that her expression was evil and that great lines marred her features and that black pits lay under her eyes. They let the strange woman pass, and she made her way to the dry earth. There, known as Sura or the wine goddess, she has dwelt ever since.

Again they churned until there rose above the waves a pure white horse. It was the most beautifully shaped horse that has ever lived on earth before or since. It swam through the billows until it reached the shore, when it thundered out of sight at full gallop.

'Let its name be Uchaisrava,' said Indra, and the gods and the demons once more bent to the churning. Then there rose above the foam the most marvellous jewel that eyes have ever beheld. Set in a vast plate of gold were emeralds like the green pools of an Indian village and sapphires like the blue lakes in the Himalaya mountains. Vast rubies shone out of masses of diamonds huge as rocks of crystal. The Lord Vishnu stepped forward and fastened the sea jewel round his neck. There, known as Kaustubha, it has hung ever since.

Still they churned, the gods and demons, until a strange ripple spread over the waters and a terrible stench rose from it. The head and tail of the giant snake dropped gradually out of the hinds of the fainting churners. Even Vasuki's eyes became dull and his coils began to slip inertly off Mount Mandara's sides. Suddenly the god Shiva placed his mouth on the waves near the ripple, and sucking it in, saved the three worlds. For this was the terrible Vish—the poisonous fluid which overlaid the ambrosia to guard it. If the Lord Shiva had not drunk it, it would have destroyed alike the lesser gods, demons and men. As the Lord Shiva swallowed it, it burnt a deep blue mark on his throat. And he has ever since been known as Nilkantha or Blue-throat.

When the fumes of the Vish had passed away, the gods and demons churned once more. At last an aged man rose slowly through the masses of the ocean foam. In his right hand he carried a gold jar of exquisite workmanship from which issued a perfume of delicious fragrance. At the sight of the aged man, whom they knew to be Dhanwantari, the demons snatched the ambrosia from his hands, trying to rob the gods of their share. But the Lord Vishnu took it back from them. And to punish them for their greed he poured out the ambrosia to the gods only, who drank it and at once became immortal, while the demons, who drank none of it, have remained mortal to this day.

But one of the demons, Rahu by name, took the form of

a celestial, and deceiving the Lord Vishnu received a draught of ambrosia. As the demon drank, the sun-god pierced his disguise and told the Lord Vishnu of his deceit. Vishnu, lifting his discus, shore off the head of Rahu with it before the ambrosia had passed his throat. Rahu's body fell to the ground, and, being mortal, soon rotted. But his head, having taken the ambrosia, is immortal and still endures.

But because the sun-god detected him as he drank the divine liquid, and told Vishnu, Rahu's head bears to the sun-god an undying hatred. Sometimes he steals up unperceived close to the bright sun-god and with a single bite swallows him. But because Rahu has no body, the sun-god in due course reappears through his enemy's throat and once again begins to shine upon the earth in all his former splendour.

And then men gather together and say that there has been an eclipse of the sun.

18

Autumn and Spring

(*Japanese*)

A fair maiden lay asleep in a rice-field. The sun was at its height, and she was weary. Now a god looked down upon the rice-field. He knew that the beauty of the maiden came from within, that it mirrored the beauty of heavenly dreams. He knew that even now, as she smiled, she held converse with the spirit of the wind or the flowers.

The god descended and asked the dream-maiden to be his bride. She rejoiced, and they were wed. A wonderful red jewel came of their happiness.

Long, long afterwards, the stone was found by a farmer, who saw that it was a very rare jewel. He prized it highly, and always carried it about with him. Sometimes, as he looked at it in the pale light of the moon, it seemed to him that he could discern two sparkling eyes in its depths. Again, in the stillness of the night, he would awaken and think that a clear soft voice called him by name.

One day, the farmer had to carry the mid-day meal to his workers in the field. The sun was very hot, so he loaded a cow with the bowls of rice, the millet dumplings, and the beans. Suddenly, Prince Ama-boko stood in the path. He was angry, for he thought that the farmer was about to kill the cow. The prince would hear no word of denial; his wrath increased. The farmer became more and more terrified, and, finally, took the precious stone from his pocket and presented it as a peace-offering to the powerful prince. Ama-boko marvelled at the brilliancy of the jewel, and allowed the man to continue his journey.

The prince returned to his home. He drew forth the treasure, and it was immediately transformed into a goddess of surpassing beauty. Even as she rose before him, he loved her, and ere the moon waned they were wed. The goddess ministered to his every want. She prepared delicate dishes, the secret of which is known only to the gods. She made wine from the juice of a myriad herbs, wine such as mortals never taste.

But, after a time, the prince became proud and overbearing. He began to treat his faithful wife with cruel contempt. The goddess was sad, and said: 'You are not worthy of my love. I will leave you and go to my father.' Ama-boko paid no heed to these words, for he did not believe that the threat would be fulfilled. But the beautiful goddess was in earnest. She escaped from the palace and fled to Naniwa, where she is still honoured as Akaru-hime, the Goddess of Light.

Now the prince was wroth when he heard that the goddess had left him, and set out in pursuit of her. But when he neared Naniwa, the gods would not allow his vessel to enter the haven. Then he knew that his priceless red jewel was lost to him for ever. He steered his ship towards the north coast of Japan, and landed at Tajima. Here he was well received, and highly esteemed on account of the treasures which he brought with him. He had costly strings of pearls, girdles of precious stones, and a mirror which the wind and the waves obeyed. Prince Ama-boko remained at Tajima, and was the father of a mighty race.

Among his children's children was a princess so renowned for her beauty that eighty suitors sought her hand. One after the other returned sorrowfully home, for none found favour in her eyes. At last, two brothers came before her, the young God of the Autumn, and the young God of the Spring. The elder of the two, the God of Autumn, first urged his suit. But the princess refused him. He went to his younger brother, and said: 'The princess does not love me, neither will you be able to win her heart.' But the Spring God was full of hope, and replied: 'I will give you a cask of rice wine if I do not win her, but if she consents to be my bride, you shall give a cask of *saké* to me.'

Now the God of Spring went to his mother, and told her all. She promised to aid him. Thereupon she wove, in a single night, a robe and sandals from the unopened buds of the lilac and white wisteria. Out of the same delicate flowers she fashioned a bow and arrows. Thus clad, the God of Spring made his way to the beautiful princess.

As he stepped before the maiden, every bud unfolded, and from the heart of each blossom came a fragrance that filled the air. The princess was overjoyed, and gave her hand to the God of the Spring.

The elder brother, the God of Autumn, was filled with rage when he heard how his brother had obtained the wondrous robe. He refused to give the promised cask of *saké*. When the mother learned that the god had broken his word, she placed stones and salt in the hollow of a bamboo cane, wrapped it round with bamboo leaves, and hung it in the smoke. Then she uttered a curse upon her first-born son: 'As the leaves wither and fade, so must you. As the salt sea ebbs, so must you. As the stone sinks, so must you.'

The terrible curse fell upon her son. While the God of Spring remains ever young, ever fragrant, ever full of mirth, the God of Autumn is old, and withered, and sad.

19

The Story of Fenris

(*Norse*)

Tyr was generally spoken of and represented as one-armed, just as Odin was called one-eyed. Various explanations are offered by different authorities; some claim that it was because he could give the victory only to one side; others, because a sword has but one blade. However this may be, the ancients preferred to account for the fact in the following way:

Loki married secretly at Jötun-heim the hideous giantess Angur-boda (anguish boding), who bore him three monstrous children—the wolf Fenris, Hel, the parti-coloured goddess of death, and Iörmungandr, a terrible serpent. He kept the existence of these monsters secret as long as he could; but they speedily grew so large that they could no longer remain confined in the cave where they had come to light. Odin, from his throne Hlidskialf, soon became aware of their existence, and also of the disquieting rapidity with which they increased in size. Fearful lest the monsters, when they had gained further strength, should invade Asgard and destroy the gods, Allfather determined to get rid of them, and striding off to Jötun-heim, he flung Hel into the depths of Nifl-heim, telling her she could reign over the nine dismal worlds of the dead. He then cast Iörmungandr into the sea, where he attained such immense proportions that at last he encircled the earth and could bite his own tail.

Into mid-ocean's dark depths hurled,
Grown with each day to giant size,
The serpent soon inclosed the world,
With tail in mouth, in circle-wise;
Held harmless still
By Odin's will.

Valhalla (J. C. Jones).

None too well pleased that the serpent should attain such fearful dimensions in his new element, Odin resolved to lead Fenris to Asgard, where he hoped, by kindly treatment, to make him gentle and tractable. But the gods one and all shrank in dismay when they saw the wolf, and none dared approach to give him food except Tyr, whom nothing daunted. Seeing that Fenris daily increased in size, strength, voracity, and fierceness, the gods assembled in council to deliberate how they might best dispose of him. They unanimously decided that as it would desecrate their peace-steads to slay him, they would bind him fast so that he could work them no harm.

With that purpose in view, they obtained a strong chain named Læding, and then playfully proposed to Fenris to bind this about him as a test of his vaunted strength. Confident in his ability to release himself, Fenris patiently allowed them to bind him fast, and when all stood aside, with a mighty effort he stretched himself and easily burst the chain asunder.

Concealing their chagrin, the gods were loud in praise of his strength, but they next produced a much stronger fetter, Droma, which, after some persuasion, the wolf allowed them to fasten around him as before. Again a short, sharp struggle sufficed to burst this bond, and it is proverbial in the North to use the figurative expressions, 'to get loose out of Læding,' and 'to dash out of Droma,' whenever great difficulties have to be surmounted.

Twice did the Æsir strive to bind,
Twice did they fetters powerless find;
Iron or brass of no avail,
Naught, save through magic, could prevail.

Valhalla (J. C. Jones).

The gods, perceiving now that ordinary bonds, however strong, would never prevail against the Fenris wolf's great strength, bade Skirnir, Frey's servant, go down to Svart-alfa-heim and bid the dwarfs fashion a bond which nothing could sever.

By magic arts the dark elves manufactured a slender silken rope from such impalpable materials as the sound of a cat's footsteps, a woman's beard, the roots of a mountain, the longings of the bear, the voice of fishes, and the spittle of birds, and when it was finished they gave it to Skirnir, assuring him that no strength would avail to break it, and that the more it was strained the stronger it would become.

Gleipnir, at last,
By Dark Elves cast,
In Svart-alf-heim, with strong spells wrought,
To Odin was by Skirnir brought:
As soft as silk, as light as air,
Yet still of magic power most rare.

Valhalla (J. C. Jones).

Armed with this bond, called Gleipnir, the gods went with Fenris to the Island of Lyngvi, in the middle of Lake Amsvartnir, and again proposed to test his strength. But although Fenris had grown still stronger, he mistrusted the bond which looked so slight. He therefore refused to allow himself to be bound, unless one of the Æsir would consent to put his hand in his mouth, and leave it there, as a pledge of good faith, and that no magic arts were to be used against him.

The gods heard the decision with dismay, and all drew back except Tyr, who, seeing that the others would not venture to comply with this condition, boldly stepped forward and thrust his hand between the monster's jaws. The gods now fastened Gleipnir securely around Fenris's neck and paws, and when they saw that his utmost efforts to free himself were fruitless, they shouted and laughed with glee. Tyr, however, could not share their joy, for the wolf, finding himself captive, bit off the god's hand at the wrist, which since then has been known as the wolf's joint.

Loki.

Be silent, Tyr!
Thou couldst never settle
A strife 'twixt two;
Of thy right hand also
I must mention make,
Which Fenris from thee took.

Tyr.

I of a hand am wanting,
But thou of honest fame;
Sad is the lack of either.
Nor is the wolf at ease:
He in bonds must abide
Until the gods' destruction.

Sæmund's Edda (Thorpe's tr.).

Deprived of his right hand, Tyr was now forced to use the maimed arm for his shield, and to wield his sword with his left hand; but such was his dexterity that he slew his enemies as before.

The gods, in spite of the wolf's struggles, drew the end of the fetter Gelgia through the rock Gioll, and fastened it to the boulder Thviti, which was sunk deep in the ground. Opening wide his fearful jaws, Fenris uttered such terrible howls that the gods, to silence him, thrust a sword into his mouth, the hilt resting upon his lower jaw and the point against his palate. The blood then began to pour out in such streams that it formed a great river, called Von. The wolf was destined to remain thus chained fast until the last day, when he would burst his bonds and would be free to avenge his wrongs.

The wolf Fenrir,
Freed from the chain,
Shall range the earth.

Death-song of Hâkon (W. Taylor's tr.).

While some mythologists see in this myth an emblem of crime restrained and made innocuous by the power of the law, others see the underground fire, which kept within bounds can injure no one, but which unfettered fills the world with destruction and woe. Just as Odin's second eye is said to rest in Mimir's well, so Tyr's second hand (sword) is found in Fenris's jaws. He has no more use for two weapons than the sky for two suns.

The worship of Tyr is commemorated in sundry places (such as Tübingen, in Germany), which bear more or less modified forms of his name. The name has also been given to the aconite, a plant known in Northern countries as 'Tyr's helm.'

20

Lohengrin and Elsa the Beautiful

(*German*)

The young Duchess of Brabant, Elsa the Beautiful, had gone into the woods hunting, and becoming separated from her attendants, sat down to rest under a wide-branching linden-tree.

She was sorely troubled, for many lords and princes were asking for her hand in marriage. More urgent than all the others was the invincible hero, Count Telramund, her former guardian, who since the death of her father had ruled over the land with masterly hand. Now the duke, her father, on his death-bed had promised Telramund that he might have Elsa for wife, should she be willing; and Telramund was continually reminding her of this. But Elsa blushed with shame at the mere thought of such a union, for Telramund was a rough warrior, as much hated for his cruelty as he was feared for his strength. To make matters worse he was now at the court of the chosen King Henry of Saxony, threatening her with war and even worse calamities.

In the shade of the linden Elsa thought of all this, and pitied her own loneliness in that no brother or friend stood at her side to help her. Then the sweet singing of birds seemed to comfort her, and she dropped into a gentle sleep. As she dreamed it seemed to her that a young knight stepped out of the depths of the forest. Holding up a small silver bell, he spoke in friendly tones:

'If you should need my help, just ring this.'

Elsa tried to take the trinket, but she could neither rise nor reach the outstretched hand. Then she awoke.

Thinking over the apparition Elsa noted a falcon circling over her head. It came nearer and finally settled on her shoulder. Around his neck hung a bell exactly like that she had seen in the dream. She loosened it, and as she did so the bird rose and flew away. But she still held the little bell in her hand, and in her soul was fresh hope and peace.

When she returned to the castle she found there a message, bidding her appear before the king in Cologne on the Rhine. Filled with confidence in the protection of higher powers, she did not hesitate to obey. In gorgeous costume, with many followers, she set out.

King Henry was a man who loved justice and exercised it, but his kingdom was in constant danger from inroads by wild Huns, and for this reason he wished to do whatever would win the favour of the powerful Count Telramund. When, however, he saw Elsa in all her beauty and innocence he hesitated in his purpose.

The plaintiff brought forward three men who testified that the duchess had entered into a secret union with one of her vassals. Only two of these men were shown to be perfidious; the testimony of the other seemed valid, though this was not enough to condemn her.

Then Telramund seized his sword, crying out that God Himself should be the judge, and that a duel should decide the matter. So a duel was arranged to take place three days later.

Elsa cast her eyes around the circle of nobles, but saw no one grasp his sword in defence of her innocence. Fear of the mighty warrior Telramund filled them all.

Remembering the little bell, she drew it forth from her pocket and rang it. The clear tones broke the stillness, grew louder and louder until they reached even the distant mountains.

'My champion will appear in the contest,' she said; whereupon the count let forth such a mocking laugh that the hearts of all were filled with intense fear.

The day of the contest was at hand. The king sat on his high throne and watched the majestic river that sent its mighty waters through the valley. Princes and brave knights were gathered together. Before them stood Telramund, clad in armour, and at his side the accused Elsa, adorned with every grace that Nature can bestow.

Three times the mighty hero challenged some one to come forward as a champion for the accused girl, but no one stirred. Then arose from the Rhine the sound of sweet music; something silvery gleamed in the distance, and as it came nearer it was plain that it was a swan with silver feathers. With a silver chain he was pulling a small ship, in which lay sleeping a knight clad in bright armour.

When the bark landed, the knight awoke, rose, and blew three times on a golden horn. This was the signal that he took up the challenge. Quickly he strode into the lists.

'Your name and descent?' cried the herald.

'My name is Lohengrin,' answered the stranger, 'my origin royal: more it is not necessary to tell.'

'Enough,' broke in the king, 'nobility is written on your brow.'

Trumpets gave the signal for the fight to begin. Telramund's strokes fell thick as hail, but suddenly the stranger knight rose and with one fearful stroke split the count's helmet and cut his head.

'God has decided,' cried the king. 'His judgment is right; but you, noble knight, will help us in the campaign against the barbarian hordes and will be the leader of the detachment which the fair duchess will send from Brabant.'

Gladly Lohengrin consented, and amid cries of delight from the assembled people he rode over to Elsa, who greeted him as her deliverer.

Lohengrin escorted Elsa back to Brabant, and on the way love awoke in their hearts, and they knew that they were destined for each other. In the castle of Antwerp they were pledged, and a few weeks later the marriage took place. As the bridal couple were leaving the cathedral, Lohengrin said to Elsa:

'One thing I must ask of you, and that is that you never inquire concerning my origin, for in the hour that you put that question must I surely part from you.'

It was not long after the ceremony that the cry to arms came from King Henry, and Elsa accompanied her husband and his troops to Cologne, where all the counts of the kingdom were assembled. Here there were many inquiries concerning Lohengrin, and when none seemed to know of his origin, some jealously claimed that he was the son of a heathen magician, and that he gained his victories by the power of black arts.

Elsa, who had heard rumours of these charges, was deeply grieved; for she knew the noble heart of her husband. He had even relieved her fears for his safety by the assurance that he was under the protection of powers higher than human.

But she could not banish the evil rumours from her mind, and forgetting the warning her husband had given her on the day of her marriage, she dropped to her knees and asked him concerning his birth.

'Dear wife,' he cried in great distress, 'now will I tell to you and to the king and to all the assembled princes, what up to this time I have kept secret; but know that the time of our parting is at hand.'

Then the hero led his trembling wife before the king and his nobles who were assembled on the banks of the Rhine.

'The son of Parsifal am I,' he said, 'the son of Parsifal, the keeper of the Holy Grail. Gladly would I have helped you, O King, in your fight against the barbarians, but an unavoidable fate calls me away. You will, however, be victorious, and under your descendants will Germany become a powerful nation.'

When he finished speaking there was a deep silence, and then, as upon his arrival, there rose the sound of music—not joyful this time, but solemn, like a chant at the grave of the dead. It came nearer and again the swan and the boat appeared.

'Farewell, dear one,' Lohengrin cried, folding his wife in his arms. 'Too dearly did I hold you and your pleasant land of earth; now a higher duty calls me.'

Weeping, Elsa clung to him; but the swan song sounded louder, like a warning. He tore himself free and stepped into the boat. Was it the ship of death and destruction, or only the ship that carried the blessed to the sacred place of the Grail? No one knew.

Elsa, lonely and sad, did not live long after the separation. Her only hope was that she would be reunited to her dear husband; and she parted willingly with her own life, as other children of earth have done when they have lost all that they held most precious.

21

The Great Fir Tree of Takasago

(*Japanese*)

The cherry tree has blossomed many times since O-Matsue lived with her father and mother on the sandy coast of the Inland Sea. The home at Takasago was sheltered by a tall fir tree of great age; a god had planted it as he passed that way. O-Matsue was beautiful, for her mother had taught her to love the sea, and the birds, the trees, and every living thing.

Her eyes were like a clear deep ocean-pool on a summer day. Her smile was as the sunshine on the surface of Lake Biwa.

The fallen needles of the fir made a soft couch on which O-Matsue sat for hours at a time, plying her shuttle, weaving robes for the peasants around. Sometimes, she would go to sea with the fishers, and peer into the depths to try and catch a glimpse of the Palace of the Ocean Bed; the fishers would tell her the story of the poor jelly-fish who lost his shell, or of the Blessed Island of Eternal Youth, whose tree could at times be discerned from the coast.

The steep shore of Sumi-no-ye is many leagues distant from Takasago, but a youth who dwelt there took a long journey. Teoyo said, 'I will see what lies beyond the mountains. I will see the country to which the heron wings his way across the plain.' He travelled through many provinces, and at last came to the land of Harima. One day he passed by Takasago. O-Matsue sat in the shade of the fir tree. She was weaving, and sang as she worked.

These are the words of her song:—

> No man so callous but he heaves a sigh
> When o'er his head the withered Cherry flowers
> Come fluttering down. Who knows? the Spring's soft
> showers
> May be but tears shed by the sorrowing sky.

Teoyo heard the sweet song, and said, 'It is like the song of a spirit,—and how beautiful the maiden is!' For some time he watched her as she wove. Then her song ceased, he moved towards her, and spoke: 'I have travelled far. I have seen many fair maidens, but not one so fair as you. Take me to your father and mother that I may speak with them.' Teoyo asked the peasants for the hand of their daughter, and they gave their consent.

There was great rejoicing. O-Matsue received many presents, and, as the wedding-day approached, a great feast was prepared. Bride and bridegroom drank thrice of three cups of *saké* which made them man and wife, and the feast went on.

Now Teoyo said, 'This country of Harima is a good land. Let us stay here with your father and mother.' O-Matsue was glad. So they dwelt with the old people under the great fir tree. At last, the father and mother died. O-Matsue and Teoyo still lived beneath the shelter of the tree. They were very happy. Summer, autumn and winter passed over the land of Harima many times. Their love was always in its spring. The 'waves of age' furrowed their brows, but their hearts remained young and tender, green as the needles of the pine. Even when their eyes had grown dim, they went to the shore to listen to the waters of the Inland Sea, or together they gathered, with rakes of bamboo, the fallen needles of the fir.

A crane came and built in the topmost branches of the tree, and for many years they watched the birds rear their young. A tortoise also dwelt beside them. O-Matsue said, 'We are blessed with a fir tree, a crane, and a tortoise. The God of Long Life has taken us under his care.'

When, at last, at the same moment, Teoyo and O-Matsue died, their spirits withdrew into the tree which had for so long been the witness of their happiness. To this day the pine tree is called 'The Pine of the Lovers.'

On moonbright nights, when the coast wind whispers in the branches of the tree, O-Matsue and Teoyo may sometimes be seen, with bamboo rakes in their hands, gathering together the needles of the fir.

Despite the storms of time, the old tree stands to this hour eternally green on the high shore of Takasago.

22

Kil Arthur

(Irish)

There was a time long ago, and if we had lived then, we shouldn't be living now.

In that time there was a law in the world that if a young man came to woo a young woman, and her people wouldn't give her to him, the young woman should get her death by the law.

There was a king in Erin at that time who had a daughter, and he had a son too, who was called Kil Arthur, son of the monarch of Erin.

Now, not far from the castle of the king there was a tinker; and one morning he said to his mother: 'Put down my breakfast for me, mother.'

'Where are you going?' asked the mother.

'I'm going for a wife.'

'Where?'

'I am going for the daughter of the king of Erin.'

'Oh! my son, bad luck is upon you. It is death to ask for the king's daughter, and you a tinker.'

'I don't care for that,' said he.

So the tinker went to the king's castle. They were at dinner when he came, and the king trembled as he saw him.

Though they were at table, the tinker went into the room.

The king asked: 'What did you come for at this time?'

'I came to marry your daughter.'

'That life and strength may leave me if ever you get my daughter in marriage! I'd give her to death before I would to a tinker.'

Now Kil Arthur, the king's son, came in, caught the tinker and hanged him, facing the front of the castle. When he was dead, they made seven parts of his body, and flung them into the sea.

Then the king had a box made so close and tight that no water could enter, and inside the box they fixed a coffin; and when they had put a bed with meat and drink into the coffin, they brought the king's daughter, laid her on the bed, closed the box, and pushed it into the open sea. The box went out with the tide and moved on the water for a long time; where it was one day it was not the next,—carried along by the waves day and night, till at last it came to another land.

Now, in the other land was a man who had spent his time in going to sea, till at length he got very poor, and said: 'I'll stay at home now, since God has let me live this long. I heard my father say once that if a man would always rise early and walk along the strand, he would get his fortune from the tide at last.'

One morning early, as this man was going along the strand, he saw the box, and brought it up to the shore, where he opened it and took out the coffin. When the lid was off the coffin, he found a woman inside alive.

'Oh!' said he, 'I'd rather have you there than the full of the box of gold.'

'I think the gold would be better for you,' said the woman.

He took the stranger to his house, and gave her food and drink. Then he made a great cross on the ground, and clasping hands with the woman, jumped over the arms of the cross, going in the same direction as the sun. This was the form of marriage in that land.

They lived together pleasantly. She was a fine woman, worked well for her husband, and brought him great wealth, so that he became richer than any man; and one day, when out walking alone, he said to himself: 'I am able to give a grand dinner now to Ri Fohin, Sladaire Mor (king under the wave, the great robber), who owns men, women, and every kind of beast.'

Then he went home and invited Ri Fohin to dinner. He came with all the men, women, and beasts he had, and they covered the country for six miles.

The beasts were fed outside by themselves, but the people in the house. When dinner was over, he asked Ri Fohin: 'Have you ever seen a house so fine and rich, or a dinner so good, as mine to-night?'

'I have not,' said Ri Fohin.

Then the man went to each person present. Each gave the same answer, and said, 'I have never seen such a house nor such a dinner.'

He asked his wife, and she said: 'My praise is no praise here; but what is this to the house and the feasting of my father, the king of Erin?'

'Why did you say that?' asked the man, and he went a second and a third time to the guests and to his wife. All had the same answers for him. Then he gave his wife a flip of the thumb on her ear, in a friendly way, and said: 'Why don't you give good luck to my house; why do you give it a bad name?'

Then all the guests said: 'It is a shame to strike your wife on the night of a feast.'

Now the man was angry and went out of his house. It was growing dark, but he saw a champion coming on a black steed between earth and air; and the champion, who was no other than Kil Arthur, his brother-in-law, took him up and bore him away to the castle of the king of Erin.

When Kil Arthur arrived they were just sitting down to dinner in the castle, and the man dined with his father-in-law.

After dinner the king of Erin had cards brought and asked his son-in-law: 'Do you ever play with these?'

'No, I have never played with the like of them.'

'Well, shuffle them now,' said the king. He shuffled; and as they were enchanted cards and whoever held them could never lose a game he was the best player in the world, though he had never played a game before in his life.

The king said, 'Put them in your pocket, they may do you good.' Then the king gave him a fiddle, and asked:

'Have you ever played on the like of this?'

'Indeed I have not,' said the man.

'Well, play on it now,' said the king.

He played, and never in his life had he heard such music.

'Keep it,' said the king; 'as long as you don't let it from you, you're the first musician on earth. Now I'll give you something else. Here is a cup which will always give you every kind of drink you can wish for; and if all the men in the world were to drink out of it they could never empty it. Keep these three things; but never raise hand on your wife again.'

The king of Erin gave him his blessing; then Kil Arthur took him up on the steed, and going between earth and sky he was soon back at his own home.

Now Ri Fohin had carried off the man's wife and all that he had while he was at dinner with the King of Erin. Going out on the road the king's son-in-law began to cry: 'Oh, what shall I do; what shall I do!' and as he cried, who should come but Kil Arthur on his steed, who said, 'Be quiet, I'll go for your wife and goods.'

Kil Arthur went, and killed Ri Fohin and all his people and beasts,—didn't leave one alive. Then he brought back his sister to her husband, and stayed with them for three years.

One day he said to his sister: 'I am going to leave you. I don't know what strength I have; I'll walk the world now till I know is there a man in it as good as myself.'

Next morning he bade good-bye to his sister, and rode away on his black-haired steed, which overtook the wind before and outstripped the wind behind. He travelled swiftly till evening, spent the night in a forest, and the second day hurried on as he had the first.

The second night he spent in a forest; and next morning as he rose from the ground he saw before him a man covered with blood from fighting, and the clothes nearly torn from his body.

'What have you been doing?' asked Kil Arthur.

'I have been playing cards all night. And where are you going?' inquired the stranger of Kil Arthur.

'I am going around the world to know can I find a man as good as myself.'

'Come with me,' said the stranger, 'and I'll show you a man who couldn't find his match till he went to fight the main ocean.'

Kil Arthur went with the ragged stranger till they came to a place from which they saw a giant out on the ocean beating the waves with a club.

Kil Arthur went up to the giant's castle, and struck the pole of combat such a blow that the giant in the ocean heard it above the noise of his club as he pounded the waves.

'What do you want?' asked the giant in the ocean, as he stopped from the pounding.

'I want you to come in here to land,' said Kil Arthur, 'and fight with a better man than yourself.'

The giant came to land, and standing near his castle said to Kil Arthur: 'Which would you rather fight with,—grey stones or sharp weapons?'

'Grey stones,' said Kil Arthur.

They went at each other, and fought the most terrible battle that either of them had ever seen till that day. At last Kil Arthur pushed the giant to his shoulders through solid earth.

'Take me out of this,' cried the giant, 'and I'll give you my sword of light that never missed a blow, my Druidic rod of most powerful enchantment, and my healing draught which cures every sickness and wound.'

'Well,' said Kil Arthur, 'I'll go for your sword and try it.'

He went to the giant's castle for the sword, the rod, and the healing draught. When he returned the giant said: 'Try the sword on that tree out there.'

'Oh,' said Kil Arthur, 'there is no tree so good as your own neck,' and with that he swept off the head of the giant; took it, and went on his way till he came to a house. He went in and put the head on a table; but that instant it disappeared,—went away of itself. Food and drink of every kind came on the table. When Kil Arthur had eaten and the table was cleared by some invisible power, the giant's head bounded on to the table, and with it a pack of cards.

'Perhaps this head wants to play with me,' thought Kil Arthur, and he cut his own cards and shuffled them.

The head took up the cards and played with its mouth as well as any man could with his hands. It won all the time,—wasn't playing fairly. Then Kil Arthur thought: 'I'll settle this;' and he took the cards and showed how the head had taken five points in the game that didn't belong to it. Then the head sprang at him, struck and beat him till he seized and hurled it into the fire.

As soon as he had the head in the fire a beautiful woman stood before him, and said: 'You have killed nine of my brothers, and this was the best of the nine. I have eight more brothers who go out to fight with four hundred men each day, and they kill them all; but next morning the four hundred are alive again and my brothers have to do battle anew. Now my mother and these eight brothers will be here soon; and they'll go down on their bended knees and curse you who killed my nine brothers, and I'm afraid your blood will rise within you when you hear the curses, and you'll kill my eight remaining brothers.'

'Oh,' said Kil Arthur, 'I'll be deaf when the curses are spoken; I'll not hear them.' Then he went to a couch and lay down. Presently the mother and eight brothers came, and cursed Kil Arthur with all the curses they knew. He heard them to the end, but gave no word from himself.

Next morning he rose early, girded on his nine-edged sword, went forth to where the eight brothers were going to fight the four hundred, and said to the eight: 'Sit down, and I'll fight in your place.'

Kil Arthur faced the four hundred, and fought with them alone; and exactly at midday he had them all dead. 'Now some one,' said he, 'brings these to life again. I'll lie down among them and see who it is.'

Soon he saw an old hag coming with a brush in her hand, and an open vessel hanging from her neck by a string. When she came to the four hundred she dipped the brush into the vessel and sprinkled the liquid which was in it over the bodies of the men. They rose up behind her as she passed along.

'Bad luck to you,' said Kil Arthur, 'you are the one that keeps them alive;' then he seized her. Putting one of his feet on her two ankles, and grasping her by the head and shoulders, he twisted her body till he put the life out of her.

When dying she said: 'I put you under a curse, to keep on this road till you come to the 'ram of the five rocks,' and tell him you have killed the hag of the heights and all her care.'

He went to the place where the ram of the five rocks lived and struck the pole of combat before his castle. Out came the ram, and they fought till Kil Arthur seized his enemy and dashed the brains out of him against the rocks.

Then he went to the castle of the beautiful woman whose nine brothers he had killed, and for whose eight brothers he had slain the four hundred. When he appeared the mother rejoiced; the eight brothers blessed him and gave him their sister in marriage; and Kil Arthur took the beautiful woman to his father's castle in Erin, where they both lived happily and well.

23

The Father of Gods and Men

(Norse)

Odin, Wuotan, or Woden was the highest and holiest god of the Northern races. He was the all-pervading spirit of the universe, the personification of the air, the god of universal wisdom and victory, and the leader and protector of princes and heroes. As all the gods were supposed to be descended from him, he was surnamed Allfather, and as eldest and chief among them he occupied the highest seat in Asgard. Known by the name of Hlidskialf, this chair was not only an exalted throne, but also a mighty watch-tower, from whence he could overlook the whole world and see at a glance all that was happening among gods, giants, elves, dwarfs, and men.

From the hall of Heaven he rode away
To Lidskialf, and sate upon his throne,
The mount, from whence his eye surveys the world.
And far from Heaven he turned his shining orbs
To look on Midgard, and the earth, and men.

Balder Dead (Matthew Arnold).

None but Odin and his wife and queen Frigga were privileged to use this seat, and when they occupied it they generally gazed towards the south and west, the goal of all the hopes and excursions of the Northern nations. Odin was generally represented as a tall, vigorous man, about fifty years of age, either with dark curling hair or with a long grey beard and bald head. He was clad in a suit of grey, with a blue hood, and his muscular body was enveloped in a wide blue mantle flecked with grey—an emblem of the sky with its fleecy clouds. In his hand Odin generally carried the infallible spear Gungnir, which was so sacred that an oath sworn upon its point could never be broken, and on his finger or arm he wore the marvellous ring, Draupnir, the emblem of fruitfulness, precious beyond compare. When seated upon his throne or armed for the fray, to mingle in which he would often descend to earth, Odin wore his eagle helmet; but when he wandered peacefully about the earth in human guise, to see what men were doing, he generally donned a broad-brimmed hat, drawn low over his forehead to conceal the fact that he possessed but one eye.

Two ravens, Hugin (thought) and Munin (memory), perched upon his shoulders as he sat upon his throne, and these he sent out into the wide world every morning, anxiously watching for their return at nightfall, when they whispered into his ears news of all they had seen and heard. Thus he was kept well informed about everything that was happening on earth.

Hugin and Munin
Fly each day
Over the spacious earth.
I fear for Hugin
That he come not back,
Yet more anxious am I for Munin.

Norse Mythology (R. B. Anderson).

At his feet crouched two wolves or hunting hounds, Geri and Freki, animals which were therefore considered sacred to him, and of good omen if met by the way. Odin always fed these wolves with his own hands from meat set before him. He required no food at all for himself, and seldom tasted anything except the sacred mead.

> Geri and Freki
> The war-wont sates,
> The triumphant sire of hosts;
> But on wine only
> The famed in arms
> Odin, ever lives.
>
> *Lay of Grimnir (Thorpe's tr.).*

When seated in state upon his throne, Odin rested his feet upon a footstool of gold, the work of the gods, all of whose furniture and utensils were fashioned either of that precious metal or of silver.

Besides the magnificent hall Glads-heim, where stood the twelve seats occupied by the gods when they met in council, and Valaskialf, where his throne, Hlidskialf, was placed, Odin had a third palace in Asgard, situated in the midst of the marvellous grove Glasir, whose shimmering leaves were of red gold.

24

The Discovery of Flax

(Norse)

There was once a peasant who daily left his wife and children in the valley to take his sheep up the mountain to pasture; and as he watched his flock grazing on the mountain-side, he often had opportunity to use his cross-bow and bring down a chamois, whose flesh would furnish his larder with food for many a day.

While pursuing a fine animal one day he saw it disappear behind a boulder, and when he came to the spot, he was amazed to see a doorway in the neighbouring glacier, for in the excitement of the pursuit he had climbed higher and higher, until he was now on top of the mountain, where glittered the everlasting snow.

The shepherd boldly passed through the open door, and soon found himself in a wonderful jewelled cave hung with stalactites, in the centre of which stood a beautiful woman, clad in silvery robes, and attended by a host of lovely maidens crowned with Alpine roses. In his surprise, the shepherd sank to his knees, and as in a dream heard the queenly central figure bid him choose anything he saw to carry away with him. Although dazzled by the glow of the precious stones around him, the shepherd's eyes constantly reverted to a little nosegay of blue flowers which the gracious apparition held in her hand, and he now timidly proffered a request that it might become his. Smiling with pleasure, Holda, for it was she, gave it to him, telling him he had chosen wisely and would live as long as the flowers did not droop and fade. Then, giving the shepherd a measure of seed which she told him to sow in his field, the goddess bade him begone; and as the thunder pealed and the earth shook, the poor man found himself out upon the mountain-side once more, and slowly wended his way home to his wife, to whom he told his adventure and showed the lovely blue flowers and the measure of seed.

The woman reproached her husband bitterly for not having brought some of the precious stones which he so glowingly described, instead of the blossoms and seed; nevertheless the man proceeded to sow the latter, and he found to his surprise that the measure supplied seed enough for several acres.

Soon the little green shoots began to appear, and one moonlight night, while the peasant was gazing upon them, as was his wont, for he felt a curious attraction to the field which he had sown, and often lingered there wondering what kind of grain would be produced, he saw a misty form hover above the field, with hands outstretched as if in blessing. At last the field blossomed, and countless little blue flowers opened their calyxes to the golden sun. When the flowers had withered and the seed was ripe, Holda came once more to teach the peasant and his wife how to harvest the flax—for such it was—and from it to spin, weave, and bleach linen. As the people of the neighbourhood willingly purchased both linen and flax-seed, the peasant and his wife soon grew very rich indeed, and while he ploughed, sowed, and harvested, she spun, wove, and bleached the linen. The man lived to a good old age, and saw his grandchildren and great-grandchildren grow up around him. All this time his carefully treasured bouquet had remained fresh as when he first brought it home, but one day he saw that during the night the flowers had drooped and were dying.

Knowing what this portended, and that he too must die,

the peasant climbed the mountain once more to the glacier, and found again the doorway for which he had often vainly searched. He entered the icy portal, and was never seen or heard of again, for, according to the legend, the goddess took him under her care, and bade him live in her cave, where his every wish was gratified.

25

The Fool and the Birch Tree

(Russian)

In a certain country there once lived an old man who had three sons. Two of them had their wits about them, but the third was a fool. The old man died and his sons divided his property among themselves by lot. The sharp-witted ones got plenty of all sorts of good things, but nothing fell to the share of the Simpleton but one ox—and that such a skinny one!

Well, fair-time came round, and the clever brothers got ready to go and transact business. The Simpleton saw this, and said:

'I'll go, too, brothers, and take my ox for sale.'

So he fastened a cord to the horn of the ox and drove it to the town. On his way he happened to pass through a forest, and in the forest there stood an old withered Birch-tree. Whenever the wind blew the Birch-tree creaked.

'What is the Birch creaking about?' thinks the Simpleton. 'Surely it must be bargaining for my ox? Well,' says he, 'if you want to buy it, why buy it. I'm not against selling it. The price of the ox is twenty roubles. I can't take less. Out with the money!'

The Birch made no reply, only went on creaking. But the Simpleton fancied that it was asking for the ox on credit. 'Very good,' says he, 'I'll wait till to-morrow!' He tied the ox to the Birch, took leave of the tree, and went home. Presently in came the clever brothers, and began questioning him:

'Well, Simpleton! sold your ox?'

'I've sold it.'

'For how much?'

'For twenty roubles.'

'Where's the money?'

'I haven't received the money yet. It was settled I should go for it to-morrow.'

'There's simplicity for you!' say they.

Early next morning the Simpleton got up, dressed himself, and went to the Birch-tree for his money. He reached the wood; there stood the Birch, waving in the wind, but the ox was not to be seen. During the night the wolves had eaten it.

'Now, then, neighbor!' he exclaimed, 'pay me my money. You promised you'd pay me to-day.'

The wind blew, the Birch creaked, and the Simpleton cried:

'What a liar you are! Yesterday you kept saying, 'I'll pay you to-morrow,' and now you make just the same promise. Well, so be it, I'll wait one day more, but not a bit longer. I want the money myself.'

When he returned home, his brothers again questioned him closely:

'Have you got your money?'

'No, brothers; I've got to wait for my money again.'

'Whom have you sold it to?'

'To the withered Birch-tree in the forest.'

'Oh, what an idiot!'

On the third day the Simpleton took his hatchet and went to the forest. Arriving there, he demanded his money; but the Birch-tree only creaked and creaked. 'No, no, neighbor!' says he. 'If you're always going to treat me to promises, there'll be no getting anything out of you. I don't like such joking; I'll pay you out well for it!'

With that he pitched into it with his hatchet, so that its chips flew about in all directions. Now, in that Birch-tree there was a hollow, and in that hollow some robbers had hidden a pot full of gold. The tree split asunder, and the Simpleton caught sight of the gold. He took as much of it as the skirts of his caftan would hold, and toiled home with it. There he showed his brothers what he had brought.

'Where did you get such a lot, Simpleton?' said they.

'A neighbour gave it me for my ox. But this isn't anything like the whole of it; a good half of it I didn't bring home with me! Come along, brothers, let's get the rest!'

Well, they went into the forest, secured the money, and carried it home.

'Now mind, Simpleton,' say the sensible brothers, 'don't tell anyone that we've such a lot of gold.'

'Never fear, I won't tell a soul!'

All of a sudden they run up against a *Diachok*, and says he:—

'What's that, brothers, you're bringing from the forest?'

The sharp ones replied, 'Mushrooms.' But the Simpleton contradicted them, saying:

'They're telling lies! we're carrying money; here, just take a look at it.'

The Diachok uttered such an 'Oh!'—then he flung himself on the gold, and began seizing handfuls of it and stuffing them into his pocket. The Simpleton grew angry, dealt him a blow with his hatchet, and struck him dead.

'Heigh, Simpleton! what have you been and done!' cried his brothers. 'You're a lost man, and you'll be the cause of our destruction, too! Wherever shall we put the dead body?'

They thought and thought, and at last they dragged it to an empty cellar and flung it in there. But later on in the evening the eldest brother said to the second one:—

'This piece of work is sure to turn out badly. When they begin looking for the Diachok, you'll see that Simpleton will tell them everything. Let's kill a goat and bury it in the cellar, and hide the body of the dead man in some other place.'

Well, they waited till the dead of night; then they killed a goat and flung it into the cellar, but they carried the Diachok to another place and there hid him in the ground. Several days passed, and then people began looking everywhere for the Diachok, asking everyone about him.

'What do you want him for?' said the Simpleton, when he was asked. 'I killed him some time ago with my hatchet, and my brothers carried him into the cellar.'

Straightway they laid hands on the Simpleton, crying, 'Take us there and show him to us.'

The Simpleton went down into the cellar, got hold of the goat's head, and asked:—

'Was your Diachok dark-haired?'

'He was.'

'And had he a beard?'

'Yes, he'd a beard.'

'And horns?'

'What horns are you talking about, Simpleton?'

'Well, see for yourselves,' said he, tossing up the head to them. They looked, saw it was a goat's, spat in the Simpleton's face, and went their ways home.

26

The First Labour–the Nemean Lion

(Greek)

It happened that a fearful lion lived in Nemea, a wild district in upper Argolis, and it devastated all the land and was the terror of the inhabitants. Eurystheus ordered Herakles to bring him the skin of this lion. So Herakles took his bow, his quiver, and heavy club and started out in search of the beast.

When he had reached a little town which is in the neighborhood of Nemea he was kindly received by a good countryman, who promised to put him on the track of the lion if he would sacrifice the animal to Zeus.

Herakles promised, and the countryman went with him to show him the way. When they reached the place where traces of the lion were seen, Herakles said to his guide: 'Remain here thirty days. If I return safely from the lion-hunt you must sacrifice a sheep to Zeus, for he is the god who will have saved me. But if I am slain by the lion you must sacrifice the sheep to me, for after my death I shall be honoured as a hero.' Having said this, Herakles went his way.

He reached the wilderness of Nemea, where he spent several days in looking for the lion, but without success. Not a trace of him could be found, nor did he fall in with any human being, for there was no one bold enough to wander around in that wilderness. Finally he spied the lion as he was about to crawl into his den.

The lion was indeed worthy of his terrible fame. His size was prodigious, his eyes shot forth flames of fire, and his tongue licked his bloody chops. When he roared, the whole desert resounded.

But Herakles stood fearlessly near a grove from whence he might approach the lion, and suddenly shot at him with his bow and arrow, hitting him squarely in the breast. The arrow glanced aside, and slipping around the lion's neck, fell on a rock behind him. When Herakles saw this he knew that the lion was proof against arrows and must be killed in some other way, and seizing his club, he gave chase to him.

The lion made for a cave which had two mouths. Herakles closed up one of the entrances with heavy rocks and entered the other. He seized the lion by the throat and then came a terrible struggle, but Herakles squeezed him in his mighty arms until he gasped for breath, and at last lay dead.

Then Herakles took up the huge body and, throwing it easily over his shoulder, returned to the place where he had left the countryman. It was on the last of the thirty appointed days, and the rustic, supposing that Herakles had come to his death through the lion, was about to offer up a sheep as a sacrifice in his honor.

He rejoiced greatly when he saw Herakles alive and victorious, and the sheep was offered up to Zeus. Herakles left the little town and went to Mykenæ to the house of his uncle and showed him the dead body of the terrible lion. Eurystheus was so greatly frightened at the sight that he hid himself within a tower whose walls were built of solid brass.

And he ordered Herakles not to enter the city again, but to stay outside of its gates until he had performed the other labors.

Herakles stripped the skin from the lion with his fingers, although it was so tough, and knowing it to be arrow-proof, took it for a cloak and wore it as long as he lived.

27

Ivan Popyalof

(Russian)

Once upon a time there was an old couple, and they had three sons. Two of these had their wits about them, but the third was a simpleton, Ivan by name, surnamed Popyalof.

For twelve whole years Ivan lay among the ashes from the stove; but then he arose, and shook himself, so that six poods of ashes fell off from him.

Now in the land in which Ivan lived there was never any day, but always night. That was a Snake's doing. Well, Ivan undertook to kill that Snake, so he said to his father, 'Father, make me a mace five poods in weight.' And when he had got the mace, he went out into the fields, and flung it straight up in the air, and then he went home. The next day he went out into the fields to the spot from which he had flung the mace on high, and stood there with his head thrown back. So when the mace fell down again it hit him on the forehead. And the mace broke in two.

Ivan went home and said to his father, 'Father, make me another mace, a ten pood one.' And when he had got it he went out into the fields, and flung it aloft. And the mace went flying through the air for three days and three nights. On the fourth day Ivan went out to the same spot, and when the mace came tumbling down, he put his knee in the way, and the mace broke over it into three pieces.

Ivan went home and told his father to make him a third

mace, one of fifteen poods weight. And when he had got it, he went out into the fields and flung it aloft. And the mace was up in the air six days. On the seventh Ivan went to the same spot as before. Down fell the mace, and when it struck Ivan's forehead, the forehead bowed under it. Thereupon he said, 'This mace will do for the Snake!'

So when he had got everything ready, he went forth with his brothers to fight the Snake. He rode and rode, and presently there stood before him a hut on fowl's legs, and in that hut lived the Snake. There all the party came to a standstill. Then Ivan hung up his gloves, and said to his brothers, 'Should blood drop from my gloves, make haste to help me.' When he had said this he went into the hut and sat down under the boarding.Presently there rode up a Snake with three heads. His steed stumbled, his hound howled, his falcon clamoured. Then cried the Snake:

'Wherefore hast thou stumbled, O Steed! hast thou howled, O Hound! hast thou clamoured, O Falcon?'

'How can I but stumble,' replied the Steed, 'when under the boarding sits Ivan Popyalof?'

Then said the Snake, 'Come forth, Ivanushka! Let us try our strength together.' Ivan came forth, and they began to fight. And Ivan killed the Snake, and then sat down again beneath the boarding.

Presently there came another Snake, a six-headed one, and him, too, Ivan killed. And then there came a third, which had twelve heads. Well, Ivan began to fight with him, and lopped off nine of his heads. The Snake had no strength left in him. Just then a raven came flying by, and it croaked:

'Krof? Krof!' Then the Snake cried to the Raven, 'Fly, and tell my wife to come and devour Ivan Popyalof.'

But Ivan cried: 'Fly, and tell my brothers to come, and then we will kill this Snake, and give his flesh to thee.'

And the Raven gave ear to what Ivan said, and flew to his

brothers and began to croak above their heads. The brothers awoke, and when they heard the cry of the Raven, they hastened to their brother's aid. And they killed the Snake, and then, having taken his heads, they went into his hut and destroyed them. And immediately there was bright light throughout the whole land.

After killing the Snake, Ivan Popyalof and his brothers set off on their way home. But he had forgotten to take away his gloves, so he went back to fetch them, telling his brothers to wait for him meanwhile. Now when he had reached the hut and was going to take away his gloves, he heard the voices of the Snake's wife and daughters, who were talking with each other. So he turned himself into a cat, and began to mew outside the door. They let him in, and he listened to everything they said. Then he got his gloves and hastened away.

As soon as he came to where his brothers were, he mounted his horse, and they all started afresh. They rode and rode; presently they saw before them a green meadow, and on that meadow lay silken cushions. Then the elder brothers said, 'Let's turn out our horses to graze here, while we rest ourselves a little.'

But Ivan said, 'Wait a minute, brothers!' and he seized his mace, and struck the cushions with it. And out of those cushions there streamed blood.

So they all went on further. They rode and rode; presently there stood before them an apple-tree, and upon it were gold and silver apples. Then the elder brothers said, 'Let's eat an apple apiece.' But Ivan said, 'Wait a minute, brothers; I'll try them first,' and he took his mace, and struck the apple-tree with it. And out of the tree streamed blood.

So they went on further. They rode and rode, and by and by they saw a spring in front of them. And the elder brothers cried, 'Let's have a drink of water.' But Ivan Popyalof cried: 'Stop, brothers!' and he raised his mace and struck the spring, and its waters became blood.

For the meadow, the silken cushions, the apple-tree, and the spring, were all of them daughters of the Snake.

After killing the Snake's daughters, Ivan and his brothers went on homewards. Presently came the Snake's Wife flying after them, and she opened her jaws from the sky to the earth, and tried to swallow up Ivan. But Ivan and his brothers threw three poods of salt into her mouth. She swallowed the salt, thinking it was Ivan Popyalof, but afterwards—when she had tasted the salt, and found out it was not Ivan—she flew after him again.

Then he perceived that danger was at hand, and so he let his horse go free, and hid himself behind twelve doors in the forge of Kuzma and Demian. The Snake's Wife came flying up, and said to Kuzma and Demian, 'Give me up Ivan Popyalof.' But they replied:

'Send your tongue through the twelve doors and take him.' So the Snake's Wife began licking the doors. But meanwhile they all heated iron pincers, and as soon as she had sent her tongue through into the smithy, they caught tight hold of her by the tongue, and began thumping her with hammers. And when the Snake's Wife was dead they consumed her with fire, and scattered her ashes to the winds. And then they went home, and there they lived and enjoyed themselves, feasting and revelling, and drinking mead and wine.

28

The Willow of Mukochima

(Japanese)

Not far from Matsue, the great city of the Province of the Gods, there once dwelt a widow and her son. Their wooden hut looked upon the Shinji Lake set in a framework of mountain peaks. Ayame was true to the old religion, the worship of the descendants of Izanagi and Izanami. Long ere the sun rose above the chain of hills, she was up, and, with Umewaki's hand clasped closely in her own, went down to the verge of the lake. First they laved their faces in the cool water, then, turning towards the east, they clapped their hands four times and saluted the sun. 'Konnichi Sama! All hail to thee, Day-Maker. Shine and bring joy to the Place of the Issuing of Clouds.' Then, having turned towards the west, mother and son blessed the holy, immemorial shrine of Kitzuki; towards the north and the south they turned and prayed to the gods, unto each one, who dwell in the blue Plain of High Heaven.

Umewaki's father had been dead many years, and the love of the mother was centred upon her son. He was in the open air from sunrise to nightfall; sometimes by Ayame's side, sometimes alone, watching the heron or the crane, or listening to the sweet call of the *yamabato*. The hut was in a remote spot, but Ayame felt that her son was safe in the keeping of the good gods.

It was a beautiful summer morning. Ayame and Umewaki awakened soon after dawn. Hand in hand they went to the shore of Lake Shinji. It still slept beneath the faintly-tinged haze. The Lady of Fire had not whispered of her approach to the soft mists that veiled the hills. Mother and son waited patiently. As the Day-Maker appeared, they cried, 'Konnichi Sama! Great Goddess, shine upon thy land. Give it beauty and peace and joy.' Then mother and son returned to the hut. Ayame plied her shuttle, and Umewaki left her to wander in the woods.

Noon came. 'My boy has met some woodcutter; he talks with him in the shade of the pine trees,' she thought. As the evening drew on, she said, 'He is with little Kime, his playmate, but I shall soon hear his soft footstep.' Night fell. 'Once only has he been so late; when he went to Matsue with the good Shijo.' She looked through the paper window, and then stepped out. The hills cast a mysterious shadow on the surface of the lake. Still there was no sign of Umewaki. The mother called his name. No response came save the echo of her own voice. Now she searched far and near. To every peasant she put the question, 'Have you seen my Umewaki?' But she always received the same answer. At last she returned home weary: 'He may be there waiting for me,' she thought. It was midnight: the hut was empty. Ayame was heavy at heart, and as she lay upon her mat she wept bitterly, and cried to the gods to give her back her son. So the night passed. In the morning she learned that a band of robbers had been seen among the mountains.

Poor Umewaki had, in truth, been stolen by the robbers. He was watched night and day, and had no chance of escape. From town to town they travelled. Through strange villages where the name of Buddha was upon the lips of the people, across great plains unsheltered by mountains. The summer passed, and autumn came. Still the men would not let Umewaki go. They treated him cruelly, and he began to pine away. Then the robbers knew that he was of no use to them. As they neared Yedo, they left him, faint and weary, on the roadside. A kind man of

Mukochima found the poor little fellow and carried him to his home. But Umewaki had not long to live. On the fifteenth day of the third month, the day sacred to the awakening of the Spring, he opened his eyes, and called to the good woman who tended him, 'Tell my dear mother that I love her, and would stay with her, but the Lady of the Great Light calls me, and I must obey.'

Ayame had left her quiet hut by the lake of Shinji to follow the men who had stolen her son. The autumn and the winter had gone by, and still she persevered. As she passed through Mukochima, she heard that a poor boy was dead, and soon found that it was her son. She went to the house where he had been cared for, and the woman gave her Umewaki's message.

In the evening, when all was quiet, Ayame crept to the graveside of her child. Near it a sacred willow was planted. The slender tree moved in the wind. There was a whispered sound: the voice of Umewaki speaking softly to the mother from his place of rest. She was happy.

Every evening she came to listen to the sighing of the willow. Every evening she lay down happy to have spoken to her son.

On the fifteenth day of the third month, the day of the awakening of the Spring, many pilgrims visit the resting-place of Umewaki. If it rains on that day, the people say, 'Umewaki weeps.'

The willow is under the protection of the gods. Storm and rain can do it no hurt.

29

The Two Jeebi

(Native American)

There lived a hunter in the north, who had a wife and one child. His lodge stood far off in the forest, several days' journey from any other. He spent his days in hunting, and his evenings in relating to his wife the incidents that had befallen him. As game was very abundant, he found no difficulty in killing as much as they wanted. Just in all his acts, he lived a peaceful and happy life.

One evening during the winter season, it chanced that he remained out longer than usual, and his wife began to fear that some accident had befallen him. It was already dark. She listened attentively, and at last heard the sound of approaching footsteps.

Not doubting that it was her husband, she went to the door and beheld two strange females. She bade them enter, and invited them to remain. She observed that they were total strangers in the country. There was something so peculiar in their looks, air and manner, that she was disturbed by their presence. They would not come near to the fire. They sat in a remote part of the lodge, shy and taciturn, and drew their garments about them in such a manner as nearly to hide their faces. So far as she could judge, they were pale, hollow-eyed, and long-visaged, very thin and emaciated.

There was but little light in the lodge, as the fire was low, and its fitful flashes, by disclosing their white faces and then dropping them in sudden darkness, served rather to increase than to dispel her fears.

'Merciful Spirit!' cried a voice from the opposite part of the lodge; 'there are two corpses clothed with garments!'

The hunter's wife turned around, but seeing nobody save her little child, staring across from under his blanket, she said to herself, 'The boy can not speak; the sounds were but the gusts of wind.' She trembled, and was ready to sink to the earth.

Her husband at this moment entered, and in some measure relieved her alarm. He threw down the carcass of a large fat deer.

'Behold what a fine and fat animal!' cried the mysterious females; and they immediately ran and pulled off pieces of the whitest fat, which they greedily devoured.

The hunter and his wife looked on with astonishment, but remained silent. They supposed that their guests might have been stricken with famine.

The next day, however, the same unusual conduct was repeated. The strange females again tore off the fat and devoured it with eagerness. The third day, the hunter thought that he would anticipate their wants by tying up a share of the hunt, and placing it apart for their express use. They accepted it, but still appeared dissatisfied, and went to the wife's portion and tore off more.

The hunter and his wife were surprised at such rude and unaccountable conduct, but they remained silent, for they respected their guests, and had observed that they had been attended with marked good luck during the sojourn of these mysterious visitors in their lodge.

In other respects, the deportment of the females was strictly unexceptionable. They were modest, distant, and silent. They never uttered a word during the day. At night they would occupy themselves in procuring wood, which they carried to the lodge, and then, restoring the implements exactly where they had found them, resume their places without speaking. They were never known to stay out until daylight. They never laughed or jested.

The winter was nearly passed away, when, one evening, the hunter was abroad later than usual. The moment he came in and laid down his day's hunt, as was his custom, before his wife, the two females seized upon the deer and began to tear off the fat in so unceremonious a way that her anger was excited. She constrained herself, however, in a good degree, but she could not conceal her feelings, though she said but little.

The strange guests observed the state of her mind, and they became uneasy, and withdrew further still into the remote gloom of the lodge. The good hunter saw the eclipse that was darkening the quiet of his lodge, and carefully inquired of its cause; but his wife denied having used any words of complaining or reproach.

They retired to their couches, and the hunter tried to compose himself to sleep, but could not, for the sighs and sobs of the two females were incessant. He arose on his couch and addressed them as follows:

'Tell me,' said he, 'what is it that gives you pain of mind and causes you to bemoan your presence here. Has my wife given you offense, or trespassed upon the rights of hospitality?'

They replied in the negative. 'We have been treated by you with kindness and affection. It is not for any slight we have received that we weep. Our mission is not to you only. We come from the other land to test mankind, and to try the sincerity of the living. Often we have heard the bereaved by death say that if the lost could be restored, they would devote their lives to make them happy. We have been moved by the bitter lamentations which have reached the place of the departed, and have come to make proof of the sincerity of those who have lost friends. We are your two dead sisters. Three moons were allotted us by the Master of Life to make the trial. More than half the time had been successfully passed, when the angry feelings of your wife indicated the irksomeness you felt at our presence, and has made us resolve on our departure.'

They continued to talk to the hunter and his wife, gave them instructions as to a future life, and pronounced a blessing upon them.

'There is one point,' they added, 'of which we wish to speak. You have thought our conduct very strange and rude in possessing ourselves of the choicest parts of your hunt. *That* was the point of trial selected to put you to. It is the wife's peculiar privilege. You love your wife. For another to usurp what belongs to her, we know to be the severest test of her goodness of heart, and consequently of your temper and feelings. We knew your manners and customs, but we came to prove you, not by complying with but by violating them. Pardon us. We are the agents of him who sent us. Peace to your dwelling. Farewell!'

When they ceased, total darkness filled the lodge. No object could be seen. The inmates heard the lodge-door open and shut, but they never saw more of the Two Spirits.

The hunter found the success which they had promised. He became celebrated in the chase, and never wanted for any thing. He had many children, all of whom grew up to manhood; and he who had lain in the lodge, a little child, while the Jeebi dwelt there, led them in all good deeds, and health, peace, and long life were the rewards of the hunter's hospitality.

30

The Ghost of Wahaula Temple

(*Hawaiian*)

Hawaiian temples were never works of art. Broken lava was always near the site upon which a temple was to be built. Rough unhewn stones were easily piled into massive walls and laid in terraces for altar and floors. Water-worn pebbles were carried from the nearest beach and strewn over the uneven floor, making a comparatively smooth place over which the naked feet of the temple dwellers passed without the injuries which would otherwise frequently come from the sharp-edged lava. Rude grass huts built on terraces were the abodes of the priests and of the high chiefs who sometimes visited the places of sacrifice. Elevated, flat-topped piles of stones were usually built at one end of the temple for the chief idols and the sacrifices placed before them. Simplicity of detail marked every step of temple erection.

No hewn pillars or arched gateways of even the most primitive designs can be found in any of the temples whether of recent date or belonging to remote antiquity. There was no attempt at ornamentation even in the images of the great gods which they worshipped. Crude, uncouth, and hideous were the images before which they offered sacrifice and prayer.

In themselves the *heiaus*, or temples, of the Hawaiian Islands have but little attraction. To-day they seem more like massive walled cattle-pens than places which had ever been used for sacred worship.

On the southeast coast of the island of Hawaii near Kalapana is one of the largest, oldest, and best preserved heiaus, or temples, in the Hawaiian Islands. It is no exception to the architectural rule for Hawaiian temples, and is worthy the name of temple only as it is intimately associated with the religious customs of the Hawaiians. Its walls are several feet thick and in places ten to twelve feet high. It is divided into rooms or pens, in one of which still lies the huge sacrificial stone upon which victims—sometimes human—were slain before the bodies were placed as offerings in front of the hideous idols leaning against the stone walls.

This heiau now bears the name Wahaula, or 'red-mouth.' In ancient times it was known as Ahaula, or 'the red assembly,' possibly denoting that at times the priests and their attendants wore red mantles in their processions or during some part of their sacred ceremonies.

This temple is said to be the oldest of all the Hawaiian heiaus—except possibly the heiau at Kohala on the northern coast of the same island. These two heiaus date back in tradition to the time of Paao, the priest from Upolu, Samoa, who was said to have built them. He was the traditional father of the priestly line which ran parallel to the royal genealogy of the Kamehamehas during several centuries until the last high priest, Hewahewa, became a follower of Jesus Christ—the Saviour of the world. This was the last heiau destroyed when the ancient *tabu*s and ceremonial rites were overthrown by the chiefs just before the coming of Christian missionaries. At that time the grass houses of the priests were burned and in these raging flames were thrown the wooden idols back of the altars and the bamboo huts of the soothsayers and the rude images on the walls, with everything combustible which belonged to the ancient order of worship. Only the walls and rough stone floors were left in the temple.

In the outer temple court was the most noted sacred grave in all the islands. Earth had been carried from the mountain-sides inland. Leaves and decaying trees added to the permanency of the soil. Here in a most unlikely place it was said that all the varieties of trees then found in the islands had been gathered by the priests—the descendants of Paao. To this day the grave stands by the temple walls, an object of superstitious awe among the natives. Many of the varieties of trees there planted have died, leaving only those which were more hardy and needed less priestly care than they received a hundred years or more ago.

The temple is built near the coast on the rough, sharp, broken rocks of an ancient lava flow. In many places in and around the temple the lava was dug out, making holes three or four feet across and from one to two feet deep. These in the days of the priesthood had been filled with earth brought in baskets from the mountains. Here they raised sweet potatoes and taro and bananas. Now the rains have washed the soil away and to the unknowing there is no sign of previous agriculture. Near these depressions and along the paths leading to Wahaula other holes were sometimes cut out of the hard fine-grained lava. When heavy rains fell, little grooves carried the drops of water to these holes and they became small cisterns. Here the thirsty messengers running from one priestly clan to another, or the traveler or worshippers coming to the sacred place, could almost always find a few drops of water to quench their thirst.

Usually these water-holes were covered with a large flat stone under which the water ran into the cistern. To this day these small water places border the path across the pahoehoe lava field which lies adjacent to the broken a-a lava upon which the Wahaula heiau is built. Many of them are still covered as in the days of the long ago.

It is not strange that legends have developed through the mists of the centuries around this rude old temple.

Wahaula was a tabu temple of the very highest rank. The native chants said,

No keia heiau oia ke kapu enaena.

['Concerning this heiau is the burning tabu.']

'*Enaena*' means 'burning with a red hot rage.' The heiau was so thoroughly 'tabu,' or '*kapu*,' that the smoke of its fires falling upon any of the people or even upon any one of the chiefs was sufficient cause for punishment by death, with the body as a sacrifice to the gods of the temple.

These gods were of the very highest rank among the Hawaiian deities. Certain days were tabu to Lono—or Rongo, as he was known in other island groups of the Pacific Ocean. Other days belonged to Ku—who was also worshipped from New Zealand to Tahiti. At other times Kane, known as Tane by many Polynesians, was held supreme. Then again Kanaloa—or Tanaroa, sometimes worshipped in Samoa and other island groups as the greatest of all their gods—had his days especially set apart for sacrifice and chant.

The Mu, or 'body-catcher,' of this heiau with his assistants seems to have been continually on the watch for human victims, and woe to the unfortunate man who carelessly or ignorantly walked where the winds blew the smoke from the temple fires. No one dared rescue him from the hands of the hunter of men—for then the wrath of all the gods was sure to follow him all the days of his life.

The people of the districts around Wahaula always watched the course of the winds with great anxiety, carefully noting the direction taken by the smoke. This smoke was the shadow cast by the deity worshipped, and was far more sacred than the shadow of the highest chief or king in all the islands.

It was always sufficient cause for death if a common man allowed his shadow to fall upon any tabu chief, i.e., a chief of especially high rank; but in this 'burning tabu,' if any man permitted the smoke or shadow of the god who was being worshipped in this temple to come near to him or overshadow him, it was a mark of such great disrespect that the god was supposed to be enaena, or red hot with rage.

Many ages ago a young chief whom we shall know by the name Kahele determined to take an especial journey around the island visiting all the noted and sacred places and becoming acquainted with the alii, or chiefs, of the other districts.

He passed from place to place, taking part with the chiefs who entertained him sometimes in the use of the *papa-hee*, or surf-board, riding the white-capped surf as it majestically swept shoreward—sometimes spending night after night in the innumerable gambling contests which passed under the name *pili waiwai*—and sometimes riding the narrow sled, or *holua*, with which Hawaiian chiefs raced down the steep grassed lanes. Then again, with a deep sense of the solemnity of sacred things, he visited the most noted of the heiaus and made contributions to the offerings before the gods. Thus the days passed, and the slow journey was very pleasant to Kahele.

In time he came to Puna, the district in which was located the temple Wahaula.

But alas! in the midst of the many stories of the past which he had heard, and the many pleasures he had enjoyed while on his journey, Kahele forgot the peculiar power of the tabu of the smoke of Wahaula. The fierce winds of the south were blowing and changing from point to point. The young man saw the sacred grove in the edge of which the temple walls could be discerned. Thin wreaths of smoke were tossed here and there from the temple fires.

Kahele hastened toward the temple. The Mu was watching his coming and joyfully marking him as a victim. The altars of the gods were desolate, and if but a particle of smoke fell upon the young man no one could keep him from the hands of the executioner.

The perilous moment came. The warm breath of one of the fires touched the young chief's cheek. Soon a blow from the club of the Mu laid him senseless on the rough stones of the outer court of the temple. The smoke of the wrath of the gods had fallen upon him, and it was well that he should lie as a sacrifice upon their altars.

Soon the body with the life still in it was thrown across the sacrificial stone. Sharp knives made from the strong wood of the bamboo let his life-blood flow down the depressions across the face of the stone. Quickly the body was dismembered and offered as a sacrifice.

For some reason the priests, after the flesh had decayed, set apart the bones for some special purpose. The legends imply that the bones were to be treated dishonorably. It may have been that the bones were folded together in the shape known as *unihipili*, or 'grasshopper' bones, i.e., folded and laid away for purposes of incantation. Such bundles of bones were put through a process of prayers and charms until at last it was thought a new spirit was created which dwelt in that bundle and gave the possessor a peculiar power in deeds of witchcraft.

The spirit of Kahele rebelled against this disposition of all that remained of his body. He wanted to be back in his native district, that he might enjoy the pleasures of the Underworld with his own chosen companions. Restlessly the spirit haunted the dark corners of the temple, watching the priests as they handled his bones.

Helplessly the ghost fumed and fretted against its condition. It did all that a disembodied spirit could do to attract the attention of the priests.

At last the spirit fled by night from this place of torment to the home which he had so joyfully left a short time before.

Kahele's father was the high chief of Kau. Surrounded by retainers, he passed his days in quietness and peace waiting for the return of his son.

One night a strange dream came to him. He heard a voice calling from the mysterious confines of the spirit-land. As he listened, a spirit form stood by his side. The ghost was that of his son Kahele.

By means of the dream the ghost revealed to the father that he had been put to death and that his bones were in great danger of dishonorable treatment.

The father awoke benumbed with fear, realizing that his son was calling upon him for immediate help. At once he left his people and journeyed from place to place secretly, not knowing where or when Kahele had died, but fully sure that the spirit of his vision was that of his son. It was not difficult to trace the young man. He had left his footprints openly all along the way. There was nothing of shame or dishonor—and the father's heart filled with pride as he hastened on.

From time to time, however, he heard the spirit voice calling him to save the bones of the body of his dead son. At last he felt that his journey was nearly done. He had followed the footsteps of Kahele almost entirely around the island, and had come to Puna—the last district before his own land of Kau would welcome his return.

The spirit voice could be heard now in the dream which nightly came to him. Warnings and directions were frequently given.

Then the chief came to the lava fields of Wahaula and lay down to rest. The ghost came to him again in a dream, telling him that great personal danger was near at hand. The chief was a very strong man, excelling in athletic and brave deeds, but in obedience to the spirit voice he rose early in the morning, secured oily nuts from a kukui-tree, beat out the oil, and anointed himself thoroughly.

Walking along carelessly as if to avoid suspicion, he drew near to the lands of the temple Wahaula. Soon a man came out to meet him. This man was an Olohe, a beardless man belonging to a lawless robber clan which infested the district, possibly assisting the man-hunters of the temple in securing victims for the temple altars. This Olohe was very strong and self-confident, and thought he would have but little difficulty in destroying this stranger who journeyed alone through Puna.

Almost all day the battle raged between the two men. Back and forth they forced each other over the lava beds. The chief's well-oiled body was very difficult for the Olohe to grasp. Bruised and bleeding from repeated falls on the rough lava, both of the combatants were becoming very weary. Then the chief made a new attack, forcing the Olohe into a narrow place from which there was no escape, and at last seizing him, breaking his bones, and then killing him.

As the shadows of night rested over the temple and its sacred grave the chief crept closer to the dreaded tabu walls. Concealing himself he waited for the ghost to reveal to him the best plan for action. The ghost came, but was compelled to bid the father wait patiently for a fit time when the secret place in which the bones were hidden could be safely visited.

For several days and nights the chief hid himself near the temple. He secretly uttered the prayers and incantations needed to secure the protection of his family gods.

One night the darkness was very great, and the priests and watchmen of the temple felt sure that no one would attempt to enter the sacred precincts. Deep sleep rested upon all the temple-dwellers.

Then the ghost of Kahele hastened to the place where the father was sleeping and aroused him for the dangerous task before him.

As the father arose he saw this ghost outlined in the darkness, beckoning him to follow. Step by step he felt his way cautiously over the rough path and along the temple walls until he saw the ghost standing near a great rock pointing at a part of the wall.

The father seized a stone which seemed to be the one most directly in the line of the ghost's pointing. To his surprise it very easily was removed from the wall. Back of it was a hollow place in which lay a bundle of folded bones. The ghost urged the chief to take these bones and depart quickly.

The father obeyed, and followed the spirit guide until safely away from the temple of the burning wrath of the gods. He carried the bones to Kau and placed them in his own secret family burial cave.

The ghost of Wahaula went down to the spirit world in great joy. Death had come. The life of the young chief had been taken for temple service and yet there had at last been nothing dishonorable connected with the destruction of the body and the passing away of the spirit.

31

Nedzumi

(Japanese)

In the Central Land of Reed-Plains dwelt two rats. Their home was in a lonely farmstead surrounded by rice fields. Here they lived happily for so many years that the other rats in the district, who had constantly to change their quarters, believed that their neighbours were under the special protection of Fukoruku Jin, one of the Seven Gods of Happiness, and the Patron of Long Life.

These rats had a large family of children. Every summer day they led the little ones into the rice fields, where, under shelter of the waving stalks, the young rats learned the history and cunning of their people. When work was done, they would scamper away and play with their friends until it was time to return home.

The most beautiful of these children was Nedzumi, the pride of her parents' heart. She was truly a lovely little creature, with sleek silvery skin, bright intelligent eyes, tiny upstanding ears, and pearly white teeth. It seemed to the fond father and mother that no one was great enough to marry their daughter, but, after much pondering, they decided that the most powerful being in the whole universe should be their son-in-law.

The parents discussed the weighty question with a trusted neighbour, who said, 'If you would wed your daughter to the most powerful being in the universe, you must ask the sun to marry her, for his empire knows no bounds.'

How they mounted through the skies, no rat can tell. The

sun gave them audience and listened graciously as they said, 'We would give you our daughter to wife.' He smiled and rejoined, 'Your daughter is indeed beautiful, and I thank you for coming so far to offer her to me. But, tell me, why have you chosen me out of all the world?' The rats made answer, 'We would marry our Nedzumi to the mightiest being, and you alone wield world-wide sway.' Then the sun replied, 'Truly my kingdom is vast, but oftentimes, when I would illumine the world, a cloud floats by and covers me. I cannot pierce the cloud; therefore you must go to him if your wish is to be attained.'

In no way discouraged, the rats left the sun and came to a cloud as he rested after a flight through the air. The cloud received them less cordially than the sun, and replied to their offer, with a look of mischief in his dusky eyes, 'You are mistaken if you think that I am the most powerful being. It is true that I sometimes hide the sun, but I cannot withstand the force of the wind. When he begins to blow I am driven away, and torn in pieces. My strength is not equal to the power of the wind.'

A little saddened, the rats, intent on their daughter's future prosperity, waylaid the wind as he swept through a pine forest. He was about to awaken the plain beyond, to stir the grass and the flowers into motion. The two anxious parents made known their mission. This was the whispered reply of the wind: 'It is true that I have strength to drive away the clouds, but I am powerless against the wall which men build to keep me back. You must go to him if you would have the mightiest being in the world for your son-in-law. Indeed I am not so mighty as the wall.'

The rats, still persistent in their quest, came to the wall and told their story. The wall answered, 'True, I can withstand the wind, but the rat undermines me and makes holes through my very heart. To him you must go if you would wed your daughter to the most powerful being in the world. I cannot overcome the rat.'

And now the parent rats returned to their home in the farmstead. Nedzumi, their beautiful daughter with the silken coat and sparkling eyes, rejoiced when she heard that she was to marry one of her own people, for her heart had already been given to a playfellow of the rice fields. They were married, and lived for many years as king and queen of the rat world.

32

Geirrod and Agnar

(Norse)

Odin, as has already been stated, took great interest in the affairs of mortals, and, we are told, was specially fond of watching King Hrauding's handsome little sons, Geirrod and Agnar, when they were about eight and ten years of age respectively. One day these little lads went fishing, and a storm suddenly arose which blew their boat far out to sea, where it finally stranded upon an island, upon which dwelt a seeming old couple, who in reality were Odin and Frigga in disguise. They had assumed these forms in order to indulge a sudden passion for the close society of their *protégés*. The lads were warmly welcomed and kindly treated, Odin choosing Geirrod as his favourite, and teaching him the use of arms, while Frigga petted and made much of little Agnar. The boys tarried on the island with their kind protectors during the long, cold winter season; but when spring came, and the skies were blue, and the sea calm, they embarked in a boat which Odin provided, and set out for their native shore. Favoured by gentle breezes, they were soon wafted thither; but as the boat neared the strand Geirrod quickly sprang out and pushed it far back into the water, bidding his brother sail away into the evil spirit's power. At that self-same moment the wind veered, and Agnar was indeed carried away, while his brother hastened to his father's palace with a lying tale as to what had happened to his brother. He was joyfully received as one from the dead, and in due time he succeeded his father upon the throne.

Years passed by, during which the attention of Odin had been claimed by other high considerations, when one day, while the divine couple were seated on the throne Hlidskialf, Odin suddenly remembered the winter's sojourn on the desert island, and he bade his wife notice how powerful his pupil had become, and taunted her because her favourite Agnar had married a giantess and had remained poor and of no consequence. Frigga quietly replied that it was better to be poor than hardhearted, and accused Geirrod of lack of hospitality—one of the most heinous crimes in the eyes of a Northman. She even went so far as to declare that in spite of all his wealth he often ill-treated his guests.

When Odin heard this accusation he declared that he would prove the falsity of the charge by assuming the guise of a Wanderer and testing Geirrod's generosity. Wrapped in his cloud-hued raiment, with slouch hat and pilgrim staff,—

> Wanderer calls me the world,
> Far have I carried my feet,
> On the back of the earth
> I have boundlessly been,—
>
> *Wagner (Forman's tr.).*

Odin immediately set out by a roundabout way, while Frigga, to outwit him, immediately despatched a swift messenger to warn Geirrod to beware of a man in wide mantle and broad-brimmed hat, as he was a wicked enchanter who would work him ill.

When, therefore, Odin presented himself before the king's palace he was dragged into Geirrod's presence and questioned roughly. He gave his name as Grimnir, but refused to tell whence he came or what he wanted, so as this reticence confirmed the suspicion suggested to the mind of Geirrod, he allowed his love of cruelty full play, and commanded that the stranger should be bound between two fires, in such wise that the flames played around him without quite touching him, and he remained thus eight days and nights, in obstinate silence, without food. Now Agnar had returned secretly to his brother's palace, where he occupied a menial position, and one night when all was still, in pity for the suffering of the unfortunate captive, he conveyed to his lips a horn of ale. But for this Odin would have had nothing to drink—the most serious of all trials to the god.

At the end of the eighth day, while Geirrod, seated upon his throne, was gloating over his prisoner's sufferings, Odin began to sing—softly at first, then louder and louder, until the hall re-echoed with his triumphant notes—a prophecy that the king, who had so long enjoyed the god's favour, would soon perish by his own sword.

The fallen by the sword
Ygg shall now have;
Thy life is now run out:
Wroth with thee are the Dísir:
Odin thou now shalt see:
Draw near to me if thou canst.

Sæmund's Edda (Thorpe's tr.).

As the last notes died away the chains dropped from his hands, the flames flickered and went out, and Odin stood in the midst of the hall, no longer in human form, but in all the power and beauty of a god.

On hearing the ominous prophecy Geirrod hastily drew his sword, intending to slay the insolent singer; but when he beheld the sudden transformation he started in dismay, tripped, fell upon the sharp blade, and perished as Odin had just foretold. Turning to Agnar, who, according to some accounts, was the king's son, and not his brother, for these old stories are often strangely confused, Odin bade him ascend the throne in reward for his humanity, and, further to repay him for the timely draught of ale, he promised to bless him with all manner of prosperity.

33

Elijah the Prophet and Nicholas

(*Russian*)

A long while ago there lived a *Moujik*. Nicholas's day he always kept holy, but Elijah's not a bit; he would even work upon it. In honour of St Nicholas he would have a taper lighted and a service performed, but about Elijah the Prophet he forgot so much as to think.

Well, it happened one day that Elijah and Nicholas were walking over the land belonging to this Moujik; and as they walked they looked—in the cornfields the green blades were growing up so splendidly that it did one's heart good to look at them.

'Here'll be a good harvest, a right good harvest!' says Nicholas, 'and the Moujik, too, is a good fellow sure enough, both honest and pious: one who remembers God and thinks about the Saints! It will fall into good hands—'

'We'll see by-and-by whether much will fall to his share!' answered Elijah; 'when I've burnt up all his land with lightning, and beaten it all flat with hail, then this Moujik of yours will know what's right, and will learn to keep Elijah's day holy.'

Well, they wrangled and wrangled; then they parted asunder. St Nicholas went off straight to the Moujik and said:

'Sell all your corn at once, just as it stands, to the Priest of Elijah. If you don't, nothing will be left of it: it will all be beaten flat by hail.'

Off rushed the Moujik to the Priest.

'Won't your Reverence buy some standing corn? I'll sell my whole crop. I'm in such pressing need of money just now. It's a case of pay up with me! Buy it, Father! I'll sell it cheap.'

They bargained and bargained, and came to an agreement. The Moujik got his money and went home.

Some little time passed by. There gathered together, there came rolling up, a stormcloud; with a terrible raining and hailing did it empty itself over the Moujik's cornfields, cutting down all the crop as if with a knife—not even a single blade did it leave standing.

Next day Elijah and Nicholas walked past. Says Elijah:

'Only see how I've devastated the Moujik's cornfield!'

'The Moujik's! No, brother! Devastated it you have splendidly, only that field belongs to the Elijah Priest, not to the Moujik.'

'To the Priest! How's that?'

'Why, this way. The Moujik sold it last week to the Elijah Priest, and got all the money for it. And so, methinks, the Priest may whistle for his money!'

'Stop a bit!' said Elijah. 'I'll set the field all right again. It shall be twice as good as it was before.'

They finished talking, and went each his own way. St Nicholas returned to the Moujik, and said:

'Go to the Priest and buy back your crop—you won't lose anything by it.'

The Moujik went to the Priest, made his bow, and said:

'I see, your Reverence, God has sent you a misfortune—the hail has beaten the whole field so flat you might roll a ball over it. Since things are so, let's go halves in the loss. I'll take my field back, and here's half of your money for you to relieve your distress.'

The Priest was rejoiced, and they immediately struck hands on the bargain.

Meanwhile—goodness knows how—the Moujik's ground began to get all right. From the old roots shot forth new tender stems. Rain-clouds came sailing exactly over the cornfield and gave the soil to drink. There sprang up a marvellous crop—tall and thick. As to weeds, there positively was not one to be seen. And the ears grew fuller and fuller, till they were fairly bent right down to the ground.

Then the dear sun glowed, and the rye grew ripe—like so much gold did it stand in the fields. Many a sheaf did the Moujik gather, many a heap of sheaves did he set up; and now he was beginning to carry the crop, and to gather it together into ricks.

At that very time Elijah and Nicholas came walking by again. Joyfully did the Prophet gaze on all the land, and say:

'Only look, Nicholas! what a blessing! Why, I have rewarded the Priest in such wise, that he will never forget it all his life.'

'The Priest? No, brother! the blessing indeed is great, but this land, you see, belongs to the Moujik. The Priest hasn't got anything whatsoever to do with it.'

'What are you talking about?'

'It's perfectly true. When the hail beat all the cornfield flat, the Moujik went to the Priest and bought it back again at half price.'

'Stop a bit!' says Elijah. 'I'll take the profit out of the corn. However many sheaves the Moujik may lay on the threshing-floor, he shall never thresh out of them more than a peck at a time.'

'A bad piece of work!' thinks St Nicholas. Off he went at once to the Moujik.

'Mind,' says he, 'when you begin threshing your corn, never put more than one sheaf at a time on the threshing-floor.'

The Moujik began to thresh: from every sheaf he got a peck of grain. All his bins, all his storehouses, he crammed with rye; but still much remained over. So he built himself new barns, and filled them as full as they could hold.

Well, one day Elijah and Nicholas came walking past his homestead, and the Prophet began looking here and there, and said:

'Do you see what barns he's built? has he got anything to put into them?'

'They're quite full already,' answers Nicholas.

'Why, wherever did the Moujik get such a lot of grain?'

'Bless me! Why, every one of his sheaves gave him a peck of grain. When he began to thresh he never put more than one sheaf at a time on the threshing-floor.'

'Ah, brother Nicholas!' said Elijah, guessing the truth, 'it's you who go and tell the Moujik everything!'

'What an idea! that I should go and tell—'

'As you please; that's your doing! But that Moujik sha'n't forget me in a hurry!'

'Why, what are you going to do to him?'

'What I shall do, that I won't tell you,' replies Elijah.

'There's a great danger coming,' thinks St Nicholas, and he goes to the Moujik again, and says:

'Buy two tapers, a big one and a little one, and do thus and thus with them.'

Well, next day the Prophet Elijah and St Nicholas were walking along together in the guise of wayfarers, and they met the Moujik, who was carrying two wax tapers—one, a big rouble one, and the other, a tiny copeck one.

'Where are you going, Moujik?' asked St Nicholas.

'Well, I'm going to offer a rouble taper to Prophet Elijah; he's been ever so good to me! When my crops were ruined by the hail, he bestirred himself like anything, and gave me a plentiful harvest, twice as good as the other would have been.'

'And the copeck taper, what's that for?'

'Why, that's for Nicholas!' said the peasant and passed on.

'There now, Elijah!' says Nicholas, 'you say I go and tell everything to the Moujik—surely you can see for yourself how much truth there is in that!'

Thereupon the matter ended. Elijah was appeased and didn't threaten to hurt the Moujik any more. And the Moujik led a prosperous life, and from that time forward he held in equal honor Elijah's Day and Nicholas's Day.

34

Aïdes

(Greek)

Aïdes, Aïdoneus, or Hades, was the son of Cronus and Rhea, and the youngest brother of Zeus and Poseidon. He was the ruler of that subterranean region called Erebus, which was inhabited by the shades or spirits of the dead, and also by those dethroned and exiled deities who had been vanquished by Zeus and his allies. Aïdes, the grim and gloomy monarch of this lower world, was the successor of Erebus, that ancient primeval divinity after whom these realms were called.

The early Greeks regarded Aïdes in the light of their greatest foe, and Homer tells us that he was 'of all the gods the most detested,' being in their eyes the grim robber who stole from them their nearest and dearest, and eventually deprived each of them of their share in terrestrial existence. His name was so feared that it was never mentioned by mortals, who, when they invoked him, struck the earth with their hands, and in sacrificing to him turned away their faces.

The belief of the people with regard to a future state was, in the Homeric age, a sad and cheerless one. It was supposed that when a mortal ceased to exist, his spirit tenanted the shadowy outline of the human form it had quitted. These shadows, or shades as they were called, were driven by Aïdes into his dominions, where they passed their time, some in brooding over the vicissitudes of fortune which they had experienced on earth, others in regretting the lost pleasures they had enjoyed in life, but all in a condition of semi-consciousness, from which the intellect could only be roused to full activity by drinking of the blood of the sacrifices offered to their shades by living friends, which, for a time, endowed them with their former mental vigour. The only beings supposed to enjoy any happiness in a future state were the heroes, whose acts of daring and deeds of prowess had, during their life, reflected honour on the land of their birth; and even these, according to Homer, pined after their career of earthly activity. He tells us that when Odysseus visited the lower world at the command of Circe, and held communion with the shades of the heroes of the Trojan war, Achilles assured him that he would rather be the poorest day-labourer on earth than reign supreme over the realm of shades.

The early Greek poets offer but scanty allusions to Erebus. Homer appears purposely to envelop these realms in vagueness and mystery, in order, probably, to heighten the sensation of awe inseparably connected with the lower world. In the Odyssey he describes the entrance to Erebus as being beyond the furthermost edge of Oceanus, in the far west, where dwelt the Cimmerians, enveloped in eternal mists and darkness.

In later times, however, in consequence of extended intercourse with foreign nations, new ideas became gradually introduced, and we find Egyptian theories with regard to a future state taking root in Greece, which become eventually the religious belief of the whole nation. It is now that the poets and philosophers, and more especially the teachers of the Eleusinian Mysteries, begin to inculcate the doctrine of the future reward and punishment of good and bad deeds. Aïdes, who had hitherto been regarded as the dread enemy of mankind, who delights in his grim office, and keeps the shades imprisoned in his dominions after withdrawing them from the joys of existence, now receives them with hospitality and friendship, and Hermes replaces him as conductor of shades to Hades. Under this new aspect Aïdes usurps the functions of a totally different divinity called Plutus (the god of riches), and is henceforth regarded as the giver of wealth to mankind, in the shape of those precious metals which lie concealed in the bowels of the earth.

The later poets mention various entrances to Erebus, which were for the most part caves and fissures. There was one in the mountain of Taenarum, another in Thesprotia, and a third, the most celebrated of all, in Italy, near the pestiferous Lake Avernus, over which it is said no bird could fly, so noxious were its exhalations.

In the dominions of Aïdes there were four great rivers, three of which had to be crossed by all the shades. These three were Acheron (sorrow), Cocytus (lamentation), and Styx (intense darkness), the sacred stream which flowed nine times round these realms.

The shades were ferried over the Styx by the grim, unshaven old boatman Charon, who, however, only took those whose bodies had received funereal rites on earth, and who had brought with them his indispensable toll, which was a small coin or obolus, usually placed under the tongue of a dead person for this purpose. If these conditions had not been fulfilled, the unhappy shades were left behind to wander up and down the banks for a hundred years as restless spirits.

On the opposite bank of the Styx was the tribunal of Minos, the supreme judge, before whom all shades had to appear, and who, after hearing full confession of their actions whilst on earth, pronounced the sentence of happiness or misery to which their deeds had entitled them. This tribunal was guarded by the terrible triple-headed dog Cerberus, who, with his three necks bristling with snakes, lay at full length on the ground;—a formidable sentinel, who permitted all shades to enter, but none to return.

The happy spirits, destined to enjoy the delights of Elysium, passed out on the right, and proceeded to the golden palace where Aïdes and Persephone held their royal court, from whom they received a kindly greeting, ere they set out for the Elysian Fields which lay beyond. This blissful region was replete with all that could charm the senses or please the imagination; the air was balmy and fragrant, rippling brooks flowed peacefully through the smiling meadows, which glowed with the varied hues of a thousand flowers, whilst the groves resounded with the joyous songs of birds. The occupations and amusements of the happy shades were of the same nature as those which they had delighted in whilst on earth. Here the warrior found his horses, chariots, and arms, the musician his lyre, and the hunter his quiver and bow.

In a secluded vale of Elysium there flowed a gentle, silent stream, called Lethe (oblivion), whose waters had the effect of dispelling care, and producing utter forgetfulness of former events. According to the Pythagorean doctrine of the transmigration of souls, it was supposed that after the shades had inhabited Elysium for a thousand years they were destined to animate other bodies on earth, and before leaving Elysium they drank of the river Lethe, in order that they might enter upon their new career without any remembrance of the past.

The guilty souls, after leaving the presence of Minos, were conducted to the great judgment-hall of Hades, whose massive walls of solid adamant were surrounded by the river Phlegethon, the waves of which rolled flames of fire, and lit up, with their lurid glare, these awful realms. In the interior sat the dread judge Rhadamanthus, who declared to each comer the precise torments which awaited him in Tartarus. The wretched sinners were then seized by the Furies, who scourged them with their whips, and dragged them along to the great gate, which closed the opening to Tartarus, into whose awful depths they were hurled, to suffer endless torture.

Tartarus was a vast and gloomy expanse, as far below Hades as the earth is distant from the skies. There the Titans, fallen from their high estate, dragged out a dreary and monotonous existence; there also were Otus and Ephialtes, those giant sons of Poseidon, who, with impious hands, had attempted to scale Olympus and dethrone its mighty ruler. Principal among the sufferers in this abode of gloom were Tityus, Tantalus, Sisyphus, Ixion, and the Danaïdes.

TITYUS, one of the earth-born giants, had insulted Hera on her way to Peitho, for which offence Zeus flung him into Tartarus, where he suffered dreadful torture, inflicted by two vultures, which perpetually gnawed his liver.

TANTALUS was a wise and wealthy king of Lydia, with whom the gods themselves condescended to associate; he was even permitted to sit at table with Zeus, who delighted in his conversation, and listened with interest to the wisdom of his observations. Tantalus, however, elated at these distinguished marks of divine favour, presumed upon his position, and used unbecoming language to Zeus himself; he also stole nectar and ambrosia from the table of the gods, with which he regaled his friends; but his greatest crime consisted in killing his own son Pelops, and serving him up at one of the banquets to the gods, in order to test their omniscience. For these heinous offences he was condemned by Zeus to eternal punishment in Tartarus, where, tortured with an ever-burning thirst, he was plunged up to the chin in water, which, as he stooped to drink, always receded from his parched lips. Tall trees, with spreading branches laden with delicious fruits, hung temptingly over his head; but no sooner did he raise himself to grasp them, than a wind arose, and carried them beyond his reach.

SISYPHUS was a great tyrant who, according to some accounts, barbarously murdered all travellers who came into his dominions, by hurling upon them enormous pieces of rock. In punishment for his crimes he was condemned to roll incessantly a huge block of stone up a steep hill, which, as soon as it reached the summit, always rolled back again to the plain below.

IXION was a king of Thessaly to whom Zeus accorded the privilege of joining the festive banquets of the gods; but, taking advantage of his exalted position, he presumed to aspire to the favour of Hera, which so greatly incensed Zeus, that he struck him with his thunderbolts, and commanded Hermes to throw him into Tartarus, and bind him to an ever-revolving wheel.

The DANAÏDES were the fifty daughters of Danaus, king of Argos, who had married their fifty cousins, the sons of Ægyptus. By the command of their father, who had been warned by an oracle that his son-in-law would cause his death, they all killed their husbands in one night, Hypermnestra alone excepted. Their punishment in the lower world was to fill with water a vessel full of holes,—a never-ending and useless task.

Aïdes is usually represented as a man of mature years and stern majestic mien, bearing a striking resemblance to his brother Zeus; but the gloomy and inexorable expression of the face contrasts forcibly with that peculiar benignity which so characterizes the countenance of the mighty ruler of heaven. He is seated on a throne of ebony, with his queen, the grave and sad Persephone, beside him, and wears a full beard, and long flowing black hair, which hangs straight down over his forehead; in his hand he either bears a two-pronged fork or the keys of the lower world, and at his feet sits Cerberus. He is sometimes seen in a chariot of gold, drawn by four black horses, and wearing on his head a helmet made for him by the Cyclops, which rendered the wearer invisible. This helmet he frequently lent to mortals and immortals.

Aïdes, who was universally worshipped throughout Greece, had temples erected to his honour in Elis, Olympia, and also at Athens.

His sacrifices, which took place at night, consisted of black sheep, and the blood, instead of being sprinkled on the altars or received in vessels, as at other sacrifices, was permitted to run down into a trench, dug for this purpose. The officiating priests wore black robes, and were crowned with cypress.

The narcissus, maiden-hair, and cypress were sacred to this divinity.

35

Uranus and Gæa

(Greek)

The ancient Greeks had several different theories with regard to the origin of the world, but the generally accepted notion was that before this world came into existence, there was in its place a confused mass of shapeless elements called Chaos. These elements becoming at length consolidated (by what means does not appear), resolved themselves into two widely different substances, the lighter portion of which, soaring on high, formed the sky or firmament, and constituted itself into a vast, overarching vault, which protected the firm and solid mass beneath.

Thus came into being the two first great primeval deities of the Greeks, Uranus and Ge or Gæa.

Uranus, the more refined deity, represented the light and air of heaven, possessing the distinguishing qualities of light, heat, purity, and omnipresence, whilst Gæa, the firm, flat, life-sustaining earth, was worshipped as the great all-nourishing mother. Her many titles refer to her more or less in this character, and she appears to have been universally revered among the Greeks, there being scarcely a city in Greece which did not contain a temple erected in her honour; indeed Gæa was held in such veneration that her name was always invoked whenever the gods took a solemn oath, made an emphatic declaration, or implored assistance.

Uranus, the heaven, was believed to have united himself in

marriage with Gæa, the earth; and a moment's reflection will show what a truly poetical, and also what a logical idea this was; for, taken in a figurative sense, this union actually does exist. The smiles of heaven produce the flowers of earth, whereas his long-continued frowns exercise so depressing an influence upon his loving partner, that she no longer decks herself in bright and festive robes, but responds with ready sympathy to his melancholy mood.

The first-born child of Uranus and Gæa was Oceanus, the ocean stream, that vast expanse of ever-flowing water which encircled the earth. Here we meet with another logical though fanciful conclusion, which a very slight knowledge of the workings of nature proves to have been just and true. The ocean is formed from the rains which descend from heaven and the streams which flow from earth. By making Oceanus therefore the offspring of Uranus and Gæa, the ancients, if we take this notion in its literal sense, merely assert that the ocean is produced by the combined influence of heaven and earth, whilst at the same time their fervid and poetical imagination led them to see in this, as in all manifestations of the powers of nature, an actual, tangible divinity.

But Uranus, the heaven, the embodiment of light, heat, and the breath of life, produced offspring who were of a much less material nature than his son Oceanus. These other children of his were supposed to occupy the intermediate space which divided him from Gæa. Nearest to Uranus, and just beneath him, came Aether (Ether), a bright creation representing that highly rarified atmosphere which immortals alone could breathe. Then followed Aër (Air), which was in close proximity to Gæa, and represented, as its name implies, the grosser atmosphere surrounding the earth which mortals could freely breathe, and without which they would perish. Aether and Aër were separated from each other by divinities called Nephelae. These were their restless and wandering sisters, who existed in the form of clouds, ever floating between Aether and Aër. Gæa also produced the mountains, and Pontus (the sea). She united herself with the latter, and their offspring were the sea-deities Nereus, Thaumas, Phorcys, Ceto, and Eurybia.

Co-existent with Uranus and Gæa were two mighty powers who were also the offspring of Chaos. These were Erebus (Darkness) and Nyx (Night), who formed a striking contrast to the cheerful light of heaven and the bright smiles of earth. Erebus reigned in that mysterious world below where no ray of sunshine, no gleam of daylight, nor vestige of health-giving terrestrial life ever appeared. Nyx, the sister of Erebus, represented Night, and was worshipped by the ancients with the greatest solemnity.

Uranus was also supposed to have been united to Nyx, but only in his capacity as god of light, he being considered the source and fountain of all light, and their children were Eos (Aurora), the Dawn, and Hemera, the Daylight. Nyx again, on her side was also doubly united, having been married at some indefinite period to Erebus.

In addition to those children of heaven and earth already enumerated, Uranus and Gæa produced two distinctly different races of beings called Giants and Titans. The Giants personified brute strength alone, but the Titans united to their great physical power intellectual qualifications variously developed. There were three Giants, Briareus, Cottus, and Gyges, who each possessed a hundred hands and fifty heads, and were known collectively by the name of the Hecatoncheires, which signified hundred-handed. These mighty Giants could shake the universe and produce earthquakes; it is therefore evident that they represented those active subterranean forces to which allusion has been made in the opening chapter. The Titans were twelve in number; their names were: Oceanus, Ceos, Crios, Hyperion, Iapetus, Cronus, Theia, Rhea, Themis, Mnemosyne, Phœbe, and Tethys.

Now Uranus, the chaste light of heaven, the essence of all that is bright and pleasing, held in abhorrence his crude, rough, and turbulent offspring, the Giants, and moreover feared that their great power might eventually prove hurtful to himself. He therefore hurled them into Tartarus, that portion of the lower world which served as the subterranean dungeon of the gods. In order to avenge the oppression of her children, the Giants, Gæa instigated a conspiracy on the part of the Titans against Uranus, which was carried to a successful issue by her son Cronus. He wounded his father, and from the blood of the wound which fell upon the earth sprang a race of monstrous beings also called Giants. Assisted by his brother-Titans, Cronus succeeded in dethroning his father, who, enraged at his defeat, cursed his rebellious son, and foretold to him a similar fate. Cronus now became invested with supreme power, and assigned to his brothers offices of distinction, subordinate only to himself. Subsequently, however, when, secure of his position, he no longer needed their assistance, he basely repaid their former services with treachery, made war upon his brothers and faithful allies, and, assisted by the Giants, completely defeated them, sending such as resisted his all-conquering arm down into the lowest depths of Tartarus.

36

Maluae and the Underworld

(Hawaiian)

This is a story from Manoa Valley, back of Honolulu. In the upper end of the valley, at the foot of the highest mountains on the island Oahu, lived Maluae. He was a farmer, and had chosen this land because rain fell abundantly on the mountains, and the streams brought down fine soil from the decaying forests and disintegrating rocks, fertilizing his plants.

Here he cultivated bananas and taro and sweet potatoes. His bananas grew rapidly by the sides of the brooks, and yielded large bunches of fruit from their tree-like stems; his taro filled small walled-in pools, growing in the water like water-lilies, until the roots were matured, when the plants were pulled up and the roots boiled and prepared for food; his sweet potatoes—a vegetable known among the ancient New Zealanders as *ku-maru*, and supposed to have come from Hawaii—were planted on the drier uplands.

Thus he had plenty of food continually growing, and ripening from time to time. Whenever he gathered any of his food products he brought a part to his family temple and placed it on an altar before the gods Kane and Kanaloa, then he took the rest to his home for his family to eat.

He had a boy whom he dearly loved, whose name was Kaa-lii (rolling chief). This boy was a careless, rollicking child.

One day the boy was tired and hungry. He passed by the

temple of the gods and saw bananas, ripe and sweet, on the little platform before the gods. He took these bananas and ate them all.

The gods looked down on the altar expecting to find food, but it was all gone and there was nothing for them. They were very angry, and ran out after the boy. They caught him eating the bananas, and killed him. The body they left lying under the trees, and taking out his ghost threw it into the Underworld.

The father toiled hour after hour cultivating his food plants, and when wearied returned to his home. On the way he met the two gods. They told him how his boy had robbed them of their sacrifices and how they had punished him. They said, 'We have sent his ghost body to the lowest regions of the Underworld.'

The father was very sorrowful and heavy hearted as he went on his way to his desolate home. He searched for the body of his boy, and at last found it. He saw too that the story of the gods was true, for partly eaten bananas filled the mouth, which was set in death.

He wrapped the body very carefully in *kapa* cloth made from the bark of trees. He carried it into his rest-house and laid it on the sleeping-mat. After a time he lay down beside the body, refusing all food, and planning to die with his boy. He thought if he could escape from his own body he would be able to go down where the ghost of his boy had been sent. If he could find that ghost he hoped to take it to the other part of the Underworld, where they could be happy together.

He placed no offerings on the altar of the gods. No prayers were chanted. The afternoon and evening passed slowly. The gods waited for their worshipper, but he came not. They looked down on the altar of sacrifice, but there was nothing for them.

The night passed and the following day. The father lay by the side of his son, neither eating nor drinking, and longing only for death. The house was tightly closed.

Then the gods talked together, and Kane said: 'Maluae eats

no food, he prepares no *awa* to drink, and there is no water by him. He is near the door of the Underworld. If he should die, we would be to blame.'

Kanaloa said: 'He has been a good man, but now we do not hear any prayers. We are losing our worshipper. We in quick anger killed his son. Was this the right reward? He has called us morning and evening in his worship. He has provided fish and fruits and vegetables for our altars. He has always prepared awa from the juice of the yellow awa root for us to drink. We have not paid him well for his care.'

Then they decided to go and give life to the father, and permit him to take his ghost body and go down into Po, the dark land, to bring back the ghost of the boy. So they went to Maluae and told him they were sorry for what they had done.

The father was very weak from hunger, and longing for death, and could scarcely listen to them.

When Kane said, 'Have you love for your child?' the father whispered: 'Yes. My love is without end.' 'Can you go down into the dark land and get that spirit and put it back in the body which lies here?'

'No,' the father said, 'no, I can only die and go to live with him and make him happier by taking him to a better place.'

Then the gods said, 'We will give you the power to go after your boy and we will help you to escape the dangers of the land of ghosts.'

Then the father, stirred by hope, rose up and took food and drink. Soon he was strong enough to go on his journey.

The gods gave him a ghost body and also prepared a hollow stick like bamboo, in which they put food, battle-weapons, and a piece of burning lava for fire.

Not far from Honolulu is a beautiful modern estate with fine roads, lakes, running brooks, and interesting valleys extending back into the mountain range. This is called by the very ancient name Moanalua (two lakes). Near the seacoast of this estate was one of the most noted ghost localities of the islands. The ghosts after wandering over the island Oahu would come to this place to find a way into their real home, the Underworld, or, as the Hawaiians usually called it, Po.

Here was a ghostly breadfruit-tree named Lei-walo, possibly meaning 'the eight wreaths' or 'the eighth wreath'—the last wreath of leaves from the land of the living which would meet the eyes of the dying.

The ghosts would leap or fly or climb into the branches of this tree, trying to find a rotten branch upon which they could sit until it broke and threw them into the dark sea below.

Maluae climbed up the breadfruit-tree. He found a branch upon which some ghosts were sitting waiting for it to fall. His weight was so much greater than theirs that the branch broke at once, and down they all fell into the land of Po.

He needed merely to taste the food in his hollow cane to have new life and strength. This he had done when he climbed the tree; thus he had been able to push past the fabled guardians of the pathway of the ghosts in the Upper-World. As he entered the Underworld he again tasted the food of the gods and he felt himself growing stronger and stronger.

He took a magic war-club and a spear out of the cane given by the gods. Ghostly warriors tried to hinder his entrance into the different districts of the dark land. The spirits of dead chiefs challenged him when he passed their homes. Battle after battle was fought. His magic club struck the warriors down, and his spear tossed them aside.

Sometimes he was warmly greeted and aided by ghosts of kindly spirit. Thus he went from place to place, searching for his boy, finding him at last, as the Hawaiians quaintly expressed it, 'down in the *papa-ku*' (the established foundation of Po), choking and suffocating from the bananas of ghost-land which he was compelled to continually force into his mouth.

The father caught the spirit of the boy and started back toward the Upper-world, but the ghosts surrounded him. They tried to catch him and take the spirit away from him. Again the father partook of the food of the gods. Once more he wielded his war-club, but the hosts of enemies were too great. Multitudes arose on all sides, crushing him by their overwhelming numbers.

At last he raised his magic hollow cane and took the last portion of food. Then he poured out the portion of burning lava which the gods had placed inside. It fell upon the dry floor of the Underworld. The flames dashed into the trees and the shrubs of ghost-land. Fire-holes opened in the floor and streams of lava burst out.

Backward fled the multitudes of spirits. The father thrust the spirit of the boy quickly into the empty magic cane and rushed swiftly up to his home-land. He brought the spirit to the body lying in the rest-house and forced it to find again its living home.

Afterward the father and the boy took food to the altars of the gods, and chanted the accustomed prayers heartily and loyally all the rest of their lives.

37

How Milu Became the King of Ghosts

(*Hawaiian*)

Lono was a chief living on the western side of the island Hawaii. He had a very red skin and strange-looking eyes. His choice of occupation was farming. This man had never been sick. One time he was digging with the *oo*, a long sharp-pointed stick or spade. A man passed and admired him. The people said, 'Lono has never been sick.' The man said, 'He will be sick.'

Lono was talking about that man and at the same time struck his oo down with force and cut his foot. He shed much blood, and fainted, falling to the ground. A man took a pig, went after the stranger, and let the pig go, which ran to this man. The stranger was Kamaka, a god of healing. He turned and went back at the call of the messenger, taking some *popolo* fruit and leaves in his cloak. When he came to the injured man he asked for salt, which he pounded into the fruit and leaves and placed in coco cloth and bound it on the wound, leaving it a long time. Then he went away.

As he journeyed on he heard heavy breathing, and turning saw Lono, who said, 'You have helped me, and so I have left my lands in the care of my friends, directing them what to do, and have hastened after you to learn how to heal other people.'

The god said, 'Lono, open your mouth!' This Lono did, and the god spat in his mouth, so that the saliva could be taken into every part of Lono's body. Thus a part of the god became a part of Lono, and he became very skillful in the use of all healing remedies. He learned about the various diseases and the medicines needed for each. The god and Lono walked together, Lono receiving new lessons along the way, passing through the districts of Kau, Puna, Hilo, and then to Hamakua.

The god said, 'It is not right for us to stay together. You can never accomplish anything by staying with me. You must go to a separate place and give yourself up to healing people.'

Lono turned aside to dwell in Waimanu and Waipio Valleys and there began to practice healing, becoming very noted, while the god Kamaka made his home at Ku-kui-haele.

This god did not tell the other gods of the medicines that he had taught Lono. One of the other gods, Kalae, was trying to find some way to kill Milu, and was always making him sick. Milu, chief of Waipio, heard of the skill of Lono. Some had been sick even to death, and Lono had healed them. Therefore Milu sent a messenger to Lono who responded at once, came and slapped Milu all over the body, and said: 'You are not ill. Obey me and you shall be well.'

Then he healed him from all the sickness inside the body caused by Kalae. But there was danger from outside, so he said: 'You must build a *ti*-leaf house and dwell there quietly for some time, letting your disease rest. If a company should come by the house making sport, with a great noise, do not go out, because when you go they will come up and get you for your death. Do not open the ti leaves and look out. The day you do this you shall die.'

Some time passed and the chief remained in the house, but one day there was the confused noise of many people talking and shouting around his house. He did not forget the command of Lono. Two birds were sporting in a wonderful way in the sky above the forest. This continued all day until it was dark.

Then another long time passed and again Waipio was full of

resounding noises. A great bird appeared in the sky resplendent in all kinds of feathers, swaying from side to side over the valley, from the top of one precipice across to the top of another, in grand flights passing over the heads of the people, who shouted until the valley re-echoed with the sound.

Milu became tired of that great noise and could not patiently obey his physician, so he pushed aside some of the ti leaves of his house and looked out upon the bird. That was the time when the bird swept down upon the house, thrusting a claw under Milu's arm, tearing out his liver. Lono saw this and ran after the bird, but it flew swiftly to a deep pit in the lava on one side of the valley and dashed inside, leaving blood spread on the stones. Lono came, saw the blood, took it and wrapped it in a piece of tapa cloth and returned to the place where the chief lay almost dead. He poured some medicine into the wound and pushed the tapa and blood inside. Milu was soon healed.

The place where the bird hid with the liver of Milu is called to this day *Ke-ake-o-Milu* ('The liver of Milu'). When this death had passed away he felt very well, even as before his trouble.

Then Lono told him that another death threatened him and would soon appear. He must dwell in quietness.

For some time Milu was living in peace and quiet after this trouble. Then one day the surf of Waipio became very high, rushing from far out even to the sand, and the people entered into the sport of surf-riding with great joy and loud shouts. This noise continued day by day, and Milu was impatient of the restraint and forgot the words of Lono. He went out to bathe in the surf.

When he came to the place of the wonderful surf he let the first and second waves go by, and as the third came near he launched himself upon it while the people along the beach shouted uproariously. He went out again into deeper water, and again came in, letting the first and second waves go first. As he came to the shore the first and second waves were hurled back from the shore in a great mass against the wave upon which he was riding. The two great masses of water struck and pounded Milu, whirling and crowding him down, while the surf-board was caught in the raging, struggling waters and thrown out toward the shore. Milu was completely lost in the deep water.

The people cried: 'Milu is dead! The chief is dead!' The god Kalae thought he had killed Milu, so he with the other poison-gods went on a journey to Mauna Loa. Kapo and Pua, the poison-gods, or gods of death, of the island Maui, found them as they passed, and joined the company. They discovered a forest on Molokai, and there as kupua spirits, or ghost bodies, entered into the trees of that forest, so the trees became the kupua bodies. They were the medicinal or poison qualities in the trees.

Lono remained in Waipio Valley, becoming the ancestor and teacher of all the good healing priests of Hawaii, but Milu became the ruler of the Underworld, the place where the spirits of the dead had their home after they were driven away from the land of the living. Many people came to him from time to time.

He established ghostly sports like those which his subjects had enjoyed before death. They played the game *kilu* with polished cocoanut shells, spinning them over a smooth surface to strike a post set up in the centre. He taught *konane*, a game commonly called 'Hawaiian checkers,' but more like the Japanese game of 'Go.' He permitted them to gamble, betting all the kinds of property found in ghost-land. They boxed and wrestled; they leaped from precipices into ghostly swimming-pools; they feasted and fought, sometimes attempting to slay each other. Thus they lived the ghost life as they had lived on earth. Sometimes the ruler was forgotten and the ancient Hawaiians called the Underworld by his name—Milu. The New Zealanders frequently gave their Underworld the name '*Miru*.' They also supposed that the ghosts feasted and sported as they had done while living.

38

The Smith and the Demon

(Russian)

Once upon a time there was a Smith, and he had one son, a sharp, smart, six-year-old boy. One day the old man went to church, and as he stood before a picture of the Last Judgment he saw a Demon painted there—such a terrible one!—black, with horns and a tail.

'O my!' says he to himself. 'Suppose I get just such another painted for the smithy.' So he hired an artist, and ordered him to paint on the door of the smithy exactly such another demon as he had seen in the church. The artist painted it. Thenceforward the old man, every time he entered the smithy, always looked at the Demon and said, 'Good morning, fellow-countryman!' And then he would lay the fire in the furnace and begin his work.

Well, the Smith lived in good accord with the Demon for some ten years. Then he fell ill and died. His son succeeded to his place as head of the household, and took the smithy into his own hands. But he was not disposed to show attention to the Demon as the old man had done. When he went into the smithy in the morning, he never said 'Good morrow' to him; instead of offering him a kindly word, he took the biggest hammer he had handy, and thumped the Demon with it three times right on the forehead, and then he would go to his work. And when one of God's holy days came round, he would go to church and offer each saint a taper; but he would go up to the Demon and spit in his face. Thus three years went by, he all the while favouring the Evil One every morning either with a spitting or with a hammering. The Demon endured it and endured it, and at last found it past all endurance. It was too much for him.

'I've had quite enough of this insolence from him!' thinks he. 'Suppose I make use of a little diplomacy, and play him some sort of a trick!'

So the Demon took the form of a youth, and went to the smithy.

'Good day, uncle!' says he.

'Good day!'

'What should you say, uncle, to taking me as an apprentice? At all events, I could carry fuel for you, and blow the bellows.'

The Smith liked the idea. 'Why shouldn't I?' he replied. 'Two are better than one.'

The Demon began to learn his trade; at the end of a month he knew more about smith's work than his master did himself, was able to do everything that his master couldn't do. It was a real pleasure to look at him! There's no describing how satisfied his master was with him, how fond he got of him. Sometimes the master didn't go into the smithy at all himself, but trusted entirely to his journeyman, who had complete charge of everything.

Well, it happened one day that the master was not at home, and the journeyman was left all by himself in the smithy.

Presently he saw an old lady driving along the street in her carriage, whereupon he popped his head out of doors and began shouting:—

'Heigh, sirs! Be so good as to step in here! We've opened a new business here; we turn old folks into young ones.'

Out of her carriage jumped the lady in a trice, and ran into the smithy.

'What's that you're bragging about? Do you mean to say it's true? Can you really do it?' she asked the youth.

'We haven't got to learn our business!' answered the Demon. 'If I hadn't been able to do it, I wouldn't have invited people to try.'

'And how much does it cost?' asked the lady.

'Five hundred roubles altogether.'

'Well, then, there's your money; make a young woman of me.'

The Demon took the money; then he sent the lady's coachman into the village.

'Go,' says he, 'and bring me here two buckets full of milk.'

After that he took a pair of tongs, caught hold of the lady by the feet, flung her into the furnace, and burnt her up; nothing was left of her but her bare bones.

When the buckets of milk were brought, he emptied them into a large tub, then he collected all the bones and flung them into the milk. Just fancy! at the end of about three minutes the lady emerged from the milk—alive, and young, and beautiful!

Well, she got into her carriage and drove home. There she went straight to her husband, and he stared hard at her, but didn't know she was his wife.

'What are you staring at?' says the lady. 'I'm young and elegant, you see, and I don't want to have an old husband! Be off at once to the smithy, and get them to make you young; if you don't, I won't so much as acknowledge you!'

There was no help for it; off set the seigneur. But by that time the Smith had returned home, and had gone into the smithy. He looked about; the journeyman wasn't to be seen. He searched and searched, he enquired and enquired, never a thing came of it; not even a trace of the youth could be found. He took to his work by himself, and was hammering away, when at that moment up drove the seigneur, and walked straight into the smithy.

'Make a young man of me,' says he.

'Are you in your right mind, Barin? How can one make a

young man of you?'

'Come, now! you know all about that.'

'I know nothing of the kind.'

'You lie, you scoundrel! Since you made my old woman young, make me young too; otherwise, there will be no living with her for me.'

'Why I haven't so much as seen your good lady.'

'Your journeyman saw her, and that's just the same thing. If he knew how to do the job, surely you, an old hand, must have learnt how to do it long ago. Come, now, set to work at once. If you don't, it will be the worse for you. I'll have you rubbed down with a birch-tree towel.'

The Smith was compelled to try his hand at transforming the seigneur. He held a private conversation with the coachman as to how his journeyman had set to work with the lady, and what he had done to her, and then he thought:—

'So be it! I'll do the same. If I fall on my feet, good; if I don't, well, I must suffer all the same!'

So he set to work at once, stripped the seigneur naked, laid hold of him by the legs with the tongs, popped him into the furnace, and began blowing the bellows. After he had burnt him to a cinder, he collected his remains, flung them into the milk, and then waited to see how soon a youthful seigneur would jump out of it. He waited one hour, two hours. But nothing came of it. He made a search in the tub. There was nothing in it but bones, and those charred ones.

Just then the lady sent messengers to the smithy, to ask whether the seigneur would soon be ready. The poor Smith had to reply that the seigneur was no more.

When the lady heard that the Smith had only turned her husband into a cinder, instead of making him young, she was tremendously angry, and she called together her trusty servants, and ordered them to drag him to the gallows. No sooner said than done. Her servants ran to the Smith's house, laid hold of him, tied his hands together, and dragged him off to the gallows. All of a sudden there came up with them the youngster who used to live with the Smith as his journeyman, who asked him:—

'Where are they taking you, master?'

'They're going to hang me,' replied the Smith, and straightway related all that had happened to him.

'Well, uncle!' said the Demon, 'swear that you will never strike me with your hammer, but that you will pay me the same respect your father always paid, and the seigneur shall be alive, and young, too, in a trice.'

The Smith began promising and swearing that he would never again lift his hammer against the Demon, but would always pay him every attention. Thereupon the journeyman hastened to the smithy, and shortly afterwards came back again, bringing the seigneur with him, and crying to the servants:

'Hold! hold! Don't hang him! Here's your master!'

Then they immediately untied the cords, and let the Smith go free.

From that time forward the Smith gave up spitting at the Demon and striking him with his hammer. The journeyman disappeared, and was never seen again. But the seigneur and his lady entered upon a prosperous course of life, and if they haven't died, they're living still.

39

The Tale of the Pole Star

(Indian)

Once upon a time there lived a great king in India whose name was Uttanpad. He had two wives, one named Suniti and the other Suruchi. The former had a beautiful nature and the latter a beautiful face. And just like other kings in other parts of the world, King Uttanpad neglected the queen with the beautiful nature to grow every day more in love with the queen with the beautiful face.

Now by Suruchi King Uttanpad had a little boy called Uttam and by Suniti he had a little boy called Dhruv. Uttam was six and Dhruv was five and each of them inherited the qualities of his mother. King Uttanpad loved them both but because of Suruchi's jealousy he dared not fondle Dhruv in her presence. One day the king was telling the two little boys a story and had Dhruv on his knee. Queen Suruchi entered the room, and furious at the sight, gave Dhruv a push so that he fell over backwards. Prince Dhruv pleaded that he was King Uttanpad's son just as much as Uttam was. But Queen Suruchi grew very angry and bade him go and pray to the gods. For until they pitied him and let him be born again as her son, King Uttanpad would never take him on his knee again.

Little Dhruv went to his mother Suniti and told her what had happened. Suniti told him to pray to the god Krishna. So little Dhruv said that he would go into the forest and pray to

Krishna and when he had done so he would return and tell her. But once he had entered the forest he prayed and prayed and prayed so that he never thought of returning, and lived on roots and water. And as he prayed years passed by until the god Krishna, pleased with the boy's devotion, revealed himself and offered him a boon. 'Take me with you, O Lord, back to heaven,' said Dhruv. 'No,' said Krishna, 'that cannot be. You have yet to go to your father's country and reign over it and bring it happiness. In due time I shall send for you.' Dhruv consented. And the god Krishna sent the great sage Narada to lead him back to his father's town. Narada took the prince's hand in his and led him back to King Uttanpad's city.

For many years the king had mourned for Dhruv as one long dead. But when Narada sent word to him that Prince Dhruv had returned, the king made great preparations to welcome him. Seated in a golden howdah carried by the king's own elephant and shaded by the royal umbrella, Prince Dhruv was borne back to his father's palace. And as he passed through the streets, all the maidens, peeping at him through the chinks in the walls or from the corners of the windows, wondered at the handsome prince. And all the matrons and aged dames showered flowers on him from their balconies and roofs. For all were overjoyed at his return except only Prince Uttam and his mother Queen Suruchi. For Prince Uttam had grown into a selfish, jealous man and he was furious that his brother should receive such favour from the king and such honour from the people. And Queen Suruchi hated Prince Dhruv as a possible rival to her own son. Thus although the king and Queen Suniti and the nobles and the ministers welcomed Prince Dhruv and tried to outbid each other in the warmth of their greeting, his brother would barely look in his direction and Queen Suruchi muttered to herself, but so loudly that the bystanders heard, 'If only the brat had died in the forest!'

Prince Dhruv did his utmost to win their love, but all to no purpose. Prince Uttam and Queen Suruchi sought every day to humiliate him. At last the king rebuked Prince Uttam. Then the young man's anger knew no bounds. He begged the king for leave to go out with an army that was about to attack a forest tribe who for some months past had revolted against the king's authority. The king gave his son leave to go and placed him at the head of the horse-soldiers but under the orders of the general. Prince Uttam, however, was vain and wayward. He would not heed the advice of his father's general. But taking his horsemen with him he marched ahead of the foot-soldiers into the forest. There the forest tribes easily lured the prince into an ambush and slew him and all the men with him. When the sad news reached the capital, King Uttanpad sent out Prince Dhruv and a band of fresh horsemen. He and the king's general fully avenged Prince Uttam's death, and with great pomp and laden with spoil and captives Prince Dhruv and the army returned in triumph.

But the loss of her son and the triumph of Prince Dhruv unsettled Queen Suruchi's mind. One day she ran out of the city and into the woods and was never heard of afterwards. Then King Uttanpad felt that the time had come for him, as an Aryan king, to resign his crown to his son. So he gave up his robes and sceptre to Prince Dhruv and in the garb of a pilgrim wandered forth into the forest and there led the life of an ascetic until death freed him.

Then King Dhruv ruled in his father's place. And for many a score of years he ruled beloved by his subjects. And his armies were always victorious and the frontiers of his kingdom daily widened and no monarch in all India was so greatly feared or honoured as he. Yet his heart was always sad. For he often thought with sighs of the happy years in which as a boy he had worshipped Krishna in the Madhu forest. And often he said to himself, 'Fool that I was to return to my father's home. How happy I should have been had I but spent my life in the woods, worshipping the god Krishna. In the end he would surely have borne me away and gathered me to his bosom.'

One day he could bear it no longer and handing over the reins of sovereignty to his son he made his way back to the Madhu forest on the banks of the Yamuna. He came at last to his old hermitage and suddenly in front of him he saw what he had never seen when he lived there before—a rugged path which rose steeply towards the North. Dhruv paused a moment, but a voice within him seemed to bid him follow the path. He did so, but it never seemed to end. It grew steeper and steeper and steeper. And King Dhruv would have fainted by the way had he not seemed to hear divine voices urging him onwards. Flowers too came floating on the breeze as if showered down by hands far above him. So he struggled on until at last he came to the abodes of the Sun and Moon.

'Stay with us, King Dhruv,' cried the Sun-god and the Moon-god. 'There is no place beyond us. So stay with us and be welcome.'

'Nay,' said King Dhruv, 'I must go until I reach the end of the path that stretches in front of me.'

And indeed the path ran right through the abodes of the Moon-god and the Sun-god and lost itself in the distance beyond. So, weary with labour and years, Dhruv climbed upwards until he came to where the seven rishis lived.

'Stay with us, bold prince,' cried the seven rishis. 'We need a mortal to whom to teach our lore.' King Dhruv bowed to the seven rishis. 'Incomparable sages,' he replied, 'if I could stay with you I gladly would, so that I could learn your priceless wisdom. But I desire to worship the god Krishna and until I find the place to which he directs me I must follow this path.' So the king went on towards the North along the path which never seemed to end. And the seven sages watched him as he went. At last they saw him reach the end of the path. For it stopped suddenly and a bottomless chasm yawned in front of Dhruv. There they saw him sit down and cast up his eyes in silent adoration of the god whom he had loved and sought.

And as the sages watched Dhruv, they saw him gradually lose his human shape and become a shining form. For as he prayed, there entered into him the spirit of the mighty god. And as they watched him, they too turned into shining forms and they too remained motionless in silent contemplation of the saintly king.

And on any cloudless night, if you look up at the sky, you will see a constellation flung like a saucepan right across it. And if you look at the far side of the saucepan and follow the direction in which the stars which form it are pointing, you will see all by itself a beautiful, clear star that points ever to the far North beyond which the god Krishna has his throne. For the saucepan-like constellation is that which Indians call the Seven Sages. But in the West it is known as the Great Bear. And the lonely star to which the seven rishis ever silently point is Dhruv.

For Dhruv is the Pole Star.

40

Bertha, the White Lady

(Norse)

In other parts of Germany, Frigga, Holda, or Ostara is known by the name of Brechta, Bertha, or the White Lady. She is best known under this title in Thuringia, where she was supposed to dwell in a hollow mountain, keeping watch over the Heimchen, souls of unborn children, and of those who died unbaptized. Here Bertha watched over agriculture, caring for the plants, which her infant troop watered carefully, for each babe was supposed to carry a little jar for that express purpose. While the goddess was duly respected and her retreat unmolested, she remained where she was; but tradition relates that she once left the country with her infant train dragging her plough, and settled elsewhere to continue her kind ministrations. Bertha is the legendary ancestress of several noble families, and she is supposed to be the same as the industrious queen of the same name, the mythical mother of Charlemagne, whose era has become proverbial, for in speaking of the Golden Age in France and Germany it is customary to say, 'in the days when Bertha spun.'

As this Bertha is supposed to have developed a very large and flat foot, from continually pressing the treadle of her wheel, she is often represented in mediæval art as a woman with a splay foot, and hence known as *la reine pédauque*.

As ancestress of the imperial house of Germany, the White Lady is supposed to appear in the palace before a death or misfortune in the family, and this superstition is still so rife in Germany, that the newspapers in 1884 contained the official report of a sentinel, who declared that he had seen her flit past him in one of the palace corridors.

As Bertha was renowned for her spinning, she naturally was regarded as the special patroness of that branch of female industry, and was said to flit through the streets of every village, at nightfall, during the twelve nights between Christmas and January 6, peering into every window to inspect the spinning of the household.

The maidens whose work had been carefully performed were rewarded by a present of one of her own golden threads or a distaff full of extra fine flax; but wherever a careless spinner was found, her wheel was broken, her flax soiled, and if she had failed to honour the goddess by eating plenty of the cakes baked at that period of the year, she was cruelly punished.

In Mecklenburg, this same goddess is known as Frau Gode, or Wode, the female form of Wuotan or Odin, and her appearance is always considered the harbinger of great prosperity. She is also supposed to be a great huntress, and to lead the Wild Hunt, mounted upon a white horse, her attendants being changed into hounds and all manner of wild beasts.

In Holland she was called Vrou-elde, and from her the Milky Way is known by the Dutch as *Vrou-elden-straat*; while in parts of Northern Germany she was called Nerthus (Mother Earth). Her sacred car was kept on an island, presumably Rügen, where the priests guarded it carefully until she appeared to take a yearly journey throughout her realm to bless the land. The goddess, her face completely hidden by a thick veil, then sat in this car, which was drawn by two cows, and she was respectfully escorted by her priests. When she passed, the people did homage by ceasing all warfare, and laying aside their weapons. They donned festive attire, and began no quarrel until the goddess had again retired to her sanctuary. Then both car and goddess were bathed in a secret lake (the Schwartze See, in Rügen), which swallowed up the slaves who had assisted at the bathing, and once more the priests resumed their watch over the sanctuary and grove of Nerthus or Hlodyn, to await her next appearance.

In Scandinavia, this goddess was also known as Huldra, and boasted of a train of attendant wood-nymphs, who sometimes sought the society of mortals, to enjoy a dance upon the village green. They could always be detected, however, by the tip of a cow's tail which trailed from beneath their long snow-white garments. These Huldra folk were the special protectors of the cattle on the mountain-sides, and were said to surprise the lonely traveller, at times, by the marvellous beauty of the melodies they sang to beguile the hours at their tasks.

41

Black, Brown and Grey

(*Irish*)

On a day Fin MacCumhail was near Tara of the Kings, south of Ballyshannon, hunting with seven companies of the Fenians of Erin.

During the day they saw three strange men coming towards them, and Fin said to the Fenians: 'Let none of you speak to them, and if they have good manners they'll not speak to you nor to any man till they come to me.'

When the three men came up, they said nothing till they stood before Fin himself. Then he asked what their names were and what they wanted. They answered:—

'Our names are Dubh, Dun, and Glasán (Black, Brown, and Grey). We have come to find Fin MacCumhail, chief of the Fenians of Erin, and take service with him.'

Fin was so well pleased with their looks that he brought them home with him that evening and called them his sons. Then he said, 'Every man who comes to this castle must watch the first night for me, and since three of you have come together, each will watch one third of the night. You'll cast lots to see who'll watch first and second.'

Fin had the trunk of a tree brought, three equal parts made of it, and one given to each of the men.

Then he said, 'When each of you begins his watch he will

set fire to his own piece of wood, and so long as the wood burns he will watch.'

The lot fell to Dubh to go on the first watch.

Dubh set fire to his log, then went out around the castle, the dog Bran with him. He wandered on, going further and further from the castle, and Bran after him. At last he saw a bright light and went towards it. When he came to the place where the light was burning, he saw a large house. He entered the house and when inside saw a great company of most strange looking men, drinking out of a single cup.

The chief of the party, who was sitting on a high place, gave the cup to the man nearest him; and when he had drunk his fill out of it, he passed it to his neighbour, and so on to the last.

While the cup was going the round of the company, the chief said, 'This is the great cup that was taken from Fin MacCumhail a hundred years ago; and as much as each man wishes to drink he always gets from it, and no matter how many men there may be, or what they wish for, they always have their fill.'

Dubh sat near the door on the edge of the crowd, and when the cup came to him he drank a little, then slipped out and hurried away in the dark; when he came to the fountain at the castle of Fin MacCumhail, his log was burned.

As the second lot had fallen on Dun, it was now his turn to watch, so he set fire to his log and went out, in the place of Dubh, with the dog Bran after him.

Dun walked on through the night till he saw a fire. He went towards it, and when he had come near he saw a large house, which he entered; and when inside he saw a crowd of strange looking men, fighting. They were ferocious, wonderful to look at, and fighting wildly.

The chief, who had climbed on the crossbeams of the house to escape the uproar and struggle, called out to the crowd below: 'Stop fighting now; for I have a better gift than the one you have lost this night.' And putting his hand behind his belt, he drew out a knife and held it before them, saying: 'Here is the wonderful knife, the small knife of division, that was stolen from Fin MacCumhail a hundred years ago, and if you cut on a bone with the knife, you'll get the finest meat in the world, and as much of it as ever your hearts can wish for.'

Then he passed down the knife and a bare bone to the man next him, and the man began to cut; and off came slices of the sweetest and best meat in the world.

The knife and the bone passed from man to man till they came to Dun, who cut a slice off the bone, slipped out unseen, and made for Fin's castle as fast as his two legs could carry him through the darkness and over the ground.

When he was by the fountain at the castle, his part of the log was burned and his watch at an end.

Now Glasán set fire to his stick of wood and went out on his watch and walked forward till he saw the light and came to the same house that Dubh and Dun had visited. Looking in he saw the place full of dead bodies, and thought, 'There must be some great wonder here. If I lie down in the midst of these and put some of them over me to hide myself, I shall be able to see what is going on.'

He lay down and pulled some of the bodies over himself. He wasn't there long when he saw an old hag coming into the house. She had but one leg, one arm, and one upper tooth, which was as long as her leg and served her in place of a crutch.

When inside the door she took up the first corpse she met and threw it aside; it was lean. As she went on she took two bites out of every fat corpse she met, and threw every lean one aside.

She had her fill of flesh and blood before she came to Glasán; and as soon as she had that, she dropped down on the floor, lay on her back, and went to sleep.

Every breath she drew, Glasán was afraid she'd drag the roof down on top of his head, and every time she let a breath out of her he thought she'd sweep the roof off the house.

Then he rose up, looked at her, and wondered at the bulk of her body. At last he drew his sword, hit her a slash, and if he did, three young giants sprang forth.

Glasán killed the first giant, the dog Bran killed the second, and the third ran away.

Glasán now hurried back, and when he reached the fountain at Fin's castle, his log of wood was burned, and day was dawning.

When all had risen in the morning, and the Fenians of Erin came out, Fin said to Dubh, 'Have you anything new or wonderful to tell me after the night's watching?'

'I have,' said Dubh; 'for I brought back the drinking-cup that you lost a hundred years ago. I was out in the darkness watching. I walked on, and the dog Bran with me till I saw a light. When I came to the light I found a house, and in the house a company feasting. The chief was a very old man, and sat on a high place above the rest. He took out the cup and said: "This is the cup that was stolen from Fin MacCumhail a hundred years ago, and it is always full of the best drink in the world; and when one of you has drunk from the cup pass it on to the next."'They drank and passed the cup till it came to me. I took it and hurried back. When I came here, my log was burned and my watch was finished. Here now is the cup for you,' said Dubh to Fin MacCumhail.

Fin praised him greatly for what he had done, and turning to Dun said: 'Now tell us what happened in your watch.'

'When my turn came I set fire to the log which you gave me, and walked on; the dog Bran following, till I saw a light. When I came to the light, I found a house in which was a crowd of people, all fighting except one very old man on a high place above the rest. He called to them for peace, and told them to be quiet. 'For,' said he, 'I have a better gift for you than the one you lost this night,' and he took out the small knife of division with a bare bone, and said: 'This is the knife that was stolen from Fin MacCumhail, a hundred years ago, and whenever you cut on the bone with the knife, you'll get your fill of the best meat on earth.'

'Then he handed the knife and the bone to the man nearest him, who cut from it all the meat he wanted, and then passed it to his neighbour. The knife went from hand to hand till it came to me, then I took it, slipped out, and hurried away. When I came to the fountain, my log was burned, and here are the knife and bone for you.'

'You have done a great work, and deserve my best praise,' said Fin. 'We are sure of the best eating and drinking as long as we keep the cup and the knife.'

'Now what have you seen in your part of the night?' said Fin to Glasán.

'I went out,' said Glasán, 'with the dog Bran, and walked on till I saw a light, and when I came to the light I saw a house, which I entered. Inside were heaps of dead men, killed in fighting, and I wondered greatly when I saw them. At last I lay down in the midst of the corpses, put some of them over me and waited to see what would happen.

'Soon an old hag came in at the door, she had but one arm, one leg, and the one tooth out of her upper jaw, and that tooth as long as her leg, and she used it for a crutch as she hobbled along. She threw aside the first corpse she met and took two bites out of the second,—for she threw every lean corpse away and took two bites out of every fat one. When she had eaten her fill, she lay down on her back in the middle of the floor and went to sleep. I rose up then to look at her, and every time she drew a breath I was in dread she would bring down the roof of the house on the top of my head, and every time she let a breath out of her, I thought she'd sweep the roof from the building, so strong was the breath of the old hag.

'Then I drew my sword and cut her with a blow, but if I did three young giants sprang up before me. I killed the first, Bran killed the second, but the third escaped. I walked away then, and when I was at the fountain outside, daylight had come and my log was burned.'

'Between you and me,' said Fin, 'it would have been as well if you had let the old hag alone. I am greatly in dread the third young giant will bring trouble on us all.'

For twenty-one years Fin MacCumhail and the Fenians of Erin hunted for sport alone. They had the best of eating from the small knife of division, and the best of drinking from the cup that was never dry.

At the end of twenty-one years Dubh, Dun, and Glasán went away, and one day, as Fin and the Fenians of Erin were hunting on the hills and mountains, they saw a Fear Ruadh (a red haired man) coming toward them.

'There is a bright looking man coming this way,' said Fin, 'and don't you speak to him.'

'Oh, what do we care for him?' asked Conan Maol.

'Don't be rude to a stranger,' said Fin.

The Fear Ruadh came forward and spoke to no man till he stood before Fin.

'What have you come for?' asked Fin.

'To find a master for twenty-one years.'

'What wages do you ask?' inquired Fin.

'No wages but this,—that if I die before the twenty-one years have passed, I shall be buried on Inis Caol (Light Island).'

'I'll give you those wages,' said Fin, and he hired the Fear Ruadh for twenty-one years.

He served Fin for twenty years to his satisfaction; but toward the end of the twenty-first year he fell into a decline, became an old man, and died.

When the Fear Ruadh was dead, the Fenians of Erin said

that not a step would they go to bury him; but Fin declared that he wouldn't break his word for any man, and must take the corpse to Inis Caol.

Fin had an old white horse which he had turned out to find a living for himself as he could on the hillsides and in the woods. And now he looked for the horse and found that he had become younger than older in looks since he had put him out. So he took the old white horse and tied a coffin, with the body of the Fear Ruadh in it, on his back. Then they started him on ahead and away he went followed by Fin and twelve men of the Fenians of Erin.

When they came to the temple on Inis Caol there were no signs of the white horse and the coffin; but the temple was open and in went Fin and the twelve.

There were seats for each man inside. They sat down and rested awhile and then Fin tried to rise but couldn't. He told the men to rise, but the twelve were fastened to the seats, and the seats to the ground, so that not a man of them could come to his feet.

'Oh,' said Fin, 'I'm in dread there is some evil trick played on us.'

At that moment the Fear Ruadh stood before them in all his former strength and youth and said: 'Now is the time for me to take satisfaction out of you for my mother and brothers,' Then one of the men said to Fin, 'Chew your thumb to know is there any way out of this.'

Fin chewed his thumb to know what should he do. When he knew, he blew the great whistle with his two hands; which was heard by Donogh Kamcosa and Diarmuid O'Duivne.

The Fear Ruadh fell to and killed three of the men; but before he could touch the fourth Donogh and Diarmuid were there, and put an end to him. Now all were free, and Fin with the nine men went back to their castle south of Ballyshannon.

42

Bokwewa, the Humpback

(Native American)

Bokwewa and his brother lived in a far-off part of the country. By such as had knowledge of them, Bokwewa, the elder, although deformed and feeble of person, was considered a manito, who had assumed the mortal shape; while his younger brother, Kwasynd, manly in appearance, active, and strong, partook of the nature of the present race of beings.

They lived off the path, in a wild, lonesome place, far retired from neighbors, and, undisturbed by cares, they passed their time, content and happy. The days glided by serenely as the river that flowed by their lodge.

Owing to his lack of strength, Bokwewa never engaged in the chase, but gave his attention entirely to the affairs of the lodge. In the long winter evenings he passed the time in telling his brother stories of the giants, spirits, weendigoes, and fairies of the elder age, when they had the exclusive charge of the world. He also at times taught his brother the manner in which game should be pursued, pointed out to him the ways of the different beasts and birds of the chase, and assigned the seasons at which they could be hunted with most success.

For a while the brother was eager to learn, and keenly attended to his duties as the provider of the lodge; but at length he grew weary of their tranquil life, and began to have a desire to show himself among men. He became restive in their retirement, and was seized with a longing to visit remote places.

One day, Kwasynd told his brother that he should leave him; that he wished to visit the habitations of men, and to procure a wife.

Bokwewa objected; but his brother overruled all that he said, and in spite of every remonstrance, he departed on his travels.

He traveled for a long time. At length he fell in with the footsteps of men. They were moving by encampments, for he saw, at several spots, the poles where they had passed. It was winter; and coming to a place where one of their company had died, he found upon a scaffold, lying at length in the cold blue air, the body of a beautiful young woman. 'She shall be my wife!' exclaimed Kwasynd.

He lifted her up, and bearing her in his arms, he returned to his brother. 'Brother,' he said, 'can not you restore her to life? Oh, do me that favor!'

He looked upon the beautiful female with a longing gaze; but she lay as cold and silent as when he had found her upon the scaffold.

'I will try,' said Bokwewa.

These words had been scarcely breathed, when the young woman rose up, opened her eyes, and looked upon Bokwewa with a smile, as if she had known him before.

To Kwasynd she paid no heed whatever; but presently Bokwewa, seeing how she lingered in her gaze upon himself, said to her, 'Sister, that is your husband,' pointing to Kwasynd.

She listened to his voice, and crossing the lodge, she sat by Kwasynd, and they were man and wife.

For a long time they all lived contentedly together. Bokwewa was very kind to his brother, and sought to render his days happy. He was ever within the lodge, seeking to have it in readiness against the return of Kwasynd from the hunt. And by following his directions, which were those of one deeply skilled in the chase, Kwasynd always succeeded in returning with a good store of meat.

But the charge of the two brothers was greatly lightened by the presence of the spirit-wife; for without labor of the hand, she ordered the lodge, and as she willed, every thing took its place, and was at once in proper array. The wish of her heart seemed to control whatever she looked upon, and it obeyed her desire.

But it was still more to the surprise of her husband Kwasynd that she never partook of food, nor shared in any way the longings and appetites of a mortal creature. She had never been seen arranging her hair, like other females, or at work upon her garments, and yet they were ever seemly, and without blemish or disorder.

Behold her at any hour, she was ever beautiful, and she seemed to need no ornament, nor nourishment, nor other aid, to give grace or strength to her looks.

Kwasynd, when the first wonder of her ways had passed, payed little heed to her discourse; he was engrossed with the hunt, and chose rather to be abroad, pursuing the wild game, or in the lodge, enjoying its savory spoil, than the society of his spirit-wife.

But Bokwewa watched closely every word that fell from her lips, and often forgot, like her, all mortal appetite and care of the body, in conferring with her, and noting what she had to say of spirits and fairies, of stars, and streams that never ceased to flow, and the delight of the happy hunting-grounds, and the groves of the blessed.

One day Kwasynd had gone out as usual, and Bokwewa was sitting in the lodge, on the opposite side to his brother's wife, when she suddenly exclaimed:

'I must leave you,' as a tall young man, whose face was like the sun in its brightness, entered, and taking her by the hand he led her to the door.

She made no resistance, but turning as she left the lodge,

she cast upon Bokwewa a smile of kind regard, and was at once, with her companion, gone from his view.

He ran to the door and glanced about. He saw nothing; but looking far off in the sky, he thought that he could discover, at a great distance, a shining track, and the dim figures of two who were vanishing in heaven.

When his brother returned, Bokwewa related all to him exactly as it had happened.

The face of Kwasynd changed, and was dark as the night. For several days he would not taste food. Sometimes he would fall to weeping for a long time, and now only it seemed that he remembered how gentle and beautiful had been the ways of her who was lost. At last he said that he would go in search of her.

Bokwewa tried to dissuade him from it; but he would not be turned aside from his purpose.

'Since you are resolved,' said Bokwewa, 'listen to my advice. You will have to go South. It is a long distance to the present abiding-place of your wife, and there are so many charms and temptations by the way that I fear you will be led astray and for get your errand. For the people whom you will see in the country through which you have to pass, do nothing but amuse themselves. They are very idle, gay and effeminate, and I fear that they will lead you astray. Your path is beset with dangers. I will mention one or two things which you must be on your guard against.

'In the course of your journey you will come to a large grape-vine lying across your path. You must not even taste its fruit, for it is poisonous. Step over it. It is a snake. You will next come to something that looks like bear's fat, of which you are so fond. Touch it not, or you will be overcome by the soft habits of the idle people. It is frog's eggs. These are snares laid by the way for you.'

Kwasynd promised that he would observe the advice and

bidding his brother farewell, he set out. After traveling a long time he came to the enchanted grape-vine. It looked so tempting, with its swelling purple clusters, that he forgot his brother's warning, and tasted the fruit. He went on till he came to the frog's eggs. They so much resembled delicious bear's fat that Kwasynd tasted them. He still went on.

At length he came to a wide plain. As he emerged from the forest the sun was falling in the west, and it cast its scarlet and golden shades far over the country. The air was perfectly calm, and the whole prospect had the air of an enchanted land. Fruits and flowers, and delicate blossoms, lured the eye and delighted the senses.

At a distance he beheld a large village, swarming with people, and as he drew near he discovered women beating corn in silver mortars.

When they saw Kwasynd approaching, they cried out:

'Bokwewa's brother has come to see us.'

Throngs of men and women, in bright apparel, hurried out to meet him.

He was soon, having already yielded to temptation by the way, overcome by their fair looks and soft speeches, and he was not long afterward seen beating corn with the women, having entirely abandoned all further quest for his lost wife.

Meantime, Bokwewa, alone in the lodge, often musing upon the discourse of the spirit-wife, who was gone, waited patiently his brother's return. After the lapse of several years, when no tidings could be had, he set out in search of him, and he arrived in safety among the soft and idle people of the South. He met the same allurements by the way, and they gathered around him on his coming as they had around his brother Kwasynd; but Bokwewa was proof against their flattery. He only grieved in his heart that any should yield.

He shed tears of pity to see that his brother had laid aside the arms of a hunter, and that he was beating corn with the women, indifferent to the fate and the fortune of his lost wife.

Bokwewa ascertained that his brother's wife had passed on to a country beyond.

After deliberating for a time, and spending several days in a severe fast, he set out in the direction where he saw that a light shone from the sky.

It was far off, but Bokwewa had a stout heart; and strong in the faith that he was now on the broad path toward the happy land, he pressed forward. For many days he traveled without encountering any thing unusual. And now plains of vast extent, and rich in waving grass, began to pass before his eyes. He saw many beautiful groves, and heard the songs of countless birds.

At length he began to fail in strength for lack of food; when he suddenly reached a high ground. From this he caught the first glimpse of the other land. But it appeared to be still far off, and all the country between, partly vailed in silvery mists, glittered with lakes and streams of water. As he pressed on, Bokwewa came in sight of innumerable herds of stately deer, moose, and other animals which walked near his path, and they appeared to have no fear of man.

And now again as he wound about in his course, and faced the north once more, he beheld, coming toward him, an immense number of men, women, and children, pressing forward in the direction of the shining land.

In this vast throng Bokwewa beheld persons of every age, from the little infant, the sweet and lovely *penaisee*, or younger son, to the feeble, gray old man, stooping under the burden of his years.

All whom Bokwewa met, of every name and degree, were heavily laden with pipes, weapons, bows, arrows, kettles and other wares and implements.

One man stopped him, and complained of the weary load

he was carrying. Another offered him a kettle; another his bow and arrows; but he declined all, and, free of foot, hastened on.

And now he met women who were carrying their basket-work, and painted paddles, and little boys, with their embellished war-clubs and bows and arrows, the gift of their friends.

With this mighty throng, Bokwewa was borne along for two days and nights, when he arrived at a country so still and shining, and so beautiful in its woods and groves and plains, that he knew it was here that he should find the lost spirit-wife.

He had scarcely entered this fair country, with a sense of home and the return to things familiar strong upon him, when there appeared before him the lost spirit-wife herself, who, taking him by the hand, gave him welcome, saying, 'My brother, I am glad to see you. Welcome! welcome! You are now in your native land!'

43

The Celestial Sisters

(*Native American*)

Waupee, or the White Hawk, lived in a remote part of the forest, where animals abounded. Every day he returned from the chase with a large spoil, for he was one of the most skillful and lucky hunters of his tribe. His form was like the cedar; the fire of youth beamed from his eye; there was no forest too gloomy for him to penetrate, and no track made by bird or beast of any kind which he could not readily follow.

One day he had gone beyond any point which he had ever before visited. He traveled through an open wood, which enabled him to see a great distance. At length he beheld a light breaking through the foliage of the distant trees, which made him sure that he was on the borders of a prairie. It was a wide plain, covered with long blue grass, and enameled with flowers of a thousand lovely tints.

After walking for some time without a path, musing upon the open country, and enjoying the fra grant breeze, he suddenly came to a ring worn among the grass and the flowers, as if it had been made by footsteps moving lightly round and round. But it was strange—so strange as to cause the White Hawk to pause and gaze long and fixedly upon the ground—there was no path which led to this flowery circle. There was not even a crushed leaf nor a broken twig, nor the least trace of a footstep, approaching or retiring, to be found. He thought he would hide himself and lie in wait to discover, if he could, what this strange circle meant.

Presently he heard the faint sounds of music in the air. He looked up in the direction they came from, and as the magic notes died away he saw a small object, like a little summer cloud that approaches the earth, floating down from above. At first it was very small, and seemed as if it could have been blown away by the first breeze that came along; but it rapidly grew as he gazed upon it, and the music every moment came clearer and more sweetly to his ear. As it neared the earth it appeared as a basket, and it was filled with twelve sisters, of the most lovely forms and enchanting beauty.

As soon as the basket touched the ground they leaped out, and began straightway to dance, in the most joyous manner, around the magic ring, striking, as they did so, a shining ball, which uttered the most ravishing melodies, and kept time as they danced.

The White Hawk, from his concealment, entranced, gazed upon their graceful forms and movements. He admired them all, but he was most pleased with the youngest. He longed to be at her side, to embrace her, to call her his own; and unable to remain longer a silent admirer, he rushed out and endeavored to seize this twelfth beauty who so enchanted him. But the sisters, with the quickness of birds, the moment they descried the form of a man, leaped back into the basket, and were drawn up into the sky.

Lamenting his ill-luck, Waupee gazed longingly upon the fairy basket as it ascended and bore the lovely sisters from his view. 'They are gone,' he said, 'and I shall see them no more.'

He returned to his solitary lodge, but he found no relief to his mind. He walked abroad, but to look at the sky, which had withdrawn from his sight the only being he had ever loved, was painful to him now.

The next day, selecting the same hour, the White Hawk went back to the prairie, and took his station near the ring; in order to deceive the sisters, he assumed the form of an opossum, and sat among the grass as if he were there engaged in chewing the cud. He had not waited long when he saw the cloudy basket descend, and heard the same sweet music falling as before. He crept slowly toward the ring; but the instant the sisters caught sight of him they were startled, and sprang into their car. It rose a short distance when one of the elder sisters spoke:

'Perhaps,' she said, 'it is come to show us how the game is played by mortals.'

'Oh no,' the youngest replied; 'quick, let us ascend.'

And all joining in a chant, they rose out of sight.

Waupee, casting off his disguise, walked sorrowfully back to his lodge—but ah, the night seemed very long to lonely White Hawk! His whole soul was filled with the thought of the beautiful sister.

Betimes, the next day, he returned to the haunted spot, hoping and fearing, and sighing as though his very soul would leave his body in its anguish. He reflected upon the plan he should follow to secure success. He had already failed twice; to fail a third time would be fatal. Near by he found an old stump, much covered with moss, and just then in use as the residence of a number of mice, who had stopped there on a pilgrimage to some relatives on the other side of the prairie. The White Hawk was so pleased with their tidy little forms that he thought he, too, would be a mouse, especially as they were by no means formidable to look at, and would not be at all likely to create alarm.

He accordingly, having first brought the stump and set it near the ring, without further notice became a mouse, and peeped and sported about, and kept his sharp little eyes busy with the others; but he did not forget to keep one eye up toward the sky, and one ear wide open in the same direction.

It was not long before the sisters, at their customary hour, came down and resumed their sport.

'But see,' cried the younger sister, 'that stump was not there before.'

She ran off, frightened, toward the basket. Her sisters only smiled, and gathering round the old tree-stump, they struck it, in jest, when out ran the mice, and among them Waupee. They killed them all but one, which was pursued by the younger sister. Just as she had raised a silver stick which she held in her hand to put an end to it, too, the form of the White Hawk arose, and he clasped his prize in his arms. The other eleven sprang to their basket, and were drawn up to the skies.

Waupee exerted all his skill to please his bride and win her affections. He wiped the tears from her eyes; he related his adventures in the chase; he dwelt upon the charms of life on the earth. He was constant in his attentions, keeping fondly by her side, and picking out the way for her to walk as he led her gently toward his lodge. He felt his heart glow with joy as he entered it, and from that moment he was one of the happiest of men.

Winter and summer passed rapidly away, and as the spring drew near with its balmy gales and its many-colored flowers, their happiness was increased by the presence of a beautiful boy in their lodge. What more of earthly blessing was there for them to enjoy?

Waupee's wife was a daughter of one of the stars; and as the scenes of earth began to pall upon her sight, she sighed to revisit her father. But she was obliged to hide these feelings from her husband. She remembered the charm that would carry her up, and while White Hawk was engaged in the chase, she took occasion to construct a wicker basket, which she kept concealed. In the mean time, she collected such rarities from the earth as she thought would please her father, as well as the most dainty kinds of food.

One day when Waupee was absent, and all was in readiness, she went out to the charmed ring, taking with her her little son.

As they entered the car she commenced her magical song, and the basket rose. The song was sad, and of a lowly and mournful cadence, and as it was wafted far away by the wind, it caught her husband's ear. It was a voice which he well knew, and he instantly ran to the prairie.

Though he made breathless speed, he could not reach the ring before his wife and child had ascended beyond his reach. He lifted up his voice in loud appeals, but they were unavailing. The basket still went up. He watched it till it became a small speck, and finally it vanished in the sky. He then bent his head down to the ground, and was miserable.

Through a long winter and a long summer Waupee bewailed his loss, but he found no relief. The beautiful spirit had come and gone, and he should see it no more!

He mourned his wife's loss sorely, but his son's still more; for the boy had both the mother's beauty and the father's strength.

In the mean time his wife had reached her home in the stars, and in the blissful employments of her father's house she had almost forgotten that she had left a husband upon the earth. But her son, as he grew up, resembled more and more his father, and every day he was restless and anxious to visit the scene of his birth. His grandfather said to his daughter, one day:

'Go, my child, and take your son down to his father, and ask him to come up and live with us. But tell him to bring along a specimen of each kind of bird and animal he kills in the chase.'

She accordingly took the boy and descended.

The White Hawk, who was ever near the enchanted spot, heard her voice as she came down the sky. His heart beat with impatience as he saw her form and that of his son, and they were soon clasped in his arms.

He heard the message of the Star, and he began to hunt with the greatest activity, that he might collect the present with all dispatch. He spent whole nights, as well as days, in searching for every curious and beautiful animal and bird. He only preserved a foot, a wing, or a tail of each.

When all was ready, Waupee visited once more each favorite spot—the hill-top whence he had been used to see the rising sun; the stream where he had sported as a boy; the old lodge, now looking sad and solemn, which he was to sit in no more; and last of all, coming to the magic circle, he gazed widely around him with tearful eyes, and, taking his wife and child by the hand, they entered the car and were drawn up—into a country far beyond the flight of birds, or the power of mortal eye to pierce.

Great joy was manifested upon their arrival at the starry plains. The Star Chief invited all his people to a feast; and when they had assembled, he proclaimed aloud that each one might continue as he was, an inhabitant of his own dominions, or select of the earthly gifts such as he liked best. A very strange confusion immediately arose; not one but sprang forward. Some chose a foot, some a wing, some a tail, and some a claw. Those who selected tails or claws were changed into animals, and ran off; the others assumed the form of birds, and flew away. Waupee chose a white hawk's feather. His wife and son followed his example, and each one became a white hawk. He spread his wings, and, followed by his wife and son, descended with the other birds to the earth, where he is still to be found, with the brightness of the starry plains in his eye, and the freedom of the heavenly breezes in his wings.

44

The Sun-Goddess

(Japanese)

Ama-terasu, the Sun-Goddess, was seated in the Blue Plain of Heaven. Her light came as a message of joy to the celestial deities. The orchid and the iris, the cherry and the plum blossom, the rice and the hemp fields answered to her smile. The Inland Sea was veiled in soft rich colour.

Susa-no-o, the brother of Ama-terasu, who had resigned his ocean sceptre and now reigned as the Moon-God, was jealous of his sister's glory and world-wide sway. The Heaven-Illuminating Spirit had but to whisper and she was heard throughout her kingdom, even in the depths of the clear pool and in the heart of the crystal. Her rice-fields, whether situated on hill-side, in sheltered valley, or by running stream, yielded abundant harvests, and her groves were laden with fruit. But the voice of Susa-no-o was not so clear, his smile was not so radiant. The undulating fields which lay around his palace were now flooded, now parched, and his rice crops were often destroyed. The wrath and jealousy of the Moon-God knew no bounds, yet Ama-terasu was infinitely patient and forgave him many things.

Once, as was her wont, the Sun-Goddess sat in the central court of her glorious home. She plied her shuttle. Celestial weaving maidens surrounded a fountain whose waters were fragrant with the heavenly lotus-bloom: they sang softly of the clouds and the wind and the lift of the sky. Suddenly, the body of a piebald horse fell through the vast dome at their feet: the 'Beloved of the Gods' had been 'flayed with a backward flaying' by the envious Susa-no-o. Ama-terasu, trembling at the horrible sight, pricked her finger with the weaving shuttle, and, profoundly indignant at the cruelty of her brother, withdrew into a cave and closed behind her the door of the Heavenly Rock Dwelling.

The universe was plunged in darkness. Joy and goodwill, serenity and peace, hope and love, waned with the waning light. Evil spirits, who heretofore had crouched in dim corners, came forth and roamed abroad. Their grim laughter and discordant tones struck terror into all hearts.

Then it was that the gods, fearful for their safety and for the life of every beautiful thing, assembled in the bed of the tranquil River of Heaven, whose waters had been dried up. One and all knew that Ama-terasu alone could help them. But how allure the Heaven-Illuminating Spirit to set foot in this world of darkness and strife? Each god was eager to aid, and a plan was finally devised to entice her from her hiding-place.

Ame-no-ko uprooted the holy *sakaki* trees which grow on the Mountain of Heaven, and planted them around the entrance of the cave. High on the upper branches were hung the precious string of curved jewels which Izanagi had bestowed upon the Sun-Goddess. From the middle branches drooped a mirror wrought of the rare metals of the celestial mine. Its polished surface was as the dazzling brilliancy of the sun. Other gods wove, from threads of hemp and paper mulberry, an imperial robe of white and blue, which was placed, as an offering for the goddess, on the lower branches of the *sakaki*. A palace was also built, surrounded by a garden in which the Blossom-God called forth many delicate plants and flowers.

Now all was ready. Ame-no-ko stepped forward, and, in a loud voice, entreated Ama-terasu to show herself. His appeal was in vain. The great festival began. Uzume, the goddess of mirth, led the dance and song. Leaves of the spindle tree crowned her head; club-moss, from the heavenly Mount Kagu, formed her sash; her flowing sleeves were bound with the creeper-vine; and in her hand she carried leaves of the wild bamboo and waved a wand of sun-grass hung with tiny melodious bells. Uzume blew on a bamboo flute, while the eight hundred myriad deities accompanied her on wooden clappers and instruments formed of bow-strings, across which were rapidly drawn stalks of reed and grass. Great fires were lighted around the cave, and, as these were reflected in the face of the mirror, 'the long-singing birds of eternal night' began to crow as if the day dawned. The merriment increased. The dance grew wilder and wilder, and the gods laughed until the heavens shook as if with thunder.

Ama-terasu, in her quiet retreat, heard, unmoved, the crowing of the cocks and the sounds of music and dancing, but when the heavens shook with the laughter of the gods, she peeped from her cave and said: 'What means this? I thought heaven and earth were dark, but now there is light. Uzume dances and all the gods laugh.' Uzume answered: 'It is true that I dance and that the gods laugh, because in our midst is a goddess whose splendour equals your own. Behold!' Ama-terasu gazed into the mirror, and wondered greatly when she saw therein a goddess of exceeding beauty. She stepped from her cave and forthwith a cord of rice-straw was drawn across the entrance. Darkness fled from the Central Land of Reed-Plains, and there was light. Then the eight hundred myriad deities cried: 'O, may the Sun-Goddess never leave us again.'

45

Twardowski, the Polish Faust

(Polish)

Toward the close of the eighteenth century there was pointed out to visitors in the old town of Krakau the house of the magician Twardowski, who quite properly was called the Faust of Poland, because of his dealings with the Evil One.

In his youth Twardowski had followed the study of medicine, and with such industry, such eagerness and such a clear mind did he practice his profession that it was not long before he was the most celebrated doctor in all Poland. But Twardowski was not satisfied with this. He craved greater and still greater power.

At last one day, as he was reading, he found in an old book of magic that for which he had long been seeking—the formula for summoning the devil. When night came a storm had risen, but caring not for that he hurried away to the lonely mountain Kremenki. There, in a rudely constructed hut, he began his incantations.

Before long there was an earthquake; great rocks were loosened, the ground opened at Twardowski's feet and flames leaped out; and in the flames appeared the Evil One himself, in the form of a man, clad in a red cloak with the well-known pointed red cap.

'What do you wish?' the devil asked.

'The power of your most secret wisdom,' was the answer.

'And how is this to be done?'

'You shall make me the most celebrated of all the learned men of the century, and shall besides give me such happiness as no man has ever enjoyed upon this earth before.'

'So be it,' said the devil. 'But on condition that at the end of seven years I gain possession of your soul.'

'You may take me,' answered Twardowski, 'but only in Rome may you have power over me. Thither, at the end of seven years, will I go.'

The devil hesitated over this clause, but thinking of the fun he could have in the holy city, finally agreed. Leaning against the wall of stone he wrote the compact, which Twardowski, making a slight wound in his arm, signed with his own blood.

When Twardowski descended from the mountain and made his way, book under arm, through the valley, he heard the bells in all the towers of the city ringing out clearly and solemnly on the still night air. He listened, wondering at the unaccustomed noise, then hurried into the town, inquiring from every one he met what the occasion was. But no one seemed to have heard the sound.

Then a deep feeling of sadness came over him as he realized the meaning of the bells. They were the funeral knell of his own soul.

When morning came, however, doubts were forgotten, and Twardowski was glad to have the devil at his command. The first thing that he demanded was to have all the silver of Poland gathered together in one place and covered over with great mounds of sand.

Similar requests followed, and it was not long before the devil repented of his bargain. One day it would please Twardowski to fly without wings through the air; on another, to the delight of the crowd, to gallop backward on a cock; on another to float in a boat without a rudder or sail, accompanied by some maiden who for the moment had inflamed his heart. One day, by the use of his magic mirror, he set fire to the castle of an enemy a mile away. This last feat made him greatly feared by people far and wide.

At last the seven years were up. The devil appeared to Twardowski and said:

'Twardowski, the time of our pact is over, and I command you to fulfil your promise and go to Rome.'

'What shall I do there?'

'Give me your immortal soul,' was the answer.

'Do you think I am a fool?' asked Twardowski.

'You gave me your promise to go to Rome after seven years.'

'That I have already done,' said Twardowski, 'and I did not promise to stay in Rome.'

'Noble deceiver!' exclaimed the Evil One.

'Stupid devil!' cried Twardowski.

Then after a struggle the devil vanished and Twardowski returned home.

For over a year he pored incessantly over his books of magic, until at last he found a formula for warding off death. Then he called his disciple Famulus to him and explained that he was going to test the formula.

'You have always obliged me without question,' said Twardowski, 'and I expect you to now. Take this knife and thrust it into my heart.'

'God forbid!' cried Famulus.

'Why are you frightened? I know what I am doing. Take the knife and kill me, as the parchment directs.'

'I cannot.'

'You must,' insisted Twardowski.

'It is impossible!'

'No more exclamations. Do as I tell you.'

'Oh, oh, oh!' wailed Famulus.

'Strike!' thundered Twardowski, 'or I will kill you this instant.'

Then Famulus did as he was bid and forced the blade into his master's heart.

Twardowski uttered a low cry, fell, and was soon dead.

Famulus dropped trembling into a chair and covered his face with his hands. Then he remembered that he must read the remainder of the parchment in order to find out what he must do to restore the body to life.

Then he set about the task, severed the limbs of the dead body, and worked and brewed and distilled until the elixir described in the parchment was prepared.

With the elixir he rubbed the members of the master's body, put them together, and laid the corpse in a coffin. This he buried on the following night, explaining to Twardowski's friends that such had been the master's wish.

Now the parchment stated that the body must remain in the grave seven years, seven months, seven days and seven hours; so Famulus could do nothing but wait. At last the time had expired, and on a snowy, cold December night he found his way to the grave. He dug out the coffin, brushed off the snow and earth, opened the casket and found—not the body of Twardowski, but that of a child who lay sleeping in a bed of fragrant violets.

'The child is like Twardowski,' Famulus thought, and he gathered him up under his cloak and carried him home. The next morning the child was the size of a twelve-year old; and after seven weeks he was a full-grown man.

Twardowski, who now seemed quite himself, only younger, and stronger, thanked Famulus and resumed again his study of magic. He desired, above all things, to be freed forever from his compact with the devil. This, he read in one of the books, he might do if he would brave the terrors of the Underworld.

So Twardowski determined to enter the gates of hell. At his magic speech the ground opened and he began the path of descent. Blue flames lighted the way. Deeper and deeper he went through dark and winding passages. At last he reached the Underworld itself, and many awful sights did he behold.

And the farther he went the more frightened did he become. He could not help feeling that the devil had plotted something against him. Finally he found himself in a small room, and cast a hasty glance around, looking for a means of escape.

Seeing a child in a cradle in one corner of the room he seized it hastily, threw his cloak around it, and was about to leave when the door opened and the Evil One entered.

He made a respectful bow and said, 'Will you be good enough to go with me now?'

'Why so?' asked Twardowski, obstinately.

'Because of our agreement.'

'But,' said the magician, 'only in Rome have you power over me.'

'Yes,' replied the devil, 'and Rome is the name of this house.'

'You think to trick me by a pun; but you cannot. I carry this talisman of innocence,' and throwing aside his cloak, he disclosed the sleeping child.

Anger showed in the face of the devil; but he stepped nearer to Twardowski and said softly:

'What are you thinking of, Twardowski? Have you forgotten your promise? The nobleman's word is sacred to him.'

Pride awoke in the breast of the magician.

'I must keep my word,' he said, laying the child back in the crib, and surrendering himself.

On the shoulders of the devil two wings appeared, like the wings of a bat. He seized Twardowski and flew away with him, mounting higher and higher into the night. The magician was so terrified and suffered such anguish in the clutches of the Evil One that in a few moments he was changed into an old man, but he did not lose consciousness. At last so high were they that cities appeared like flies and Krakau with its mighty turrets like two spiders. Deeply moved, Twardowski looked down upon the scene of all his struggles and all his joys.

But higher and higher they went—higher than any eagle has ever flown—and more lonely and more fearful did it seem to Twardowski. Only occasionally bright stars passed by them, or fiery meteors, leaving a long streak of light behind.

At last they came to the moon, which stared at them with dead eyes. Then a song that Twardowski had read in his mother's hymn book rose to his lips. And as he repeated mechanically the prayer his mother had taught him an angel suddenly appeared and said:

'Satan, let Twardowski go; and you, Twardowski, hang you there between heaven and earth, to atone for your sin until the Last Judgment. Then will you be reunited with your mother in heaven. The prayer which you remembered in your hour of need has saved you.'

And so, according to the story, Twardowski is suspended in the vault of heaven to this very day.

46

Theseus and the Centaur

(Greek)

Theseus, the hero king of Athens, had a reputation for great strength and bravery; but Pirithous, the son of Ixion, one of the most famous heroes of antiquity, wished to put him to the test. He therefore drove the cattle which belonged to Theseus away from Marathon, and when he heard that Theseus, weapon in hand, was following him, then, indeed, he had what he desired. He did not flee, but turned around to meet him.

When the two heroes were near enough to see each other, each was so filled with admiration for the beautiful form and the bravery of his opponent that, as if at a given signal, both threw down their weapons and hastened toward each other. Pirithous extended his hand to Theseus and proposed that the latter act as arbitrator for the settlement of the dispute about the cattle: whatever satisfaction Theseus would demand Pirithous would willingly give.

'The only satisfaction which I desire,' answered Pirithous, 'is that you instead of my enemy become my friend and comrade in arms.'

Then the two heroes embraced each other and swore eternal friendship.

Soon after this Pirithous chose the Thessalian princess, Hippodamia, from the race of Lapithæ, for his bride, and invited Theseus to the wedding. The Lapithæ, among whom the ceremony took place, were a famous family of Thessalians, rugged mountaineers, in some respects resembling animals—the first mortals who had learned to manage a horse. But the bride, who had sprung from this race, was not at all like the men of her people. She was of noble form, with delicate youthful face, so beautiful that all the guests praised Pirithous for his good fortune.

The assembled princes of Thessaly were at the wedding feast, and also the Centaurs, relatives of Pirithous. The Centaurs were half men, the offspring which a cloud, assuming the form of the goddess Hera, had born to Ixion, the father of Pirithous. They were the eternal enemies of the Lapithæ. Upon this occasion, however, and for the sake of the bride, they had forgotten past grudges and come together to the joyful celebration. The noble castle of Pirithous resounded with glad tumult; bridal songs were sung; wine and food abounded. Indeed, there were so many guests that the palace would not accommodate all. The Lapithæ and Centaurs sat at a special table in a grotto shaded by trees.

For a long time the festivities went on with undisturbed happiness. Then the wine began to stir the heart of the wildest of the Centaurs, Eurytion, and the beauty of the Princess Hippodamia awoke in him the mad desire of robbing the bridegroom of his bride. Nobody knew how it came to pass; nobody noticed the beginning of the unthinkable act; but suddenly the guests saw the wild Eurytion lifting Hippodamia from her feet, while she struggled and cried for help. His deed was the signal for the rest of the drunken Centaurs to do likewise, and before the strange heroes and the Lapithæ could leave their places, every one of the Centaurs had roughly seized one of the Thessalian princesses who served at the court of the king or who had assembled as guests at the wedding.

The castle and the grotto resembled a besieged city; the cry of the women sounded far and wide. Quickly friends and relatives sprang from their places.

'What delusion is this, Eurytion,' cried Theseus, 'to vex Pirithous while I still live, and by so doing arouse the anger of two heroes?' With these words he forced his way through the crowd and tore the stolen bride from the struggling robber.

Eurytion said nothing, for he could not excuse his deed, but he lifted his hand toward Theseus and gave him a rough knock in the chest. Then Theseus, who had no weapon at hand, seized an iron jug of embossed workmanship which stood near by and flung it into the face of his opponent with such force that the Centaur fell backward on the ground, while brains and blood oozed from the wound in his head.

'To arms!' the cry arose from all sides. At first beakers, flasks and bowls flew back and forth. Then one sacrilegious monster grabbed the oblations from the neighbouring apartments. Another tore down the lamp which burned over the table, while still another fought with a sacrificial deer which had hung on one side of the grotto. A frightful slaughter ensued. Rhoetus, the most wicked of the Centaurs after Eurytion, seized the largest brand from the altar and thrust it into the gaping wound of one of the fallen Lapithæ, so that the blood hissed like iron in a furnace. In opposition to him rose Dryas, the bravest of the Lapithæ, and seizing a glowing log from the fire, thrust it into the Centaur's neck. The fate of this Centaur atoned for the death of his fallen companion, and Dryas turned to the raging mob and laid five of them low.

Then the spear of the brave hero Pirithous flew forth and pierced a mighty Centaur, Petraeus, just as he was about to uproot a tree to use it for a club. The spear pinned him against the knotted oak. A second, Dictys, fell at the stroke of the Greek hero, and in falling snapped off a mighty ash tree; a third, wishing to avenge him, was crushed by Theseus with an oak club.

The most beautiful and youthful of the Centaurs was Cyllarus. His long hair and beard were golden; his smile was friendly; his neck, shoulders, hands and breast were as beautiful as if formed by an artist. Even the lower part of his body, the part which resembled a horse, was faultless, pitch-black in colour, with legs and tail of lighter dye. He had come to the feast with his wife, the beautiful Centaur, Hylonome, who at the table had leaned gracefully against him and even now united with him in the raging fight. He received from an unknown hand a light wound near his heart, and sank dying in the arms of his wife. Hylonome nursed his dying form, kissed him and tried to retain the fleeting breath. When she saw that he was gone she drew a dagger from her breast and stabbed herself.

For a long time still the fight between the Lapithæ and the Centaurs continued, but at last night put an end to the tumult. Then Pirithous remained in undisturbed possession of his bride, and on the following morning Theseus departed, bidding farewell to his friend. The common fight had quickly welded the fresh tie of their brotherhood into an indestructible bond.

47

Osseo, the Son of the Evening Star

(Native American)

There once lived an Indian in the north who had ten daughters, all of whom grew up to womanhood. They were noted for their beauty, especially Oweenee, the youngest, who was very independent in her way of thinking. She was a great admirer of romantic places, and spent much of her time with the flowers and winds and clouds in the open air. Though the flower were homely, if it was fragrant—though the wind were rough, if it was healthful—and though the cloud were dark, if it embosomed the fruitful rain, she knew how, in spite of appearances, to acknowledge the good qualities concealed from the eye. She paid very little attention to the many handsome young men who came to her father's lodge for the purpose of seeing her.

Her elder sisters were all sought in marriage, and one after the other they went off to dwell in the lodges of their husbands; but Oweenee was deaf to all proposals of the kind. At last she married an old man called Osseo, who was scarcely able to walk, and who was too poor to have things like others. The only property he owned in the world was the walking-staff which he carried in his hand. Though thus poor and homely, Osseo was a devout and good man; faithful in all his duties, and obedient in all things to the Good Spirit. Of course they jeered and laughed at Oweenee on all sides, but she seemed to be quite happy, and said to them, 'It is my choice and you will see in the end who has acted the wisest.'

They made a special mock of the walking-staff, and scarcely an hour in the day passed that they had not some disparaging reference to it. Among themselves they spoke of Osseo of the walking-staff, in derision, as the owner of the big woods, or the great timber-man.

'True,' said Oweenee, 'it is but a simple stick; but as it supports the steps of my husband, it is more precious to me than all the forests of the north.'

A time came when the sisters, and their husbands, and their parents were all invited to a feast. As the distance was considerable, they doubted whether Osseo, so aged and feeble, would be able to undertake the journey; but in spite of their friendly doubts, he joined them, and set out with a good heart.

As they walked along the path they could not help pitying their young and handsome sister who had such an unsuitable mate. She, however, smiled upon Osseo, and kept with him by the way the same as if he had been the comeliest bridegroom in all the company. Osseo often stopped and gazed upward; but they could perceive nothing in the direction in which he looked, unless it was the faint glimmering of the evening star. They heard him muttering to himself as they went along, and one of the elder sisters caught the words, 'Pity me, my father!'

'Poor old man,' said she; 'he is talking to his father. What a pity it is that he would not fall and break his neck, that our sister might have a young husband.'

Presently as they came to a great rock where Osseo had been used to breathe his morning and his evening prayer, the star emitted a brighter ray, which shone directly in his face. Osseo, with a sharp cry, fell trembling to the earth, where the others would have left him, but his good wife raised him up, and he sprang forward on the path, and with steps light as the reindeer he led the party, no longer decrepit and infirm, but a beautiful young man. On turning around to look for his wife, behold she had become changed, at the same moment, into an aged and feeble woman, bent almost double, and walking with the staff which he had cast aside.

Osseo immediately joined her, and with looks of fondness and the tenderest regard, bestowed on her every endearing attention, and constantly addressed her by the term of *ne-ne-moosh-a*, or my sweetheart.

As they walked along, whenever they were not gazing fondly in each other's face, they bent their looks on heaven, and a light, as if of far-off stars, was in their eyes.

On arriving at the lodge of the hunter with whom they were to feast, they found the banquet ready, and as soon as their entertainer had finished his harangue—in which he told them his feasting was in honor of the Evening or Woman's Star—they began to partake of the portion dealt out, according to age and character, to each one of the guests. The food was very delicious, and they were all happy but Osseo, who looked at his wife, and then gazed upward, as if he was looking into the substance of the sky. Sounds were soon heard, as if from far-off voices in the air, and they became plainer and plainer, till he could clearly distinguish some of the words.

'My son, my son,' said the voice; 'I have seen your afflictions, and pity your wants. I come to call you away from a scene that is stained with blood and tears. The earth is full of sorrows. Wicked spirits, the enemies of mankind, walk abroad, and lie in wait to ensnare the children of the sky. Every night they are lifting their voices to the Power of Evil, and every day they make themselves busy in casting mischief in the hunter's path. You have long been their victim, but you shall be their victim no more. The spell you were under is broken. Your evil genius is overcome. I have cast him down by my superior strength, and it is this strength I now exert for your happiness. Ascend, my son; ascend into the skies, and partake of the feast I have prepared for you in the stars, and bring with you those you love.

'The food set before you is enchanted and blessed. Fear not to partake of it. It is endowed with magic power to give immortality to mortals, and to change men to spirits. Your bowls and kettles shall no longer be wood and earth. The one shall become silver, and the other pure gold. They shall shine like fire, and glisten like the most beautiful scarlet. Every female shall also change her state and looks, and no longer be doomed to laborious tasks. She shall put on the beauty of the star-light, and become a shining bird of the air. She shall dance, and not work. She shall sing, and not cry.

'My beams,' continued the voice, 'shine faintly on your lodge, but they have power to transform it into the lightness of the skies, and decorate it with the colors of the clouds. Come, Osseo, my son, and dwell no longer on earth. Think strongly on my words, and look steadfastly at my beams. My power is now at its height. Doubt not, delay not. It is the voice of the Spirit of the Stars that calls you away to happiness and celestial rest.'

The words were intelligible to Osseo, but his companions thought them some far-off sounds of music, or birds singing in the woods. Very soon the lodge began to shake and tremble, and they felt it rising into the air. It was too late to run out, for they were already as high as the tops of the trees. Osseo looked around him as the lodge passed through the topmost boughs, and behold! their wooden dishes were changed into shells of a scarlet color, the poles of the lodge to glittering rods of silver, and the bark that covered them into the gorgeous wings of insects.

A moment more and his brothers and sisters, and their parents and friends, were transformed into birds of various plumage. Some were jays, some partridges and pigeons, and others gay singing birds, who hopped about, displaying their many-colored feathers, and singing songs of cheerful note.

But his wife, Oweenee, still kept her earthly garb, and exhibited all the indications of extreme old age. He again cast his eyes in the direction of the clouds, and uttered the peculiar cry which had given him the victory at the rock. In a moment the youth and beauty of his wife returned; her dingy garments assumed the shining appearance of green silk, and her staff was changed into a silver feather.

The lodge again shook and trembled, for they were now passing through the uppermost clouds, and they immediately after found themselves in the Evening Star, the residence of Osseo's father.

'My son,' said the old man, 'hang that cage of birds which you have brought along in your hand at the door, and I will inform you why you and your wife have been sent for.'

Osseo obeyed, and then took his seat in the lodge.

'Pity was shown to you,' resumed the King of the Star, 'on account of the contempt of your wife's sister, who laughed at her ill fortune, and ridiculed you while you were under the power of that wicked spirit whom you overcame at the rock. That spirit lives in the next lodge, being the small star you see on the left of mine, and he has always felt envious of my family because we had greater power, and especially that we had committed to us the care of the female world. He failed in many attempts to destroy your brothers and sisters-in-law, but succeeded at last in transforming yourself and your wife into decrepit old persons. You must be careful and not let the light of his beams fall on you, while you are here, for therein lies the power of his enchantment. A ray of light is the bow and arrow he uses.'

Osseo lived happy and contented in the parental lodge, and in due time his wife presented him with a son, who grew up rapidly, and in the very likeness of Osseo himself. He was very quick and ready in learning every thing that was done in his grandfather's dominions, but he wished also to learn the art of hunting, for he had heard that this was a favorite pursuit below. To gratify him, his father made him a bow and arrows, and he then let the birds out of the cage that he might practice in shooting. In this pastime he soon became expert, and the very first day he brought down a bird; but when he went to pick it up, to his amazement it was a beautiful young woman, with the arrow sticking in her breast. It was one of his younger aunts.

The moment her blood fell upon the surface of that pure and spotless planet, the charm was dissolved. The boy immediately found himself sinking, although he was partly upheld by something like wings until he passed through the lower clouds, and he then suddenly dropped upon a high, breezy island in a large lake. He was pleased, on looking up, to see all his aunts and uncles following him in the form of birds, and he soon discovered the silver lodge, with his father and mother, descending, with its waving tassels fluttering like so many insects' gilded wings. It rested on the loftiest cliffs of the island, and there they fixed their residence. They all resumed their natural shapes, but they were diminished to the size of fairies; and as a mark of homage to the King of the Evening Star, they never failed on every pleasant evening during the summer season to join hands and dance upon the top of the rocks. These rocks were quickly observed by the Indians to be covered, in moonlight evenings, with a larger sort of *Ininees*, or little men, and were called *Mish-in-e-mok-in-ok-ong*, or Little Spirits, and the island is named from them to this day.

Their shining lodge can be seen in the summer evenings, when the moon beams strongly on the pinnacles of the rocks; and the fishermen who go near those high cliffs at night, have even heard the voices of the happy little dancers. And Osseo and his wife, as fondly attached to each other as ever, always lead the dance.

48

The Star-Lovers

(Japanese)

Shokujo, daughter of the Sun, dwelt with her father on the banks of the Silver River of Heaven, which we call the Milky Way. She was a lovely maiden, graceful and winsome, and her eyes were tender as the eyes of a dove. Her loving father, the Sun, was much troubled because Shokujo did not share in the youthful pleasures of the daughters of the air. A soft melancholy seemed to brood over her, but she never wearied of working for the good of others, and especially did she busy herself at her loom; indeed she came to be called the Weaving Princess.

The Sun bethought him, that if he could give his daughter in marriage, all would be well; her dormant love would be kindled into a flame that would illumine her whole being and drive out the pensive spirit which oppressed her. Now there lived, hard by, one Kingen, a right honest herdsman, who tended his cows on the borders of the Heavenly Stream. The Sun-King proposed to bestow his daughter on Kingen, thinking in this way to provide for her happiness and at the same time to keep her near him. Every star beamed approval, and there was joy in the heavens.

The love that bound Shokujo and Kingen to one another was a great love. With its awakening, Shokujo forsook her former occupations, nor did she any longer labour industriously at the loom, but laughed, and danced, and sang, and made merry from morn till night. The Sun-King was sorely grieved, for he had not foreseen so great a change. Anger was in his eyes, and he said, 'Kingen is surely the cause of this, therefore I will banish him to the other side of the River of Stars.'

When Shokujo and Kingen heard that they were to be parted, and could thenceforth, in accordance with the King's decree, meet but once a year, and that upon the seventh night of the seventh month, their hearts were heavy. The leave-taking between them was a sad one, and great tears stood in Shokujo's eyes as she bade farewell to her lover-husband. In answer to the behest of the Sun-King, myriads of magpies flocked together, and, outspreading their wings, formed a bridge, on which Kingen crossed the River of Heaven. The moment that his foot touched the opposite bank, the birds dispersed with noisy chatter, leaving poor Kingen a solitary exile. He looked wistfully towards the weeping figure of Shokujo, who stood on the threshold of her now desolate home.

Long and weary were the succeeding days, spent as they were by Kingen in guiding his oxen and by Shokujo in plying her shuttle.

The Sun-King was gladdened by his daughter's industry. When night fell and the heavens were bright with countless lights, the lovers were wont, standing on the banks of the celestial stream, to waft across it sweet and tender messages, while each uttered a prayer for the speedy coming of the wondrous night.

The long-hoped-for month and day drew nigh, and the hearts of the lovers were troubled lest rain should fall: for the Silver River, full at all times, is at that season often in flood, and the bird-bridge might be swept away.

The day broke cloudlessly bright. It waxed and waned, and one by one the lamps of heaven were lighted. At nightfall the magpies assembled, and Shokujo, quivering with delight, crossed the slender bridge and fell into the arms of her lover. Their transport of joy was as the joy of the parched flower, when the raindrop falls upon it; but the moment of parting soon came, and Shokujo sorrowfully retraced her steps.

Year follows year, and the lovers still meet in that far-off starry land on the seventh night of the seventh month, save when rain has swelled the Silver River and rendered the crossing impossible. The hope of a permanent reunion still fills the hearts of the Star-Lovers, and is to them as a sweet fragrance and a beautiful vision.

49

Pallas-Athene

(Greek)

Pallas-Athene, goddess of Wisdom and Armed Resistance, was a purely Greek divinity; that is to say, no other nation possessed a corresponding conception. She was supposed, as already related, to have issued from the head of Zeus himself, clad in armour from head to foot. The miraculous advent of this maiden goddess is beautifully described by Homer in one of his hymns: snow-capped Olympus shook to its foundation; the glad earth re-echoed her martial shout; the billowy sea became agitated; and Helios, the sun-god, arrested his fiery steeds in their headlong course to welcome this wonderful emanation from the godhead. Athene was at once admitted into the assembly of the gods, and henceforth took her place as the most faithful and sagacious of all her father's counsellors. This brave, dauntless maiden, so exactly the essence of all that is noble in the character of 'the father of gods and men,' remained throughout chaste in word and deed, and kind at heart, without exhibiting any of those failings which somewhat mar the nobler features in the character of Zeus. This direct emanation from his own self, justly his favourite child, his better and purer counterpart, received from him several important prerogatives. She was permitted to hurl the thunderbolts, to prolong the life of man, and to bestow the gift of prophecy; in fact Athene was the only divinity whose authority was equal to that of Zeus himself, and when he had ceased to visit the earth in person she was empowered by him to act as his deputy. It was her especial duty to protect the state and all peaceful associations of mankind, which she possessed the power of defending when occasion required. She encouraged the maintenance of law and order, and defended the right on all occasions, for which reason, in the Trojan war she espouses the cause of the Greeks and exerts all her influence on their behalf. The Areopagus, a court of justice where religious causes and murders were tried, was believed to have been instituted by her, and when both sides happened to have an equal number of votes she gave the casting-vote in favour of the accused. She was the patroness of learning, science, and art, more particularly where these contributed directly towards the welfare of nations. She presided over all inventions connected with agriculture, invented the plough, and taught mankind how to use oxen for farming purposes. She also instructed mankind in the use of numbers, trumpets, chariots, &c., and presided over the building of the Argo, thereby encouraging the useful art of navigation. She also taught the Greeks how to build the wooden horse by means of which the destruction of Troy was effected.

The safety of cities depended on her care, for which reason her temples were generally built on the citadels, and she was supposed to watch over the defence of the walls, fortifications, harbours, &c. A divinity who so faithfully guarded the best interests of the state, by not only protecting it from the attacks of enemies, but also by developing its chief resources of wealth and prosperity, was worthily chosen as the presiding deity of the state, and in this character as an essentially political goddess she was called Athene-Polias.

The fact of Athene having been born clad in armour, which merely signified that her virtue and purity were unassailable, has given rise to the erroneous supposition that she was the presiding goddess of war; but a deeper study of her character in all its bearings proves that, in contradistinction to her brother Ares, the god of war, who loved strife for its own sake, she only takes up arms to protect the innocent and deserving against tyrannical oppression. It is true that in the Iliad we frequently see her on the battlefield fighting valiantly, and protecting her favourite heroes; but this is always at the command of Zeus, who even supplies her with arms for the purpose, as it is supposed that she possessed none of her own. A marked feature in the representations of this deity is the ægis, that wonderful shield given to her by her father as a further means of defence, which, when in danger, she swung so swiftly round and round that it kept at a distance all antagonistic influences; hence her name Pallas, from *pallo*, I swing. In the centre of this shield, which was covered with dragon's scales, bordered with serpents, and which she sometimes wore as a breastplate, was the awe-inspiring head of the Medusa, which had the effect of turning to stone all beholders.

In addition to the many functions which she exercised in connection with the state, Athene presided over the two chief departments of feminine industry, spinning and weaving. In the latter art she herself displayed unrivalled ability and exquisite taste. She wove her own robe and that of Hera, which last she is said to have embroidered very richly; she also gave Jason a cloak wrought by herself, when he set forth in quest of the Golden Fleece. Being on one occasion challenged to a contest in this accomplishment by a mortal maiden named Arachne, whom she had instructed in the art of weaving, she accepted the challenge and was completely vanquished by her pupil. Angry at her defeat, she struck the unfortunate maiden on the forehead with the shuttle which she held in her hand; and Arachne, being of a sensitive nature, was so hurt by this indignity that she hung herself in despair, and was changed by Athene into a spider. This goddess is said to have invented the flute, upon which she played with considerable talent, until one day, being laughed at by the assembled gods and goddesses for the contortions which her countenance assumed during these musical efforts, she hastily ran to a fountain in order to convince herself whether she deserved their ridicule. Finding to her intense disgust that such was indeed the fact, she threw the flute away, and never raised it to her lips again.

Athene is usually represented fully draped; she has a serious and thoughtful aspect, as though replete with earnestness and wisdom; the beautiful oval contour of her countenance is adorned by the luxuriance of her wealth of hair, which is drawn back from the temples and hangs down in careless grace; she looks the embodiment of strength, grandeur, and majesty; whilst her broad shoulders and small hips give her a slightly masculine appearance.

When represented as the war-goddess she appears clad in armour, with a helmet on her head, from which waves a large plume; she carries the ægis on her arm, and in her hand a golden staff, which possessed the property of endowing her chosen favourites with youth and dignity.

Athene was universally worshipped throughout Greece, but was regarded with special veneration by the Athenians, she being the guardian deity of Athens. Her most celebrated temple was the Parthenon, which stood on the Acropolis at Athens, and contained her world-renowned statue by Phidias, which ranks second only to that of Zeus by the same great artist. This colossal statue was 39 feet high, and was composed of ivory and gold; its majestic beauty formed the chief attraction of the temple. It represented her standing erect, bearing her spear and shield; in her hand she held an image of Nike, and at her feet there lay a serpent.

The tree sacred to her was the olive, which she herself produced in a contest with Poseidon. The olive-tree thus called into existence was preserved in the temple of Erectheus, on the Acropolis, and is said to have possessed such marvellous vitality, that when the Persians burned it after sacking the town it immediately burst forth into new shoots.

The principal festival held in honour of this divinity was the Panathenæa.

The owl, cock, and serpent were the animals sacred to her, and her sacrifices were rams, bulls, and cows.

50

The Cid

(Spanish)

Unlike some of the other heroes told about in this book, the Cid was a real man, whose name was Rodrigo Diaz, or Ruydiez. He was born in Burgos in the eleventh century and won the name of 'Cid,' which means 'Conqueror,' by defeating five Moorish kings. This happened after Spain had been in the hands of the Arabs for more than three hundred years, so it is small wonder that the Spaniards looked upon their hero as a very remarkable man.

When Rodrigo was still a youth, his father, Diego Laynez, was grossly insulted by Don Gomez. The custom in those days was to avenge such an insult by slaying the offender; but Diego was too old and feeble to bear arms. When he finally told his son of the wrong, Rodrigo sought out Don Gomez and challenged him to fight. So bravely and skilfully did Rodrigo manage his weapons that he slew his father's enemy. Then he cut off the head and carried it to Diego.

Soon after this Diego bade his son do homage at King Ferdinand's court. Rodrigo appeared before the king, but his bearing was so defiant that Ferdinand was frightened, and banished him.

Rodrigo departed with three hundred followers, encountered some Moors, who were invading Castile, defeated them and took five of their kings captive, releasing them only after they had promised to pay tribute and to refrain from further warfare. It was these kings who first called him 'Cid.'

In return for his brave service Rodrigo was restored to favour and given place among the king's courtiers.

One day Dona Ximena, daughter of Don Gomez, appeared and demanded justice from the king. Recognizing Rodrigo among the courtiers, she called to him to slay her also. But both demand and cry were unheeded, for the king had been too well served by Rodrigo to listen to any accusation against him.

Three times the maiden returned with the same request, and each time she came she heard greater praise of the young hero. At last she decided to alter her demand. A fourth time she returned, consenting to forego all thoughts of vengeance if the king would order the young hero to marry her. The Cid was very willing, for he had learned to love the girl, admiring her beauty and spirit.

The marriage was celebrated with great pomp and the king gave Rodrigo four cities as a marriage portion. Rodrigo, vowing that he would not be worthy of his wife until he had won five battles, after a pious pilgrimage to the shrine of the patron saint, hastened off to Calahorra, a frontier town claimed by two kings—the kings of Castile and Oregon.

It had been decided that the dispute over the town should be settled by combat. Rodrigo became the champion of Ferdinand of Castile. The other champion, Martin Gonzalez, began, as soon as the combat opened, to taunt the Cid.

'Never again will you mount your favourite steed Babieça,' he said, 'never will you return to your castle; never will you see your beloved Ximena again.'

But the Cid was undaunted, and had soon laid his enemy low. Great praise then was given to the Cid—so great that the knights of Castile were jealous and plotted to kill him. But the Moorish kings whom he had captured and released warned him in time to avert the danger.

Then the Cid aided Ferdinand in defeating the hostile Moors in Estremadura, after a siege of Coimbra lasting seven months. Several other victories over his country's enemies were added to this, and then Rodrigo returned to his beloved wife.

But not for long was he permitted to remain in the quiet of home. Henry III, Emperor of Germany, complained to the Pope that King Ferdinand had refused to acknowledge his superiority. The Pope sent a message to Ferdinand, demanding homage and tribute. The demand angered both Ferdinand and the Cid.

'Never yet have we done homage,' cried the Cid, 'and shall we now bow to a stranger?'

A proud refusal was then sent to the Pope, and he, knowing of no better way to settle the dispute, bade Henry send a champion to meet Rodrigo. The emperor's champion was, of course, defeated, and all of Ferdinand's enemies were so awed by the outcome of the fight that none ever again demanded homage or tribute. Rodrigo was, indeed, a very useful subject. When Ferdinand died, he was succeeded by his son, Don Sancho. The latter, planning a visit to Rome, selected the Cid to accompany him. Arriving, they found that in the preparations that had been made for their reception a lower seat had been prepared for Don Sancho than for the King of France. The Cid would not suffer such a slight, and became so violent that the Pope excommunicated him. Nevertheless, the seats were made of equal height, and the Cid, who was a good Catholic, humbled himself before the Pope and was forgiven.

It was an age of great wars, and the Cid aided his king in many a brave fight. At last, in the siege of Zamora, the king was treacherously murdered, and, as he had no sons, Don Alfonso, his brother, succeeded. When he arrived at Zamora the Cid refused to acknowledge Alfonso until he should swear that he had no part in the murder. The king, angered by the Cid's attitude, plotted revenge. Opportunity came during a war with the Moors, and the Cid was banished upon a slight pretext.

'I obey, O king,' replied the Cid, when he heard the decree. 'I am more ready to serve you than you are to reward me. I pray that you may never more in battle need the right arm and sword that so often served your father.'

Then the Cid rode away, through a crowd of weeping people, and camped outside of the city until he could make definite plans. The people longed to bring him food or offer him shelter, but they feared the displeasure of the king. One old man, however, crept outside of the city with food, declaring that he cared 'not a fig' for Alfonso's commands.

The Cid needed money, and to get it he pledged two locked coffers to some Jews. The Jews in those days were much despised by the Christians, though usually very wealthy. The men, thinking that the boxes contained vast treasures, when in reality they were filled with sand, advanced the Cid 600 marks of gold. Then the hero bade farewell to his wife and children and rode away, vowing that he would return, covered with glory and carrying with him rich spoils.

Within two weeks' time the Cid and his little band of followers had captured two Moorish strongholds and carried off much spoil. The Cid then prepared a truly royal present and sent it to the king. Alfonso, upon receiving the gift, pardoned the Cid, and published an edict permitting all who wished to join in the fight against the Moors to join Rodrigo and his band.

Toledo, thanks to the valour of the Cid, soon fell into the hands of Alfonso, but a misunderstanding arose and the king insulted the Cid. The latter, in great rage, left the army and made a sudden raid on Castile. Then the Moors, knowing that the Cid had departed, took courage and captured Valencia. But the Cid, hearing of the disaster, promptly returned, recaptured the city, and sent a message to Alfonso asking for his wife and daughters. At the same time he sent more than the promised sum of money to the Jews, who up to this time had not learned that the coffers were filled with sand. To the messenger he said:

'Tell them, that although they can find nothing in the coffers but sand, they will find that the pure gold of my truth lies beneath the sand.'

As the Cid was now master of Valencia, and of vast wealth, his daughters were sought in marriage by many suitors, and the marriage of both girls was celebrated with great splendour. But the Counts of Carrion, their husbands, were not brave men like the Cid, and after lingering at Valencia in idleness for two years, their weakness was clearly shown.

One evening while the Cid was sleeping, a lion broke loose from his private menagerie and entered the room where he lay. The two princes, who were playing in the room, fled, one in his haste falling into an empty vat, and the other taking refuge behind the Cid's couch. The roaring of the lion wakened the Cid, and jumping up he seized his sword, caught the lion by the mane, led it back to its cage, and calmly returned to his place.

The cowardly conduct of the Counts of Carrion roused the anger of the Cid's followers, and in the siege of Valencia that followed their conduct brought only contempt. When the Moors were finally driven away the counts asked permission to return home with their brides and gifts.

So the Cid parted from his daughters, weeping at the loss. The procession started. The first morning the counts sent their escorts ahead, and, left alone with their wives, stripped them of their garments, beat them and kicked them, and left them for dead. But Felez Muñoz, a loyal follower of the Cid's, riding back, found the two wives, bound up their wounds and obtained shelter for them in the house of a poor man whose wife and daughters promised to nurse them. Then he rode on to tell the Cid. The Cid swore that he would be avenged, and as Alfonso was responsible for the marriage, he applied to him for redress.

The king, who had long since forgiven the Cid and learned to value his services, was very angry. A battle was finally arranged. The Counts of Carrion and their uncle were defeated and banished, and the Cid returned in triumph to Valencia. Here his daughters' second marriage took place.

The Moors returned five years later, and the Cid was prepared to meet them when he received a vision of St Peter, predicting that he would die within thirty days, but that even though dead he would triumph over his enemy. He accordingly made preparations for his death, and after appointing a successor, he gave instructions that none should weep over his death, and that his body when embalmed should be set upon his horse, Babieça, and that, with his sword Tizona in his hand, he should be led on a certain day against the enemy.

The hero died and his successor together with his wife Ximena strove to carry out his instructions. A battle was planned, and the Cid, strapped upon his war horse, rode in the van. The Moors, filled with terror, fled before him.

After the victory the body was placed in the Church of San Pedro de Cardeña, where for ten years it remained seated, in plain view of all.